DRAGONS OF INTROVERTIA

By

James and Bit Barringer

ISBN 9798648847545

Cover design by Jaka Prawira
http://ellinsworth.co/

www.DragonsOfIntrovertia.com

FROM THE AUTHORS

First of all, THANK YOU! Whether you're an introvert yourself or you just love a good fantasy adventure, thank you so much for allowing us to take you on a journey. We had fun writing this series, and we hope you have fun reading it!

We began writing this series in early 2019, but the first book was published square in the middle of 2020. Again that backdrop, we became more convinced than ever of the need for hopeful and optimistic fiction. Bleak and miserable dystopias, with book covers in shades of gray and brown, ought to be dead. Open-hearted young adult fiction – the stuff that inspires you and helps you to keep hope alive – is a defiant proclamation that light overcomes, even if things look dark right now.

We hope you'll read this series with a smile!

James and Bit

Book 1: *Dragons of Introvertia*
Book 2: *The Wind Before Rain*
Book 3: *A Fury Like Thunder*
Book 4: *Tranquility Storm*
Book 5: *The Dawn After Darkness* [Summer 2021]
Book 6: *The Opening Night Wedding* [Fall 2021]
Untitled Books 7-9 [upcoming]

Table of Contents

ONE

Lightning flashed in the darkening sky, and Mazaren flinched as deafening thunder rocked the battlefield. Far above, his dragon, Arjera, wheeled hard to the right and swooped down toward the evil sorcerer and his armies. No one knew why the spellcaster had attacked the Kingdom of Introvertia, or what he hoped to accomplish by laying waste to the peaceful Introvertian way of life. If Mazaren had his way, the sorcerer wouldn't live long enough for anyone to find out.

Mazaren reached out with his mind and instantly his thoughts were one with Arjera's. He could feel the dragon's intense focus, and some faint fear at the back of her mind. Through her eyes he could see the sorcerer looking up. Terror was clearly written on the man's face. In the next moment a spear of dark purple energy shot up from the magician's staff, and Arjera reacted even before Mazaren realized what had happened, rolling over on her right wing. In the next instant she had leveled off her dive and cut loose with a spray of flame from her mouth.

Mazaren broke his connection with the dragon. A hundred yards away he could see her pulling up once more, leaving a trail of fire behind her. He could hear the

1

distant screams of the sorcerer's army, the men who had been tricked into following an evil man by his promises of wealth or power. Already they were breaking and beginning to flee into the twilight.

But the Introvertian army was only thirty yards away, and Mazaren heard Commander Onara give the command to charge. The light infantry broke into a run, laying waste to the haphazard defense put up by the magician's mercenaries. Of the spellcaster himself, though, there was no sign.

Suddenly Mazaren felt Arjera reaching out to him, and he locked minds with her once more. She had seen the man fleeing, using the cover of darkness as he stumbled toward the river off to the west. Mazaren told her to attack again and took off at a full sprint, holding his scana short sword against his side to keep it from slapping his leg as he ran. He was no mage, and he didn't know what he planned to do if he found himself in single combat against a man who could summon primal energy from thin air, but he knew he had to do something.

Lightning split the nearly-black sky as his boots pounded the rocky soil. The ground lit up for just long enough that Mazaren could see the sorcerer, now about fifty yards ahead of him. Arjera came screaming out of the darkness, fire erupting from her mouth and splashing all over the spot where the sorcerer had been standing. But Mazaren was almost sure he had seen a sparkling blue globe of protective energy enclose the spellcaster just before the fire arrived – no doubt the same thing that happened the first time Arjera attacked.

Something was wrong, though. The magician was on his knees, and was struggling to get up. Maybe he had expended too much magical energy, or maybe some of the fire had made it through his magic shield and injured him. Mazaren sped up, trying to close the distance as quickly as he could. Flaming grass and shrubs around him cast an eerie, flickering light over the battlefield. In the faint glow he could see that the sorcerer had gotten to his feet and was turning toward Mazaren with his staff in both hands.

Mazaren slowed, pulling his scana from its sheath and holding it low. "This is over," he said, trying to sound more confident that he felt.

"You wish," sneered the mage, whipping his staff over his head and extending it toward Mazaren.

Mazaren had started to dive as soon as the staff began to move, and he somersaulted away just as another spear of purple energy blew apart the dirt where he had been standing. Instantly he sprang back to his feet. Instinct made him charge directly at the sorcerer, hoping he arrived before the mage got another spell out.

He dropped his head and his shoulder crashed against the sorcerer's sternum. Both men went sprawling onto the rocks, and Mazaren heard the wood staff clattering to the ground a few yards away. But the impact had disoriented him and he didn't know whether he or the sorcerer was closer to that staff –

In the next moment he was soaring through the air, purple energy crackling around him. He smashed against the ground with an impact so hard that for a moment he wasn't sure which way was up. His legs moved on their own, though, and he found himself on his feet once more, about fifteen feet away from the sorcerer, who looked to be in even worse shape than before, as if he only had one more strong spell left in him. Where was Arjera?

"You're a fool, Mazaren Tiranna," the sorcerer said, sounding exhausted. "You could have been great in my kingdom, a dragon-companion whose name and deeds would live forever, but you've chosen death on a nameless field."

"My death doesn't matter," Mazaren said through gritted teeth. He had landed on his hip and knee, and sharp pain was beginning to radiate out from them into the rest of his body. "Introvertia will live, and you will die. Only that matters."

A furious scream erupted from the sorcerer's mouth, and a purple lance even larger than the first two launched from his staff directly at Mazaren –

Something huge swept across Mazaren's vision, followed by a thud that rocked the ground. Flame poured from whatever had landed on the ground, wrapping around the sorcerer, who hadn't thrown up his shield in time. Only then did Mazaren realize what had happened. Arjera had taken the magician's spell for him. She lay on the ground, groaning softly, as the sorcerer's scorched body fell backward, unmoving.

"Arjera!" Mazaren screamed, running around to her front and putting his hands on her cheeks. "Arjera!" He looked up frantically to see if any Introvertian soldiers had seen the fight and were coming that direction. "Help! Someone help!"

He locked minds with Arjera and felt pain, but faintly, at a great distance, as if the dragon were slipping away. "No," he whispered quietly, telling her without words how much he loved her and how much he needed her to live. "Stay with me..."

"Eza!"

Ezalen Skywing glanced up from his book, frowning in annoyance at the bad timing. "Yes, Uncle Tully?"

"We're almost at the trading circle. Come on out of the wagon."

Eza's green eyes fell longingly on the book, *Heroes of Introvertia*, before he looked out the flap of the covered wagon he'd been riding in. Uncle Tully was walking alongside the wagon, smiling in. "I know that look," Tully said. "You were at a good part and you don't want to stop reading."

"Does Arjera die?"

"I can't tell you that."

Eza couldn't stop a groan from escaping. "But I have to know..."

That got a long chuckle from Tully. "I understand the feeling, my friend. I read the book when I was about your age, and I pretended to be sick for three days in a row so I could stay home from school and read some more. It'll still be waiting for you when we get done, though."

"I have to stop reading a book to go meet strangers?" Eza asked, unable to keep the disappointment out of his voice.

"Not just any strangers, Ezalen. People from another kingdom. Introvertia is different from anywhere else in the world, and it's important that you know about other cultures and the way other kingdoms do things."

"I could read about them," Eza reasoned.

"You can learn facts from a book," Tully said. "You can't get to know people from a book. Not truly."

Distant singing, carried on an east wind, caught Eza's ear, and he tilted his head to listen. These must be the traders Uncle Tully had come to meet with. "I can't even see them," he said. "How loud are they?"

"They are very loud," admitted Tully. "There's a reason their nation is called the Kingdom of People

Yelling and Having No Concept of Personal Space."

Eza could hardly believe his ears. "It's not really called that, is it?"

"Well, no. That's an old Introvertian inside joke. The real name is Exclaimovia, but they've certainly earned the nickname fair and square. Be ready for anything."

Eza set his book down and ran his fingers along the cover before hopping out of the wagon and looking around. The forest surrounding them was full of tall pine trees, and the sky above shone blue like a gemstone. It would have been an extremely tranquil place, and Eza would have liked it very much, if it weren't for the loud people heading in his direction.

A convoy of men and horses and wagons rounded a bend in the forest road, and Eza couldn't believe what he saw. The wagons were painted in bright colors, gaudy yellows and reds. And the people – the people were wearing the same kinds of colors, loud clothes that clashed with the forest and announced their coming from hundreds of yards away. As they got closer, still shouting and carrying on, Eza noticed that even their faces had been painted, with bright purple surrounding some of their eyes and an intricate design of white and gold on another's cheek. They were a sharp contrast to the quiet calm of the Introvertian traders, who stood next to their plain wood wagons in clothes of black, gray, green, and blue, designed to accent the natural beauty of the forest.

"Tully!" a burly man shouted, approaching Eza's uncle with wide arms. To Eza's shock and horror, he wrapped Tully in a giant hug, laughing loudly as he did so, then clapped Tully on the shoulders several times. These people were *huggers*. It wasn't too late, Eza told himself; he could sprint toward the river, could lose himself among –

"And who's this little guy?" the voice boomed. Eza felt himself being lifted off the ground, alarm bells ringing in his head. Someone was hugging him. He was being hugged. His entire body shuddered, but he managed to keep himself from kicking out and injuring the man. That might have hurt Uncle Tully's chances of brokering a deal.

"That's my nephew, Ezalen," he heard his uncle saying. "You'll have to forgive him. He's never met anyone from your kingdom before. He's not used to the way you do things."

"We're a little much for you?" the man thundered, setting Eza down and grinning at him.

Eza nodded weakly. "Introvertians are not usually this..."

"Captivating? Enthralling?"

"I was going to say loud, sir."

"You are, indeed, not loud," the man agreed. "Perhaps one day you'll learn to enjoy the finer things in life."

Eza was quite sure he wouldn't enjoy *anything* this man liked.

Already he could see why these traders from the Kingdom of Yelling were not allowed in Tranquility City itself. It would hardly be Tranquility if uncivilized goons were shrieking and cackling all over the place. Eza shuddered. He didn't want to think about it.

"So what have you brought for me?" the large man shouted. "Any dragons this time?"

"No, Kalek," Tully said, "no dragons. You know we don't trade those."

"It was a joke, my friend."

Tully's smile didn't quite reach his eyes. "Of course. We have brought the usual; mountain corn from the northern regions, the last of the winter crop before the first spring harvest. It's much colder in the mountains, you understand, and so —"

"I love mountain corn!" hollered Kalek.

Eza's jaw dropped. Kalek had interrupted Uncle Tully! That simply was not done in Introvertia. Eza was fairly sure that never in all his life had he witnessed one person interrupt another. When two Introvertians were talking, one was to listen, with no thought of replying, until the other was completely finished. Then the listener was to restate what he had heard, in order to ensure he had understood it correctly, before he was permitted to reply. Everyone knew that. But this, this butting in? This cutting someone off? What kind of barbarians were these people, who did not respect the most basic rules of communication?

"Your nephew looks like he's going to be ill," Kalek observed.

"He'll be fine. The price for the corn is two nayen per bushel, unless you've brought something you'd like to trade."

"In fact," Kalek roared, "I have! Or rather I've brought the same things as before. You're sure the women of your kingdom wouldn't appreciate them?"

He gave a signal, and several rugs were dangled out the back of one wagon. Eza nearly threw up. Introvertian homes were places of calm and peace, but these garish rugs, in horrific yellow and red patterns, looked more like a warning sign the city watch would put near a bridge that had washed out.

"I'm sorry," Tully said, managing to sound as if he truly meant it. "That's simply not the style we like in our kingdom. I understand that style is popular where you're from, but if you would take some time to learn about our people and the way –"

"Bah!" shouted Kalek. "You people don't know beauty when you see it."

"Yes, yes, your kingdom's way of doing things is best, and everyone should change their thoughts and attitudes until they do it your way," Tully said. Eza had never heard such sarcasm from his uncle; Introvertians typically didn't open their mouths unless it was to say exactly what they meant. These uncultured swine from the Kingdom of People Yelling and Having No Concept of Personal Space must have been rubbing off on Uncle Tully. It was true that Tully was one of the richest people in all of Tranquility, but no amount of money could have convinced Eza to spend another minute around such rude, arrogant, and mannerless people.

Kalek was apparently done blustering, and quickly negotiated a price for five hundred bushels of mountain corn, plus smaller quantities of tomatoes, summer wheat, and red and yellow clothing dye. He seemed to have realized he was not going to sell much of his merchandise, because the majority of his wagons were empty, brought along solely so they could be loaded with the goods he had bought from Tully and the Introvertians. The transfer of goods took nearly an hour, and Eza wandered away from the road, down toward the Rapidly Flowing River that passed through Tranquility and along the edge of the Very Large Forest on its way to the Southern Ocean. The Very Large Forest was the buffer zone between Introvertia and the Kingdom of Yelling, its forty miles of flat pine lowlands ensuring that the two kingdoms stayed comfortably apart and only rarely made contact.

Eza was extremely glad for the Very Large Forest.

"Well, that's done!" exclaimed Kalek when all the goods had been transferred. "It's always a pleasure doing business with you!" He clapped Tully on the shoulders again and then turned to Eza. "And Ezalen, my boy, it was great to meet you!"

Eza could sense the man coming in for a hug, so he quickly bent down to tie his boot. Kalek's arms closed around air, but the large man didn't seem too bothered, moving on to one of the other Introvertian merchants for a flagrant violation of personal space. Eza looked down at his boots and hoped Kalek didn't notice that they had no laces.

Before long the traders from Yelling had moved off, and even the noise of their deafening songs had faded away. The sounds of the forest remained: the gentle whisper of water against the shores of the Rapidly Flowing River, sparrows singing in the trees, a woodpecker knocking happily on the hollow trunk of a juniper somewhere nearby. A light breeze from the east rustled the branches of the evergreens and a few needles drifted down toward Eza, who put out a hand and caught one. Did the loud people from Yelling even know that the forest made sounds? Did they appreciate the quiet serenity of nature, or were they just obsessed with the sound of their own voices?

Uncle Tully had an enormous smirk on his face as he approached Eza. "Are you still glad you asked to come along?"

"Yes," Eza said truthfully. "If I hadn't seen for myself, I would never have believed anyone could be so rude, so oblivious, so insensitive, so superior..."

"In their kingdom, all of those things are normal, just as peace, honesty, and personal space are normal to us. They simply don't know any better."

"I'm not disgusted that they're different," Eza said defensively. "I'm disgusted because they kept insisting their way was better. Kalek said one day we'd learn to be loud. He said our fashion sense should be more like theirs." So many thoughts were crashing around in his mind that he had to pause for a moment, and then shook his head. "I don't think the world would be a better place if people went around interrupting each other all the time."

"It wouldn't," agreed Uncle Tully. "No conversation should be dominated by the loudest and rudest any more than a society should be dominated by the most ruthless. Both of those are unjust and should not be tolerated."

"I hope I never meet another one of them."

"Here's something for your trouble," Tully said, pressing a few coins into Eza's hands.

Eza looked down, then back at his uncle, his green eyes wide. "Three nayen?"

"I figure an unauthorized hug has to be worth at least three nayen."

"Well..." Eza hedged. "If you want to give me more, I wouldn't complain..."

That earned a laugh. "Don't push it, nephew."

TWO

The road through the Very Large Forest was wide and welcoming. It followed the Rapidly Flowing River, which was sometimes very close and sometimes further away so that the gush and burble of flowing water was only a faint whisper. Far to the west, the road threaded through a point where the Impassable Mountains came within fifty yards of the river, forming a natural defensive emplacement if Exclaimovia were to ever attack Introvertia. Just past that that narrow choke point, the city of Tranquility appeared on the horizon, barely visible through the pine and fir trees, its gray stone walls and gray-and-brown houses matching the rocky soil of the forest and the trunks and branches of the trees. Eza had never been so glad to see his hometown, and he sprinted ahead of the convoy, his copy of *Heroes of Introvertia* clutched tightly in his hands and his short sandy-brown hair bobbing with each step.

The wide gates of Tranquility were open, as they almost always were. The guards, the only people in the whole Kingdom of Introvertia who had the job of making eye contact with strangers, smiled gently at Eza, and he waved back at them, not slowing as his feet pounded down the cobblestones. He was home.

15

Broad Avenue ran from one end of the city to the other, sixty feet wide and lined on both sides with tall evergreens. Just back from the trees sat restaurants and art supply shops and bakeries and schools, one- and two-story buildings made from local stone and local wood, looking like they belonged in the forest. As often as not there was a field kept empty between two buildings, with even more trees or small shrubs taking up the space, making it seem like the Very Large Forest was setting up outposts in the city itself. On the left was Cappel's Books, a stone building two stories tall, where Eza came several times a week with every spare coin he could earn or scrounge. It was also the place where he was already planning to spend all three nayen that Uncle Tully had given him.

But his father had told him to check in at home as soon as he got back, so he headed that direction instead, slowing to a walk as he breathed the fresh scent of the city. The brushing of wind through branches absorbed what little sound there already was and made the city seem even quieter – but not an ominous quiet, Eza thought, the way a dark bedroom in the small hours of the morning could be ominously quiet. This was a welcoming quiet, an announcement of peace and solitude, a promise that there would be no rude people or unauthorized huggers – Eza's entire body shuddered involuntarily – within these gates.

Just ahead was his favorite part of the entire city, the Reading Square. Broad Avenue entered one side of the square, which was so wide Eza could barely have thrown a rock from one side of it to the big dragon statue in the middle. Fir trees and flowers sprang up through carefully tended gaps in the stone paving, so that the whole of the square was under the shade of at least one branch or bough. Other streets radiated out from the sides and corners of the square; along the left side, closest to the Rapidly Flowing River, was the royal palace, the home of King Jazan and Queen Annaya. Just like the rest of Tranquility, the palace had not been built to draw attention to itself, but to fit in with its surroundings. It was solidly made of stone from the Impassable Mountains, the light gray polished so that it would almost shine in the afternoon sun.

All around the square were benches, chairs, stools, slabs, and other places where people could sit, lounge, or lie down, whatever they wanted, and simply read. There had to be five hundred people in the square now, all enjoying their own reading material – privately, but in public, satisfied in the company of others who got satisfaction from the same hobby. There was no yelling, no screaming, no loud singing. Introvertians were people who recognized the value of peace, who thrived on a few close friendships with folks who mattered to them, who disdained small talk as being insincere and shallow. If an

Introvertian was going to talk, it would be something worth saying. That was why the Reading Square was Eza's favorite place. If anyone there had something truly important to say to him, they would say it. If not, he could sit there for hours, unbothered and not bothering anyone else.

Most of the Introvertians he ran past were visibly daydreaming as they strolled, their eyes drifting over the trees or the buildings, not looking at the people who walked by. That was perfectly fine with Eza, and with everyone else in the kingdom. There was no expectation that an Introvertian would be forced to interact with anyone else. In fact, that idea was in two of the three Founding Freedoms that the entire constitution of the kingdom was based on: the Freedom to Interact and the Freedom from Interaction. The first of those meant you could talk to anybody if you wanted to and if they wanted to. The second meant that you couldn't be forced to interact with anybody. The law was beautiful in its simplicity.

That was why no one thought twice when the streets were mostly quiet. Most people preferred to keep to themselves, and Introvertia was the perfect place for that. There was only one exception.

A girl about Eza's age was skipping into the square with a book in her hand just as Eza was leaving. She wore a huge smile and happened to lock eyes with Eza, who smiled back. "I like your dress!" he said. "Thank you!" she answered happily, twirling in a circle in mid-skip and continuing into the square. That was the third freedom: the Freedom to Compliment. You couldn't interrupt someone who was doing something else, or distract someone who was deep in thought or not paying attention to you, but if you made eye contact with someone, it was always allowed – and encouraged – to say something kind. Every time Eza went out the door, he got to make a choice: he could daydream and let his eyes wander, or he could look around at the people he passed and get dozens of compliments from strangers. That was the Introvertian way, and Eza loved it.

He passed through the Music Square, the one place in Tranquility where there was guaranteed to be noise. Anyone could show up, no matter what their favorite instrument or their level of ability, and make music with the others who were there. Ezalen had never had much musical talent himself, but he understood how difficult it was to improvise on an instrument, and how each musician had to be more intent on listening to the others than on what he was going to play. That concept – listen and understand before you make noise – was really important, not just to music but to conversation as well.

After the Music Square he turned off Broad Avenue onto a quieter street, lined on both sides by two-story houses made of stone blocks. The fifth one on the left was the Skywing house, and Eza allowed himself a smile. He was home.

His father, Ezarra, was outside tending the garden in the backyard. Ezarra's bright red dragon, Neemie, was excitedly bouncing around by his side, trying not to step on the beets or the rutabagas. When the dragon saw Eza approaching, she let out a loud squeal of delight and exploded into the air.

"Hi, dad! Hi, Neemie!" Eza greeted them, just as Neemie landed on his shoulders. In the old stories, Introvertian dragons were huge, with a ten-foot wingspan and scales so tough arrows could hardly pierce them. Nowadays, for reasons Eza didn't fully understand, the only dragons he'd ever seen were about waist high to a grown man and weighed around twenty pounds.

As soon as the dragon settled on, Eza could sense her thoughts – not specific thoughts, exactly, as if he were reading Neemie's mind, but vague feelings, perceptions, movements. Neemie was happy to see Eza, as always, and even more so now that Eza could finally communicate with her. But there was something in the back of the dragon's mind, too, some worry or preoccupation that Eza couldn't put a finger on. He gently tried to reassure Neemie, but got the impression that although his efforts were appreciated, this wasn't something that a kind word or two from Eza could fix. A gentle belch of fire puffed into the afternoon warmth; dragons sometimes breathed flame, but not much at all, barely enough to start a campfire if there was proper kindling and the wood had been soaked with oil. Eza had heard stories from long ago, that dragons used to light entire cities on fire before they'd made friends with the Introvertians, but he was pretty sure those stories were just fairy tales.

"Welcome back, son," Ezarra greeted him. "What's Neemie telling you today?"

"She seems anxious about something."

"I felt the same thing," Ezarra said, pride in his voice. "You're really coming along well, if I can say so. I couldn't talk to Neemie until almost six months after I finished my Year of Silence, and yours just ended three weeks ago." Neemie, still perched on Eza's shoulders, looked down, and it seemed to Eza as if the dragon were radiating her agreement.

"It is nice to be able to talk again," Eza admitted. "Though I have to say I didn't miss it as much as I thought I would."

The Skywings were dragon-companions, one of several thousand families throughout the kingdom whose duty for generations had been to tend and befriend the dragons. But there was a catch: being able to read a dragon's mind was not something a person could simply decide to do. Every dragon-companion had to take a year-long vow of silence, from their fourteenth birthday to their fifteenth, and spend that time around dragons, using their own verbal emptiness to catch what the dragons were saying. The communication began as vague impressions, which gradually grew more certain, and eventually the companion became able to make his or her own thoughts known to the dragons as well. No one was quite sure how it worked, and most people were content to just say "magic" and smile. That was a bit of a cruel joke, considering magic had been officially banished from Introvertian society for centuries, but people said it anyway.

"How was your trip with Uncle Tully?" Ezarra asked.

"We met the traders from the Kingdom of Yelling."

"And?"

"There was yelling," Eza said lamely. "And hugging. But Uncle Tully gave me three nayen, at least."

"Mmmhmm. Have you decided what books you're going to buy with the money?"

Eza had been expecting his father to ask "What are you going to buy" and was already opening his mouth to answer "books." He blinked a few times. "Uncle Tully gave me a copy of *Heroes of Introvertia.*"

His father's eyes lit up. "One of my very favorites."

"I want to get more books like that. History books, stories of great people from the old days."

"I'm sure Mr. Cappel has just the one for you." Ezarra pulled a message out of his back pocket. "This came while you were gone. All the dragon-companions from your class have been summoned to the palace."

Eza's heart leaped. "Do you think they finally have a dragon for me?"

"We'll find out, won't we? Oh, that reminds me. Here's a list of some things I'd like you to bring home from the market. There's no rush, of course. I don't know how long you'll be at the palace." Ezarra paused. "Or at Cappel's."

"I'll try to be back for dinner," Eza said.

And so Eza's legs carried him back through the Music Square, back down Broad Avenue, and back into the Reading Square. This time he headed straight for the palace. He'd only been inside once, when taking his dragon-companion vows right before his twelfth birthday. The guards examined his letter and ushered him in, not to the throne room where he'd been the first time, but down a hallway that led to the left and then wrapped around the back of the palace.

In a room at the end of the hall was a man Eza had met before. Arzen Onanden helped oversee the dragon-breeding program to guarantee that there were always enough dragons for each student to get one, and he was also a captain in the King's Army of Introvertia. Dragons

23

hadn't been used in battle for hundreds of years, but the companion program was still part of the military, and Eza would receive a commission into the army when he graduated. Captain Onanden looked up as the guard deposited Eza in the doorway, then stood in greeting.

"Ezalen Skywing, correct?"

Eza nodded, impressed. There were probably twenty thousand companions in the whole Kingdom of Introvertia, and over a thousand his own age currently in the Dragon Academy right here in the capital city. For the man to remember Eza's name, after not seeing him for over a year, was really something.

"Please, have a seat," Captain Onanden said, motioning to a chair across from his desk.

Eza settled into it, sitting straight up, hands folded on his lap, wanting to appear like a model dragon-companion. He tried to keep eye contact with the captain, but couldn't stop his eyes from wandering over the stone walls, admiring the paintings of ancient warriors and dragons.

"I understand you passed your Year of Silence," Captain Onanden said. "Congratulations. What did you think of it?"

"I didn't miss talking as much as I thought I would, sir. I practiced with my father's dragon every day, and I'm making progress at sensing its emotions."

The captain smiled warmly. "I trust you're looking

forward to having a dragon of your own soon, right?"
Eza sat forward excitedly, unable to keep a huge grin
off his face. "Yes, sir!"

"That's what I called you here to talk about." The
other man's face grew serious. "I know you should have
one by now, since your vow ended several weeks ago.
However, we currently have a shortage of dragons. We
don't know when we'll have one to give you."

Eza's brain was paralyzed by a combination of
disappointment and confusion. "But sir," he protested, "I
read all about the program before I took my vows. I
know the dragons are raised very carefully so there are
always exactly enough for the number of companions."

"That's how it is supposed to go," Captain Onanden
allowed. "We've run into some unforeseen difficulties. I
feel bad for you, and for all the others in your companion
class, so rather than simply leave you all waiting, I
wanted to give you the news in person."

The confusion was ebbing away and disappointment
was growing in its place, making Eza want to cry – but
he couldn't do that, not here in front of an officer. He
didn't cry often, but he'd gotten his hopes up *so much* and
now...this. All he could do was swallow the enormous
lump in his throat and nod.

"I'm truly sorry," the captain said, and Eza believed he
meant it. "I hope to have better news the next time I
bring you here."

Eza could only manage another nod.

Outside the palace, with the afternoon sun beginning to head toward the horizon and golden light filtering through the branches of the pine trees, Eza put one foot in front of the other in a daze. He'd been hoping to walk out of that palace with a dragon on his shoulders; instead he was walking out with the news that not even Captain Onanden could say for sure when he'd get one – or if he'd get one at all.

Only one thing could make him feel better. He headed for Cappel's bookstore.

"Cappel's house that also happened to be a bookstore" was more accurate. Once upon a time the old man had lived in the whole building before turning his living room into a shop. Then the shop expanded into one bedroom, the other bedroom, the kitchen, the large porch he had just added on, and up the walls of the staircase, and Cappel himself had simply taken up residence on the second floor instead. That was roughly what was happening on a smaller scale in Eza's own bedroom. His father was thinking about building him a bed on stilts so they could add more bookshelves underneath, since almost no room was left on the walls.

Mr. Cappel was in his seventies, but his eyes and mind were sharp and he was quick with a smile. "Ezalen!" he exclaimed when the boy entered. "So good to see you! But you don't look as excited as you usually do. Did you drop *Collected Poems of Elzana Carrain* into the river or something?"

That got a smile out of Eza. "I really would be sad if I did that."

"Then why do you look so down, my boy?"

"They don't have a dragon for me yet."

The smile wrinkles disappeared from the corners of Cappel's eyes. "Tell me more," he said, running fingers through his short white hair.

Eza explained all that Captain Onanden had told him. The bookseller listened closely, with a look of intense concentration. When Eza had finished, Cappel rocked backwards, his eyes distant, and flatly said, "I don't believe it."

"Don't believe what?"

"That they somehow ran out of dragons. Everyone knows how tightly that program is run, how carefully the dragons are managed, how seriously the whole thing is taken. I don't see how anyone could believe they just plain counted wrong."

"You think Captain Onanden lied to me?" Eza asked in shock. "But Introvertians don't –"

"Don't open their mouths unless they're going to say something true that builds another person up, I know. I've memorized the founding charter and the constitution just like you have. So no, I don't believe the captain lied to you. But I also believe he didn't tell you the whole truth."

"Why would he hide something?" Eza murmured.

"You tell me," Cappel said, the smile returning. "Have you ever hidden something from your father?"

"Not often," Eza said truthfully. "But when I did it was because the truth would make me look bad. One time I didn't tell him how long I'd spent weeding the garden, because I had rushed through it to spend some time with my friend Shanna."

"Is that the sort of thing Captain Onanden is doing? Telling a half-truth to keep himself from looking bad?"

"No," said Eza, thinking hard. "Because the story he told me already makes him look bad. So...if he told that story to hide the truth, then the truth must make him look even worse than that."

"Very good. So what could be worse than someone being incompetent?"

"Something that's dangerous. Something that could hurt people if it got out." Eza pondered his own words. "But what could that be?"

"*Why* are they short of dragons?" Cappel nudged. "What's a *dangerous* reason they could be short of dragons?"

Eza could only think of one thing. "Some of the dragons escaped?"

"Or escaped with help."

"Stolen?" Eza said, bewildered.

28

Cappel spread his hands. "We don't have proof, Ezalen. But we do have an explanation that fits the evidence better than the explanation you were given by Captain Onanden. Is it likely that dragons were somehow lost or stolen? No. Is it likely that Captain Onanden and the dragon-breeders simply managed to miscount the number of dragons they had available? Certainly not. So the question we find ourselves with is: which do we find more likely?"

"I don't know," admitted Eza.

Cappel seemed excited, as if he were thrilled to uncover a secret plot. Suddenly Eza wondered if the old man had read too many books – if such a thing were even possible. Was he so caught up in heroes and duplicity and complex twists that he had invented a drama where there wasn't one? Was it *really* more likely that someone had managed to steal dragons – *steal* dragons! – than that the government hadn't known five years ago how large their companion program would be today? Eza certainly didn't like thinking that he couldn't trust his captain, or that he'd been deliberately misled by someone who had only ever been kind to him.

Besides, what was he supposed to do if there really had been a theft? Who was he supposed to tell that could do something about it? And would he get in trouble for knowing something that wasn't supposed to be known?

All of this was new to Eza, and he wasn't sure he liked

it, but he couldn't help a certain thrill from shooting up his back and making him shiver. What if there really *was* a plot afoot, and he and Cappel were the first two who had figured it out? What if they really did know a secret almost nobody else knew?

"Anyway," Cappel said, rubbing his hands together, "you didn't come here to be part of a conspiracy. You came here for books, or at least I assume you did."

"My uncle gave me *Heroes of Introvertia,*" Eza said, trying to pretend the previous two minutes hadn't happened. "Do you have anything else like that? Heroes and evil sorcerers and wars and all that?"

"Do I ever!" Cappel said, clapping excitedly. "Sorcery, you say! Ezalen Skywing, what if I told you there were *entire branches* of magic that nobody today even knows how to practice?"

"I would believe you," Eza told him. "I've read so many stories where cities were destroyed, where libraries were burned and magic academies torn down. There has to be so much knowledge that's been completely lost to time."

Cappel leaned closer in delight. "Some of it is not lost, but hiding. Here. Look at this."

Eza's fingers wrapped around an ancient book, whose leather cover was cracking and whose pages were well worn. "*Legends of the Artomancers,*" he read, then looked up at Mr. Cappel. "What in all the loud noises is an

Artomancer?"

"You'll find out when you read the book," Cappel said with a wave of his hand. "It's an extremely rare book, by the way. I only know of twelve copies in existence, and this one is hundreds of years old. Don't look so worried, Ezalen. I'd rather have you read it, even if it gets damaged, than have it sitting here collecting dust." He smiled reassuringly at Eza. "Between *Heroes* and this one, you'll probably have your hands full for at least a week. Why don't you come back when you're in need of more material?"

"But I have three nayen," Eza protested weakly.

"There's nothing saying you have to spend it all today," Cappel reminded him. "Read what you have and then come back for more, okay?"

"Yes, sir."

"Besides," Cappel continued, "I suspect you'll read some things in *Heroes* and *Artomancers* that will make you very curious indeed. You'll be glad you saved some money to pursue those interests."

"You're right," Eza conceded with a sigh. "My father will wonder what's wrong if I return with only one book, though."

Cappel laughed, a rich sound that filled every room of the bookstore. "It's okay to surprise people every now and then," he told Eza.

Eza handed over one of his nayen, feeling as if the

book should have cost a lot more, and slipping the other two coins back into his pocket as he took a long smell of *Legends of the Artomancers*. "Can I come back tomorrow?"

"You're welcome here anytime, Ezalen, as long as your father approves."

Cradling the book in both hands, Eza stepped out onto Broad Avenue. For the first time all day he wasn't in a hurry, and he noticed the smell of the pine needles in the spring air. Some of them had fallen to the street, making a crunchy carpet underneath Eza's boots. He stepped on a few, listening to the sound and feeling the resistance of the needles. With the setting sun shining onto his face, he suddenly felt peaceful. He'd been happy before he had begun training as a dragon-companion, and even if he never got a dragon, things would be okay. He had his books, and he had his friends, and he lived with his father in the greatest city he'd ever seen or read about. Life was good after all.

He headed off to the market, skipping lightly. Along the way he met the eyes of an older man.

"I like your book!" the man said with a smile.

"Thanks!"

THREE

Cammie Ravenwood had waited *just about long enough* for Kalek and the trading group to return. *I mean, how long does it take to trade a couple things with people who barely speak?* she thought to herself. It should just go: lift up item, nod, give something in return, nod goodbye, and boom. Done.

However, she should have realized Kalek would want to talk...a lot. She herself had been subject to hours-long stories from the burly man, but they always ended up being entertaining, so she didn't normally mind. She preferred listening anyway.

That thought made Cammie flinch. She shouldn't *prefer* to listen. She should prefer to interject with her own stories and laugh until her sides hurt. But sometimes she just couldn't – or rather, she didn't want to. It was strange, wasn't it, that an Exclaimovian would sometimes rather have peace and quiet? Was that...*wrong?*

A loud chorus of laughter and shouts dragged her attention away from her thoughts, and Cammie looked around expectantly, pushing her glasses back up her nose. Kalek was back! His entire traveling party rode in the wagons behind him, all singing and laughing thunderously. Cammie smiled as she approached his wagon, waving her arms to catch his attention.

"Cammaina!" boomed Kalek, wearing an enormous grin as she bounded up to him. She'd worn her favorite dress, bright crimson and embroidered with gold and painted with shimmering colors that melted and flowed as she moved. "Have you been waiting long?" he teased.

Cammie glared dramatically at him. "You kept me waiting on purpose, you blundering baboon!" she joked, shoving his arm and ducking when he attempted to crush her in a hug, then jumping onto the wagon and swinging her legs over the side. "Sooooo...?"

"So what?" asked Kalek with a mischievous smirk, as if he knew he was playing hard-to-get.

She gave an exasperated groan. "You're impossible! THE INTROVERTIANS!" Cammie roared this last part, grinning and standing in the wagon, almost toppling over the edge in the process. "What were they like? Did they talk at all or were they just silent the way the books say? What did they trade you? Did they have dragons?!"

"You're sixteen now," he reminded her. "Next time I'll just bring you with me."

"Ugh! Riding three hours each way in a wagon just to LOOK AT PEOPLE WHO DON'T TALK?!"

As far as Kalek knew, Cammie was always like this. She went out of her way to chat and be loud like any normal Exclaimovian ought to do in social situations –

and she was an accomplished actress, with enough experience on the stage that she always played her character flawlessly. No one, as far as she knew, had ever suspected that she might be pretending. It would be treason of the highest order if she didn't act that way, if she wasn't properly Exclaimovian – and that scared her. The price of treason...

Cammie shut that thought down as quickly as she could. She wasn't treasonous. She wasn't odd. She was just...just a girl. There had to be other Exclaimovians who felt the same way...right?

No, there aren't. There are other PEOPLE who feel the same way. They're called Introvertians.

Suddenly aware that Kalek was in the middle of answering her questions, she snapped her focus back to him. She was supposed to be paying attention so she could keep the conversation going whenever there was the slightest pause. At least, that was the unspoken rule, and there were *lots* of unspoken rules in Exclaimovia. Someone had joked to Cammie once that Exclaimovians were allergic to silence, and that was exactly what it felt like to her. Any silence in a conversation had to be covered up by small talk, by jokes, by observations about the stupidest and most meaningless things – just as long as *something* was being said. Even when Cammie was alone the whole time waiting for Kalek to return, she'd been singing to herself, whacking tree branches with sticks, stomping her feet, and generally making all the racket that her little corner of the forest would let her make.

But Kalek had been peering at her for a while as he gave his answers, looking confused at why Cammie had suddenly gone silent. Had he noticed that she'd been lost in her own thoughts, that she'd chosen daydreaming over listening and listening over talking? She kept a calm exterior, but on the inside she was cringing. *They're going to start to wonder...*

Cammie quickly took charge, trying to redirect the conversation back to Kalek. She was uncomfortable and tired, so she asked him something that she knew would keep Kalek entertained and not focused on her. "Kalek! Tell me about one of your adventures before you retired. You said you'd fought a twenty-foot dragon, right?!"

"Fifty feet, at least," he corrected, puffing out his chest with an air of superiority. This was Kalek's favorite story to tell, and it changed every time. Cammie had learned how to probe and push in just the right way to bring out someone's pride when she wanted time to herself. It was manipulative, sure...but there wasn't another way. Besides, it worked. Kalek burst into his story, acting out daring swordfights and cursing a nonexistent beast, spinning a tale so thick with lies and exaggeration that Cammie found herself wishing she hadn't asked. It was a little sickening, having to decipher truth from lie.

But that was how life was in Exclaimovia: loud and vague.

Cammie forced herself to laugh as Kalek rounded on her and thundered the punchline to a joke she hadn't been paying attention to. He guffawed so hard at his own humor that he flopped backward in the wagon, covering his stomach as his chest heaved up and down. Cammie slid to the front of the wagon, running her fingers over the fine cloth and breaking out into soft song as Kalek calmed down. A few of the other Exclaimovians joined in with Cammie so she could jump to the harmony line, while Kalek took the bass harmony.

There was no other nation in the world that sang as well as Exclaimovia did. Even the Introvertians couldn't ignore that. Normally the music was loud and fun, but other songs, like the one they were performing now, were more delicate, and in good company could even be beautiful. This was the side of Exclaimovia that Cammie enjoyed the most. They sang the rest of the way back to the capital city of Pride, exchanging jokes every now and then, and laughing when one of them sang the wrong notes or words, enjoying every minute of the the time together.

Kalek was going to the Shouting Square to sell the food he'd bought from the Introvertians, but Cammie split off from him there. Her friends were waiting for her over by Declamation Square, and they ran up to her as she arrived, bombarding her with hugs and yells of greeting. Cammie grinned back before yelping in surprise as her best friend Alair swept her up in a hug and then set her down.

She and Alair were the same age and had been inseparable since childhood; she'd never told anyone her secret about not always being comfortable in Exclaimovia, but if she ever did tell, Alair would be the one. She'd dropped a few hints just to see how he'd react, and it had seemed like he might understand – but that was a *big* secret...

Ilaria and Keiko, the twins of the group, were a year younger than her. Then there was Naomi, the smartest of them all – or at least tied with Cammie – quiet like Cammie was, but definitely still an Exclaimovian, not a traitor...

"There's the birthday girl!" Alair teased.

"My birthday was *yesterday*," Cammie corrected with her hand on her hip and a smirking smile on her face.

Naomi bounced on her toes. "How does it feel to be an *adult* now, Cammie?"

"I got there five days before her," bragged Alair.

"Oh, for the sun's sake," Cammie grumbled dramatically. "We get treated to another round of Alair's boasting. Who votes to skip it?"

"ME!" shouted the other three all at the same time.

"What is this, the High Council?" protested Alair.

"Yes, it is," Cammie told him. "And the Council has spoken."

"Fine." Alair groaned and stretched. "Ugh. We have school tomorrow."

"School gets a *yay*, not an *ugh*," giggled Naomi. "But, Cammie, you said you were leaving the city today. Did you get to meet the Silent Ones?"

"Yeah, Cammie!" Ilaria and Keiko chimed in. "Tell us!"

Cammie chuckled, having to raise her voice over the normal loudness of the square. "No! You know I didn't. I just waited for Kalek at the border."

"Booooring," yawned Alair. "What was the point of waiting by yourself for hours with nothing to do and no one to talk to?!"

Cammie turned red. She saw Alair go blank for a moment and attempt to change what he said, but it was too late; the damage had been done.

"You're right!" Cammie interjected quickly, practically screaming over the swell of voices. "It was awful! I bet Kalek kept me waiting on purpose." It was, in fact, not awful, but the lie slipped out effortlessly, as lies often had to. The time of solitude really had been nice...although Cammie had to admit she'd been a little on edge by the end. *That* was the real reason she'd been tired and grumpy in the back of Kalek's wagon. As much as she loved being alone, she'd been surrounded by noise *all her life*, and was used to the constant stimulation. Being away from the buzz of people for too long felt strange, empty somehow, like biting into a spicy egg wrap but not tasting anything.

Alair nodded, then expertly changed the topic by cracking a joke, sending the group into roaring laughter. The noon bell rang through the courtyard, and Cammie and Alair broke off from the pair as the people in the square began to file off towards their homes. While Exclaimovians were often loud and always on the move, it was a tradition for everyone to head to their homes and spend time with family for a minimum of an hour when the bell tolled through the cities. Cammie didn't need the reminder anymore, though; she had memorized the exact time of day.

Alair and Cammie lived in the same place, the capital city of Pride, while Ilaria and Keiko were from the City of the Hunt nearby, and Naomi came from Strength just to the south. All the cities and towns were connected by beaten paths and roads, and none of them were closed off to travelers except for the palace complex near the center of Pride. Even occupants of Pride had to have certain clearance to be allowed through the bronze gate in the high wall surrounding the complex.

Alair and Cammie walked towards the palace, that massive wall looming over them. On top were flags bearing Exclaimovia's crest: a golden dragon, rising above bright orange flames on a red background.

They strolled along smooth cobblestone walkways, grinning and calling out in response to the friends they passed on the way home. Children raced and skipped along the path; the adults were hand in hand or arm in arm like Cammie and Alair were. One of the other unspoken rules in Exclaimovia was that the host, usually a male of the group, exchanged small talk and entertained his guests or friends. If they were in a pair, like now, it was Alair's job to host.

"I'm sorry for earlier," he started, gently squeezing her arm. "I saw I made you uncomfortable, and I didn't mean to." It wasn't standard small talk, but Cammie appreciated it – which made her feel even more odd. She was *supposed* to enjoy small talk, but she found herself preferring when the conversation went deeper and she had the chance to discuss things that really mattered.

She didn't say that out loud, though; she merely chuckled and leaned into his side, humming softly. "It's alright. I just don't think that's the sort of thing people should joke about."

"It wasn't a joke. Why didn't you just wait for them here in the city, with us, until they got back?" Alair's eyes were on her, and he was watching intently.

Cammie was an expert at disguising her true feelings – unless someone caught her by surprise, as Alair had earlier. Now, though, she was ready for him. "If I'd known they would take so long, I'd have waited here with you – or maybe gone with them. It would have been a way better story if I'd seen the Silent Ones with my own eyes."

"Spending time with your friends would have been even better than that. You know how the expression goes. Those in good company are good people – or something."

Cammie roared with laughter. "That's not how it goes at all," she objected, then gave the correct line: "Surround yourself with good people, for you become who you are most around."

Alair sighed. "How are you so good at that?"

"At what?" she asked, falling back in step with him.

"Just – words. Language. You get perfect marks on every test without even studying."

Cammie stiffened just the smallest amount at the compliment Alair had unknowingly given her. She was always wary with compliments, like most Exclaimovians were. Compliments were often used for flattery or manipulation, and most people were very skeptical of them. It wasn't at all unusual for someone to respond to a compliment by asking, "What do you want?" She knew Alair wasn't like that, though, so she tried to receive the kind words....but something inside her just kept gagging.

She forced herself back into the moment. "Perfect

memory, remember?" Cammie tapped the side of her head with her free hand and wrinkled her nose at him teasingly.

"Not that you need it," Alair said sourly, making a face like he was thinking of his own test scores. "I could use it, though."

"You can't just *learn* perfect memory, Alair." She watched his face darken and quickly added, "But – I could certainly help you study."

"Tonight?" he asked slyly, reverting back to his normal charming demeanor.

Cammie laughed. "If you really need it."

"I DO!" he insisted loudly. "We have a test tomorrow and I'm going to fail!"

"Not with my help, you won't. Now hurry up and let's get home. I'll come by before dinner, alright?" They had arrived at a small plaza with main roads branching off in all directions; Cammie would go to the right and Alair to the left. Their houses were within walking distance of each other. So was almost everything in the city of Pride, as long as you didn't mind walking.

"Deal. I'll tell my parents. They love you."

Cammie forced her lips into a strained smile. She seriously doubted that. His parents liked her rank – her *family's* rank, her wealth, not her as a person. Maybe she was just reading too much into it. "Right," she replied. "Well, see you!" She turned and ran down the avenue, waving at a few other people who called to her as she flew past, and sprinting down the path to a large house painted mostly red, with accent panels her family had kept white for contrast. Cammie had never been much of an athlete, preferring to spend time with her nose in a book – another oddity for an Exclaimovian – and the quarter-mile back to her house was just about as far as she could run without getting winded.

In a single smooth motion she swung open her home's front door, the creaky hinges announcing her arrival before she even stepped over the threshold. Doors in Exclaimovia were never locked; friends and family simply walked in whenever they wanted, often as loudly as possible.

A woman's voice shouted from farther back in the house, "Cammaina?"

"Hi, mom!" Cammie called, shutting the door behind her and walking into the cool, lavishly decorated house. There was music echoing from one of the upper rooms – her brother Aed, probably, practicing one of his performance pieces for school.

Cammie moved into the kitchen, surveying the food laid out across the counter. Eventually she picked a pastry and took a bite. "Where's dad?"

Her mother, Aileen, sighed and turned around. "He's on his way. He had a summons from the palace today." She waggled her fingers at her daughter dramatically.

"It'll be a new family record, you know. No one's ever been later than you to lunch before."

Cammie giggled and picked up another pastry, holding one in each hand. Aileen swatted playfully at her and Cammie ducked, laughing so hard she almost choked.

"Careful," sang a deep and familiar voice from the doorway of the kitchen.

"Hey, Aed." Cammie said, clearing her throat to greet her brother. He was two years older than her and the spitting image of their mom, with blond hair, blue eyes, and freckled skin. Cammie looked more like her dad; her hair was naturally dark brown when it wasn't dyed, and her skin was slightly tanned, but her eyes were her own – one blue and one brown. She was also the only one who wore glasses...maybe because of all the time she spent reading.

Her brother smiled and took a pastry. "Don't eat them all, Cammie," he teased, waving his treat in her face as she crossed the room to give him a hug.

Cammie wrinkled her nose at him and rolled her eyes. "Says the one who eats every meal like he's never seen food in his life."

"Good point," he agreed, ruffling his sister's hair affectionately and hugging her tightly.

"Aed," Cammie whined, attempting to wriggle out of her brother's grip. Aed was strong. Being a soldier-in-training, he had to be, but it didn't help that Cammie wasn't muscular in the slightest. She'd chosen to focus on training her mind while her brother trained his body...which meant she was stuck.

Their mother was laughing at them. "Alright, you two, break it up. Aed, don't crush your sister."

Cammie was released, and she playfully stuck her tongue out at her older brother.

Aileen turned to the two of them – almost as if she had waited until Alair arrived, so that her comments would have an audience. "Cammie, what did you do all morning? I saw you with that boy, Alair, earlier..." The tone of her mother's voice spelled out exactly what she was thinking: *Are you two finally together?*

Cammie recoiled theatrically and shrieked, "NO, MOM! STOP! We're just friends – you've known him for years!"

But Aileen gave her a knowing look and a raised eyebrow.

"I promise you we're just friends," Cammie insisted.

Aed hummed loudly, looking like he was trying to suppress a smirk, and Cammie groaned inside – *not you too, Aed!* "I don't know, Cammie," he teased. "You seem pretty close with him. Are you sure he knows you're *just friends*?"

"By the sun, shut up," Cammie snarled. "Yes, he knows, you idiot." She abruptly remembered the dinner-study session she'd planned with Alair and sighed in her head, knowing what was coming. "But, um..." She stammered over her words as both her brother and mother exchanged amused, knowing glances. "I promised him I'd help him study tonight and, um..."

Aed grinned and reached over to Cammie, attempting to ruffle her hair again. "Don't worry about it, little bit. We've all been there."

"Been where?!" she demanded, dodging her brother. "NOTHING is happening! IT'S LITERALLY JUST STUDYING!" Cammie jumped over the counter, dropping her pastries on it as she did, knocking a chair on its back in the process, desperate to get away from her brother who had launched himself at her, ready to tickle her to death.

At that moment the door opened and shut with a bang. Their father waltzed into the kitchen, looking unimpressed with the level of chaos in the house, as if surprised there wasn't more. "Welcome home, Barin," Aileen said happily from across the kitchen, leaning serenely against the wall and watching her children with an amused expression.

"DADDY!" Cammie screamed hysterically, laughing so hard she could barely walk straight. "SAVE ME!" She choked on her breath, stumbling behind her father and clinging to him. Barin chuckled, like the sound of thunder, a deep rolling laugh that started in his belly and ended in his chest. It was Cammie's favorite sound in the world.

However, instead of her father holding her brother back, Barin turned and grabbed her around the middle, heaving her onto his shoulder. Cammie writhed and squealed a protest, trying to squirm away, but with no more success than she'd had with her brother. Barin held his daughter in place and Aed attacked, tickling her sides until she thought she might pass out from lack of air. Aileen laughed from a safe distance away.

"MOOOOOM!" Cammie howled, attempting to kick her brother away.

Finally Aileen stepped in; she usually played the part of mediator. "Alright, you two. Quit torturing her."

Barin and Aed relented and Cammie collapsed onto the ground against her father's leg, breathing heavily and still giggling. "Thanks..." she breathed, taking her father's hand as he helped her up.

Barin peered at his daughter for a moment, almost hesitating before saying, "That dress is beautiful on you, firebug."

Once again, Cammie stiffened. She had noticed her father tripping on his words, something he rarely did. He knew better than anyone the weight of compliments in Exclaimovia. Cammie smiled, though, knowing her father had no hidden intentions, just like Alair hadn't. He was simply saying something nice to his daughter.

"Thank you, dad," she replied, smiling up at him, then added, "Oh oh oh! Mom said you got a summons to the palace! Did you? What was it for?!" Something pierced her thoughts and she paled. "They're not wanting to call you up to active duty again, are they?"

Actress or no, she couldn't help the note of panic and almost hysterical fear that bled into her voice. Her father had served in the past wars as a general, ten years ago when the Kingdom of Ironhand had invaded from the southeast. He had almost been killed twice, and only his brilliant leadership had kept Exclaimovia from being completely overrun. Barin's legendary legacy was what had driven Aed to want to follow in his footsteps, even though Exclaimovia hadn't seen war since that invasion. Barin himself had retired three years ago, with highest honors. If they were thinking about calling him back – well, whatever kind of problem would make them think those thoughts, it had to be really bad...

Aileen had looked up in alarm and almost dropped the plate she was holding, freezing in place as she waited for an answer. Barin studied his daughter, and Cammie couldn't quite identify what was flickering behind his eyes.

"No...it's not like that," he replied after a few beats of silence. He glanced at Aed, whose eyes were ever so slightly squinted in worry, but who looked almost eager in a way. It had been Aed's dream since childhood to serve with his father. Barin smiled a little *too* forcefully. "It's nothing to worry about."

You're lying! Cammie's brain screamed in protest. She'd always been able to tell when someone was lying to her. People had certain habits, certain tells, that gave them away when they attempted to hide it. Her father had just lied to them; he had faked a smile, clasped his hands in front of him, and cleared his throat. All three of those were tells. But why lie...?

Cammie felt hurt. She'd always been top of her classes, and she was loyal (well, except for the *possible traitor to Exclaimovia* thing, she realized with a pang of guilt), and had proven herself capable in more ways than her brother ever had. So why would her father lie to her? Why would he lie to their mother? Did he think they were too weak to handle the truth?

"Well, that's good then," said Aileen with a nervous laugh. "Come now. Let's all eat and talk. Cammie..." She paused, smiling mischievously. "I believe you have something you'd like to tell your father...or shall I?"

Cammie swallowed her millions of demands and questions and felt herself flush a deep red, her face hot. "No," she replied stiffly, trying to hide the nervous laughter bubbling in her chest. "It's nothing..." She took her seat at the table, beside Aed and to the right of their father. "It's just, er – well – Alair and I are going to study tonight before dinner, so..."

She trailed off at the glint in her father's eye.

"Well," he said slowly, scratching his head and grinning. "It's about time you two got together."

Cammie shrieked unintelligibly and almost flipped the table over, her face turning even redder and her glare sucking the warmth out of the air. The rest of her family burst into laughter, but once they'd calmed down, Barin nodded.

"Of course you can go," he said. "You don't need to ask us. We trust you."

If you trust me so much, then why lie to me?

Their mother nodded. "Yes, Cammaina," she agreed. "You're much less trouble than Aed was."

"Hey!" came an indignant shout, muffled by food, from her brother. Cammie laughed a little and leaned into her brother's side.

"I told you I'm the favorite," she sang in his ear, making him swivel in his seat and attempt to protest. However, his words were dulled by the mouthful of food he accidentally choked on instead. Once again the table roared with laughter.

That afternoon of family time contained of Cammie's favorite things. They sang together; Aed taught her the harmonies to a song he had written; their father took Aed out to spar for a while; and Cammie and her mother sat out on the porch to sew and watch the men duel. Before she knew it, the sky was darkening – it always got dark *so early* this time of year, when spring was just starting to arrive – and Cammie was packing her textbooks and notes into a bag to take to Alair's house.

Her family had taken up teasing her again and she sighed, attempting to ignore it by talking over them. "I'll be back sometime tonight," she said loudly. "I don't know how long it'll take." She deliberately tried to ignore her brother, who was batting his eyelashes and pantomiming her and Alair hugging and kissing. Sometimes he really was a child, Cammie thought. She smiled and shoved Aed away, hugging her mother and father goodbye before stepping out onto the cobblestone roads to head to Alair's house.

The walk was relatively peaceful; she could hear the faint songs from other families getting ready for dinner like whispers on the wind, but the streets were mostly empty as people had gone home for mealtime. A gentle breeze floated through the air and Cammie felt content. She knew she shouldn't like this moment of peace and tranquility, but it was nice.

The calm was short-lived, however, as Cammie was still twenty feet away from Alair's doorstep when he burst out, nearly throwing the door off its hinges and wearing a look like he was about to carry her into the house. "YOU CAME!" he cried, in a voice she was sure could be heard all the way to the palace, lifting her off her feet in an enormous hug.

"Yes, I came, you idiot; now put me down," Cammie demanded, making no effort to actually get free from his hold. He carried her through the house and into the living room before releasing her.

"Why hello there, Cammaina," said a young woman, directing a crinkly-eyed smile at Cammie and offering a hug. "It's so nice to see you again. I do hope you'll join us for dinner before your study session."

Cammie smiled. "Of course. Thank you for having me."

Alair slung an arm over her shoulders and leaned into her ear. "They've been teasing me nonstop about you, so if they act stranger than normal, that's why."

Cammie began laughing. "Don't worry. I get it. My family acts like they expect us to get engaged tonight or something."

"I KNOW!" shouted Alair just as his father and two girls came in. "MY DAD – I mean, er...hi, dad." Alair laughed nervously and Cammie had to lean against a chair from laughing so hard.

"What's this about me, Alair?" the man inquired, as the two girls behind him – Alair's younger sisters, Cammie knew – giggled and whispered to each other.

"Nothing..." mumbled Alair, giving Cammie an eye roll behind his father's back.

"Well then, if it's nothing, let's eat!" his father boomed, grinning and clapping his hands joyously.

"Hope you're hungry. They went overboard," Alair murmured in Cammie's ear as they walked arm in arm towards the kitchen.

"Don't they always go overboard?" she asked, remembering the other times she'd been invited over or had just showed up in their living room after school.

"Yes," he admitted with a sigh. "But this is just...more. It's like she expected you to bring an army with you."

"Or an engagement party," Cammie teased, jabbing Alair in the side and running ahead of him into the kitchen.

"Hey!" he shouted, chasing after Cammie. When he finally caught up, her delighted laughter did *nothing* to stop his family from whispering and winking at them.

FOUR

Ezalen had always liked school; it was a chance to read and learn things, and he found that the more he learned, the more he wanted to learn. Starting at the Dragon Academy two years before had only made things better. The Academy was hosted at Carnazon Fortress, an old castle on the northeast side of Tranquility where the city met the Impassable Mountains. According to *Heroes of Introvertia*, that fortress had been the site of at least twelve major battles, from the War of Independence against Exclaimovia to the War of Five Sorcerers to the Northern War. The outer walls were pocked and scarred with damage that might have been magical in origin. The whole place was like a living book, and Eza loved exploring every corner of it – except for the few places in the basement that weren't accessible to students.

This year wasn't his favorite, though. Third-year students – those who had turned fifteen in the past year and finished their vow of silence – were supposed to have their own dragons by now, and almost none of them actually did. Most of the curriculum assumed that students would have dragons with them, and the classes had been built around hands-on techniques. With no dragons, the professors had been forced to scramble, coming up with things to teach that didn't require dragons. The first five weeks of class had been...well, they'd been okay. They'd been better than not being at school and around his friends, Eza thought. But they weren't what he'd been hoping for. Thankfully this was week five, and at the end of week six there was a two-week break before the next term of classes began. Maybe that would give the government time to sort out their problems. Maybe Eza would return from the term break and find a dragon waiting for him.

Most of the students lived at school during the week and spent the weekends at home, so on this bright and sunny Monday morning, Eza walked excitedly through Carnazon's south gate, the wide arch leading through the thick brown stone walls. Beyond the gate was the central courtyard, where a number of his classmates had already gathered to share stories and news. Eza's two best friends, Shanna Cazaran and Razan Enara, were deep in conversation to the left by the entrance to their company's barracks, and they immediately angled over to meet him.

"Eza!" Shanna said excitedly, running over to wrap him in a hug. She was so similar to Eza in appearance and personality that they were often mistaken for siblings; the only difference was her hair, which was much darker than his. "How was your weekend?"

"Great!" he said, dropping his forty-pound backpack

to the ground with an almighty thump. "Look what I got!"

He handed *Heroes of Introvertia* to Shanna and *Legends of the Artomancers* to Razan, watching their eyes get wide as they thumbed open the covers in awe. "You'll share them, won't you?" Razan asked hopefully. He was shorter than Eza and Shanna, a little more serious and a little less lighthearted. Eza hadn't liked Razan at first, but he'd also been taught not to dismiss people without truly knowing them. The two had become friends in time, united by their love of ringball and history.

"Of course!" Eza told him. "We'd better get going, though. We have to drop our things off in the barracks before class."

Shanna and Razan both reluctantly handed over the books and Eza strapped his backpack on, staggering a bit under the weight of his pleasure books, his textbooks, his tools for Survivalship class, and his soap and other necessities for the week. The castle's barracks were split into four wings, so the students were divided into four "companies" upon arrival, based on their performance on the intake test that measured aptitude and personality. Victory Company was mainly for the students who wanted to be battlefield soldiers after graduation. They were always the most competitive when it came to ringball, and the Company Games, and basically anything else that could be won. Eza was *extremely* competitive, but he'd noticed there was a big difference between him (he liked the pure joy of competing and didn't much care whether he actually won) and the Victory students (who generally got very upset if they didn't win). That might have been why he landed in Harmony Company, Victory's arch-rival, the company for students who valued camaraderie and friendship above all. Alongside Victory and Harmony was also Excellence Company; if there was an opportunity to push themselves, to achieve more than they'd thought possible, an Excellence student would be up for it. Their arch-rivals were Sun Company, the ones who valued fun and joy and laughter more than achievement or accomplishments.

Shanna and Razan were with Eza in Harmony. That had been a disappointment to Razan, who really wanted Victory Company and battlefield duty, but Eza and Shanna reminded him often that front-line soldiers could come from any company, even if most came from Victory. For their part, Eza and Shanna were happy enough just to be chosen as companions, and they didn't share Razan's enthusiasm for combat. Eza was studying to be a Ranger, the same as his father had been for a while, and Shanna wanted to give young dragons the formal training they received before being assigned to third-year students. At the end of year five, all the Dragon Academy students would officially graduate and receive their duty assignments.

The Harmony barracks were on the west side, and they sprawled to all four levels of the castle. A lounge in the middle separated the boys' from the girls' dorms, and each dorm in turn was broken up by year, with separate sections for the first- through fifth-year students, some on the main level and some up or down the stairs. The class size varied a little, but there were between thirty and forty girls and an equal number of boys for each year, for a total of around three hundred and fifty Harmony students and around fifteen hundred students total in the school. Eza had done some quick and dirty math when he was a first-year, and based on those numbers he guessed that there were a total of ten to fifteen thousand dragon companions alive in the kingdom.

Directly north of the Harmony barracks were Victory Company's, while Sun Company's were in the south wall, and Excellence Company's were across the square. A hallway wrapped around the northern rim of the second floor and connected the two sides; off it were dozens and dozens of classrooms, including the one where Professor Ozara taught History – one of Eza's very favorite subjects. Of course, he also liked Dragon Care, Military Tactics, Survivalship, Writing, Diplomacy...well, he liked them all, come to think of it, but History was his favorite.

Shanna took a left turn as they entered the lounge to drop her bag in the girls' dorm while Razan followed Eza to the right and into the boys' dorm. It was almost eight in the morning; breakfast would only be served for another hour, and then History would begin at nine sharp. Some of the boys were still in their bunks as Eza heaved his backpack over his bed. There was a smaller canvas shoulder bag inside the backpack; he stuffed his textbooks into it and clasped his survival tools to an outside loop. Suitably lightened, he bounded out the door to wait for his friends.

The lounge was well lit by large windows that opened onto the inner courtyard, and was about the size of Eza's entire house. It was rarely the site of large gatherings or raucous conversations – this was Introvertia, after all – but at almost any hour of the day or night, small groups of students could be found clustered together, laughing and discussing something of interest. One of Eza's older friends, a fifth-year named Malen, waved him over with an enormous smile.

"Eza! Victory Company challenged us to a game of ringball this afternoon. Are you in?"

Very early in Eza's first year, someone had found his greatest weakness: competition. He was as kind, polite, and unthreatening as could be, but if he had the chance to go toe to toe with somebody – anybody – in something – anything – he would jump at it. Ringball was a game most Introvertians played from the time they could walk; a rubber ball could be kicked or thrown, with different rules for how it could be moved with the feet or with the hands, the objective being to hurl it through the opponent's goal. In official games that goal was a large metal ring, but in the courtyard of Carnazon it was usually a rough circle chalked onto the opposite walls of the courtyard. Sometimes they drew a third circle onto the wall where the south gate was and a fourth circle onto the north wall by the door into the mess hall, and played every company for themselves with two or even three balls; those games were absolute chaos, and Eza loved them. There were too many students at the school for just one game, so the normal setup was for the fifth-years to play for half an hour, then the fourth-years, and so on down the line until the game was over after two and a half hours.

"I've got History and Survivalship this morning and Tactics from one to two after lunch," Eza told him. "As long as the game starts late enough, I'll be there."

"You'll be fine. The game starts at two, and the third-years will play at three. See you there!"

"Thanks!"

By then Shanna had come back into the common room. "Ringball later?" she asked, eagerness in her eyes. She usually played center forward, the main attacker, while Eza played on the right wing.

"Yeah!" said Eza, slapping hands with Shanna. "This is going to be a great day!"

Razan was dawdling for some reason, so Shanna and Eza headed to the mess hall on the first floor without him. The breakfast meal was always large and delicious, since the students did physical training in addition to their book work. Today's dish was a sweet mash of mountain corn and eggs, seasoned with spices that grew on the western slopes of the Impassable Mountains just outside Tranquility. Eza swallowed his food almost without chewing, and as he did so, he noticed Lahan Meara, from Victory Company. "Lahan!" he said, flagging the boy down. "You did a great job on your speech in Dragon Care class last week. I meant to tell you."

"Thanks!"

It occurred to Eza that the whole "friendly rivalry between companies" thing would have worked a lot better in a place that wasn't Introvertia. There was too much *friendly* and not enough *rivalry*.

Survivalship class dealt with techniques for keeping a companion and his dragon alive in the woods using only the things they'd be likely to find or scrounge. So far in his first two years Eza had learned how to find kindling, make a fire, build a fishing pole and net, construct a lean-to shelter, and dozens of other things. The third year was supposed to involve providing for a dragon's needs, but

Professor Grenalla had been forced to adapt, and the class had stayed interesting.

The professor was already at her desk when Eza entered the room fifteen minutes before class was due to begin. Eza smiled and waved at her, then spotted his friends in their usual place by the courtyard windows. Some people might have been distracted by having a window next to them, their attention able to wander at a moment's notice, but Eza had found that it helped him to concentrate. Strangely, if he wasn't near the window, he kept wondering what was going on outside; sitting next to it, and being able to see that nothing interesting was happening, set him at ease.

His notebook was out on his desk and his ink pen in his hand as soon as Professor Grenalla called the class to attention. She was barely older than Eza's father, but with permanently tanned skin and leathery hands that spoke of a life spent outdoors. When she smiled, which was often, the corners of her eyes wrinkled like Eza would have expected from someone much older than her, the same way Mr. Cappel's did. As a Ranger in the King's Army, she had distinguished herself on the northern border, keeping the outlying farming villages safe from the loose tribes and roving brigands that sat between Introvertia and the Kingdom of Claira further to the northeast. She told stories sometimes in class, on the days when she finished her lessons early, and those stories fired Eza's imagination even more than most stories tended to.

But there was a difference, wasn't there? Mazaren and Arjera were long gone, and that tale was over. The stories the professor told were true, and they were really happening today, and Eza could be in them one day. His very own dragon would come screaming out of the sapphire blue northern sky at his command and tear apart bandits who were threatening a merchant caravan, or scan the rolling plains for a child who had wandered away from her family. He'd always been told he had a vivid imagination, but when the professor spoke, it was almost like Eza could *really see* things happening right in front of his eyes, could describe the color of the bandits' horses and the pattern of their cloaks.

This lesson dealt with the proper use of a dragon as a camp scout. Again, the lesson was supposed to be conducted with a dragon on each student's shoulders, but circumstances did not permit that, so Professor Grenalla chalked some diagrams on the board, showing her class the heights and angles that would permit a dragon the best view of the widest area around a companion's campsite. "The dragon will be your eyes and ears in the sky," the professor finished, wiping chalk dust from her hands. "Use it well. You can't afford to be taken by surprise in the wild. Which reminds me..."

She reached under her desk and pulled out a stack of

roughly forty folders, one for each student in the class. An excited murmur began to ripple among the students, and Professor Grenalla held up her hand for silence. At last the class had calmed, and the professor continued. "Opening your packets, you will see the instructions for your Spring Survival Practicum. Each of you has been given a map to a location in the Very Large Forest, and a list of activities you are expected to perform and document. These range from building a fire to foraging for food to mapping your immediate surroundings. If you can borrow your family's dragon for the duration of the practicum, you are welcome to."

A week in the woods? Eza could hardly contain his excitement. He'd known this was coming, but he thought it was supposed to be later in the term. Maybe the professors had moved it up since the students could do the whole thing without needing a dragon.

He flipped open his folder and examined the map first. His location was far to the east, almost as far as the Trading Circle where he and Uncle Tully had met the folks from Yelling. That made him uneasy at first; what if more of the rude people somehow came across him while he was camping? Then he got really excited: that would add an extra challenge to the week, wouldn't it? He imagined lurking on the edge of the forest road while loud interlopers thundered around, and he saw himself hiding from them and spying on their movements. Oh yes, this was going to be *fun*.

"Where's your spot?" he asked Shanna.

"A few miles from Tranquility, down near the river." She showed him. "I'll get to eat all the fish I can catch!"

"If you can catch any," teased Razan. "You two are lucky. I got a spot just up the Impassable Mountains, only about half a mile from Tranquility. I'll still be able to see the city walls through the trees."

"That's good training," Eza reasoned. "There may be a time when you and your dragon have to spy out an enemy city."

"Huh," said Razan. "Good point. I didn't think of that."

"And Shanna, you may have to watch a river and report on the movement of ships or soldiers."

"Not the Rapidly Flowing River, though," she pointed out. "It has so much whitewater that nothing can get up or down it."

"Right, but there are other rivers, off to the north and west." None of the three of them had ever been to those farther parts of the kingdom, and certainly not to the wild lands that lay beyond the borders. The Very Large Forest, and the well maintained forest road that ran from Introvertia to the Kingdom of Yelling, was a manicured backyard by comparison. "It's going to be great," Eza told them, unable – and in fact not even trying – to hide his excitement. "We're going to be Dragon Rangers!"

"Minus the dragons," Razan said bitterly.

For the rest of the week, Eza could think of nothing else. An entire week of living by himself in the woods! And, better still, immediately after the practicum was his mid-term break, the two-week gap between class sessions that was supposed to (this was turning into a crude joke, Eza thought) provide the advanced students more time to practice with their dragons. So, if he wanted, Eza could actually take *three* weeks in the woods, which would surely earn him extra credit from Professor Grenalla. He was sure his father could find someone else to run to the market for him in the meantime.

Ezarra had been very pleased indeed to hear about his son's practicum, and had spent quite a long time telling Eza all about his own survivalship practicum, twenty years in the past. Eza listened, careful to learn everything he could, and then asked, "Dad, can I take Neemie with me?"

"I don't see why not," Ezarra said after a few moments of thought. Ezarra himself was not a Ranger or a combat soldier, obviously, as he spent his time at home and not on the frontiers or in an army barracks. He was part of the political track, the people-in-offices part of the program, tasked with keeping records of all the dragon-companion families throughout Tranquility and the outlying districts, and making sure any children from those families got their invitation to Carnazon at the proper time. It was more difficult than it sounded, Eza had come to realize. With nearly twenty thousand companions in the government's service at any time (Eza's own estimate had been a little on the low side), that was a lot of soldiers being given new assignments, a lot of people having kids and forgetting to tell the program office, a lot of companions retiring or moving or dying – and in each of those cases, the records had to be updated.

"Can I ask you a question, dad?"

"You just did," Ezarra said with a smile. "But I'll give you one more."

"What did you want to be when you graduated from Carnazon?"

Ezarra's eyes got distant and the smile faded from his face. Eza watched in alarm, wondering if he'd asked the wrong question and accidentally offended his father. Eza hated upsetting people, almost more than he hated anything else in life – not more than he hated the way those people from the Kingdom of Yelling had treated him, but close.

"I wanted to be a Ranger," Ezarra admitted, the smile returning. "I loved the woods, which is why I've taken you hiking and camping so much. I was overjoyed to find you wanted to be a Ranger yourself."

"But you took a job in an office," pressed Eza.

"I did. For you. I wanted to be here when you grew up, not be off on a hillside somewhere missing my son's fifteenth birthday. I have a lot of respect for the people who do that, you know. But for me...it just wasn't right. I put my dreams aside so you could have the life you wanted."

A lump rose in Eza's throat. "Do you regret it?" he said in a hushed whisper.

The question hung in the air as the silence stretched longer and longer. In Introvertia it was always okay to take all the time you needed to think through your answer before you opened your mouth; no one was going to start pestering you for an immediate response. The curiosity nearly broke Eza in half, though, and he forced himself to stay patient.

At last – months or years later, it seemed to Eza – his father cleared his throat. "Regret is a strong word," Ezarra said. "I don't regret a single moment of being here for you, especially after your mother died. I feel I've been the best father I could possibly have been."

"You have," Eza reassured him, hoping his eyes didn't get any wetter than they already were.

"But I will tell you that if you have a chance to live your dreams, you should do it. Take chances. Don't play it safe. I played it safe for you, so that you don't have to. Go be Ezalen Skywing. That's what the world needs, more than anything else."

"I will," promised Eza, very seriously.

"I'm going to hold you to that," Ezarra said. It was the most solemn that Eza had ever seen his father. "You're fifteen now. According to Introvertian law, you became an adult on your thirteenth birthday. You have rights and responsibilities that children don't have, and the only thing you can't do is get married until you hit the Age of First Marriage at seventeen. One of those responsibilities is to live in such a way that, when you look back on your life fifty years from now, you have nothing but smiles and satisfaction. You want to know that you made a difference, that other people's lives were better because you existed. Nothing – and I mean absolutely nothing, Eza – feels better than that."

With those words ringing in his ears, Eza left home on Friday immediately after classes ended, determined to cover the thirty miles to his campsite by dusk on Saturday.

FIVE

Cammie sat in front of her bedroom mirror a week and a half after her "study session" with Alair, carefully dabbing makeup onto her face. Like a lot of things about life in Exclaimovia, she had mixed feelings about what she was doing. Cammie *loved* makeup, but most Exclaimovians – men and women alike – wore even more makeup than Cammie needed for the theater plays she'd acted in. The style in Exclaimovia was, in Cammie's view, excessive: bright colors around the eyes, drawing attention to them, as if everyone was having a competition to see who could be the most garish. Cammie didn't like the way she looked with all that paint on her face; she didn't want to hide her face, and wished she could do something more understated, but that wasn't acceptable. *Do something different with your face,* was the rule, but if she wanted to do something *REALLY* different, something less obnoxious, she'd get strange looks. *Be different, as long as it's the same different as everyone else.*

Her conversation with Kalek bubbled up to the surface of her mind, and her perfect recall allowed her to see it as if it were happening right in front of her. The *moment* she'd acted just a little bit unusual, the *moment* she'd been just a little bit quieter than she was supposed to, she'd gotten sideways glances from him. All these unwritten rules were exhausting to her, and there were days – a *lot* of days – when she wished she could have been in a place where she didn't have to follow them anymore.

Introvertia couldn't really be as bad as everyone said, right? They couldn't *really* go their entire lives without ever talking to anyone. That *had* to be a myth. But no one she knew had ever been to Introvertia; that kingdom was closed to outsiders, and judging from what Kalek had said, any proper Exclaimovian would have been bored to tears there in less than ten minutes.

But Cammie wasn't exactly a proper Exclaimovian, was she?

She tried to shove the thought out of her mind as soon as it occurred to her; there was *no way* she could actually go visit Introvertia...could she? But she was sixteen now, an adult, as Naomi had reminded her. If she wanted to go...her parents couldn't stop her. She'd heard of several older friends going on trips to celebrate their sixteenth birthday – okay, so those trips weren't usually in the middle of the school year, but Cammie's parents loved traditions and certainly wouldn't object –

Try as she might to get rid of the idea, it just didn't want to go anywhere.

Besides, incredible stories were almost as good as

money in Exclaimovia. Forget Kalek and his stupid made-up fifty-foot dragon – if Cammie showed up with stories about seeing Introvertia with her own eyes, she'd be the talk of Pride, maybe even the whole kingdom! Suddenly she wondered why no other Exclaimovians had ever tried to sneak in and find out more about Introvertia.

Maybe they hadn't felt the need...or maybe they knew there was no way they could ever fit in with a people who didn't mind *not talking* from time to time. They'd have been found out instantly, arrested and sent home – or worse. Cammie, though, just might be the one who could pull it off.

Face hidden underneath caked-on makeup, she met Alair and her other friends for the walk to school. The morning classes were – well, they were okay, Cammie thought. She spent the whole time daydreaming about telling her family and friends stories of Introvertia, and the astonished looks on their faces as they listened intently. Alair passed the test she'd helped him study for, and she'd gotten perfect marks on it, which happened almost all the time thanks to her flawless memory. The only time she ever *didn't* get a perfect mark was if she misunderstood a question...or if she hadn't done the assigned reading because she was rehearsing for a play, which was more common than she wanted to admit.

Her final morning class dismissed shortly before noon

and the family-hour bell rang while she and Alair were walking home, arm in arm as usual. Cammie said a quick goodbye and hustled back to her house as quickly as she could; she didn't want to get another earful from her mother about being late for family time again.

But when she got home, the front door...was *locked*.

That hadn't happened in years, not since her father was still in the army. When it had happened then, though, it had only meant one thing. Her father was in a top-secret briefing inside.

Curiosity overpowered Cammie. This wasn't a coincidence, not after that lie her dad had told the week before. If there was one thing Cammie hated, it was suspense – well, also she hated being in silence for too long, but suspense was probably a close second. Impulsively she decided to find out where they were talking and spy on them.

She crept around the right side of the house, ignoring the odd looks she got from people on the street. No one was in the living room, or the guest bedroom. Aed's curtains were open – his room was an absolute mess, Cammie thought; he needed to clean *badly* – but no one was inside. The curtains on her parents' windows were closed, but Cammie listened as intently as she could, ear to the glass as she tried to tune out the noise of the crowd walking home for their family hours. She was pretty sure she couldn't hear anything.

So around to the kitchen she went, peeking up over the windowsill and immediately dropping back to the ground. Her father was seated, with his back to her, and at the other three places around the table were two other generals and a member of the Exclaimovian High Council. Cammie was in her side yard now, away from the street, so things were a little quieter. She got as close to the glass as she dared and listened in.

Barin was shaking his head in protest. "This is not right," he insisted. "There was no wisdom in such a decision. All you're going to do is antagonize the –"

"What are you going to do?" the councilman cut in. "Tell the Introvertians?"

"We should," Barin insisted, placing a palm on the table for emphasis. "We should admit this to them right away and return their dragons. Surely they know by now that *hundreds* of their dragons are missing, and when they find out we're the ones who stole them, it's going to create a diplomatic incident."

"A diplomatic incident," repeated one of the generals mockingly. "This is a great moment for Exclaimovia! There's a dragon on our *flag*, for the sun's sake, but we haven't had dragons in our kingdom for thousands of years ever since the Introvertians left to start their own nation. Now we can again! We can train our own fighting army of them! The Introvertians haven't gone to war against anybody in – well, ever, I think – but just *imagine* a sky full of dragons, swooping down on the armies of Ironhand –"

"You don't think Ironhand will invade *immediately* when they find out we're trying to make an army of dragons? We can't keep this a secret from them forever – or from the Introvertians." Barin shook his head furiously. "You should never have listened to that K-" It sounded like her father had said a name after that, but Cammie couldn't make it out.

"That's why we need you to return to active duty," the other general insisted. "Ironhand wouldn't dare come against us if they knew Barin Ravenwood was leading our armies again."

"Who's to say they wouldn't ally with Introvertia and attack us from both sides?" Barin argued.

That thought seemed not to have occurred to *any* of the other three, and they exchanged nervous looks.

"Give the dragons back," Barin said, forcefully, but so quietly that Cammie almost couldn't hear him through the window. Sometimes *not* yelling was a good way to get a point across, she had noticed.

"Out of the question," said the councilman.

Barin shook his head. "So what you're telling me is that you've made foolish decisions that put you in a horrible situation, and now you need your most famous general to come bail you out – but you won't actually listen to my advice or take any of my recommendations.

The army is still weak from the loss of so many good soldiers and officers in the last war, and here you all are, making *stupid* choices that could lead to another war, and acting like *I'm* out of line for counseling caution!"

There was silence – and Cammie couldn't help but be impressed that her father had made *three* Exclaimovians speechless.

"So...is that a no?" one of the generals ventured at last.

"It is not," Barin said immediately. "I accept the offer to return to active duty, on one condition: I return to my old rank and status as the highest-ranking general in the kingdom."

"Done," said both other generals at the same time.

"Good. Since you both report to me now, I order you to return the dragons."

Cammie slumped to the ground to keep from laughing hysterically at her father's maneuver. But the response was probably going to be important, so she choked off the laughter and peeked through the window again.

"– was the decision of the king himself," the councilman said. "We don't have the authority to overrule it."

"The king has gotten bad counsel," Barin told them. "I will try to make him see reason. For now...you're all dismissed."

Cammie lingered in the side yard until she was sure

her father's guests were gone and down the street, and then she breathed very hard for a few moments and messed up her hair, trying to make it look like she'd been rushing home. She banged open the front door – which was unlocked now – and shouted, "SORRY I'M LATE!"

Her father faked a smile – Cammie could *tell* it was fake – and came from the kitchen to wrap her up in a hug. "Welcome home, firebug."

"How was your morning, daddy?" she asked brightly, immediately regretting the words. It was the same question she asked all the time, but today she *knew* the answer, and she'd just put her father in a position where he was probably going to lie.

"Oh, you know," he said, worry showing around his eyes despite the smile on his face. "The army wants me back."

I knew that a week and a half ago, she thought to herself. "Are you thinking about it?"

The smile faded and worry was all that remained now. That scared Cammie. Her father was strong and brave. If he was uneasy, then this must be *really* bad.

"I am," he said. "The army is not the same now that I'm gone. Some things are happening, and I may be the only one who can help fix them. There's no war. Just...some things."

That had been surprisingly honest – but now Cammie was stuck, because normal-Cammie would be barraging him with questions like "What things" and "Why are you the only one" and "But you're not going to have to leave home, are you?" Since she'd snooped outside, she already knew all the details, and she didn't want to make things any more difficult for her father. Instead she just hugged him again. "I love you, daddy. And I know you'll make the right choice."

The smile was back. "I hope so, firebug."

That hour of family time was one of Cammie's finest accomplishments as an actress. She'd shrieked and cackled and interrupted her way all through lunch, not giving a single indication that she'd just learned one of the most terrible secrets imaginable. Exclaimovia – her own people – had stolen dragons from Introvertia. What if the Silent Ones got mad and invaded? That wasn't likely; they hadn't declared war in the whole history of their kingdom, she knew, and the only times they'd ever fought were when they'd been directly attacked. But what if they considered this an attack? Or what if – as her father had said – the kingdom of Ironhand decided to invade again, and the whole Introvertian army came marching through the Very Large Forest at the same time? Exclaimovia wanted to train an army of dragons – well, Introvertia already *had* one! This was wrong; this was all wrong...

Somehow she faked her way through her afternoon

classes at school, but all the pretending had left her emotionally exhausted by the time she got home. She'd even had to turn down Alair's invitation to another study session, and he hadn't been persuaded by her loud insistence that nothing was wrong. She couldn't remember ever lying to him before – hiding her big secret from him, yes, but not lying to him –

Her secret...

All the thoughts she'd had that morning crashed back together, as if they'd all been leading up to this moment. Sixteenth-birthday trip. Wanting to see Introvertia. Well – now she had something to tell them. Now she had something she *needed* to tell them. They had to know what had happened to their dragons – maybe, with her father in charge of the army, they would decide to negotiate with him rather than attack...

That just made her feel like even more of a traitor. She had found out a secret so huge that her father had *locked the door* over it, and her first instinct was to blab it to Introvertians. But – that was the right thing to do, wasn't it? "If you know the right thing and don't do it, you've done evil," she said to herself, hands behind her head as she lay in her bed staring at the ceiling. She didn't know which Exclaimovian philosopher had said the phrase, but she'd always liked the way it sounded.

Stealing dragons was *wrong*. It was so wrong that *even the people who had done it* were worried about being invaded from two sides if anyone found out. That settled it for Cammie. Her father was going to rejoin the army and do everything he could to persuade Exclaimovia to do the right thing. And Cammie...

Cammie was going to Introvertia, to try and persuade *them* to do the right thing – and forgive her people, and get her dragons back without there being a war. And, of course, come back with the most legendary stories that any Exclaimovian had ever told. Maybe she'd be famous! She could write a book, and travel around giving lectures. People would pack theaters to listen to her talk about her time among the Silent Ones!

She knew from her geography class exactly how far it was to Introvertia, and could figure out how much food she'd need to take with her, although she'd never been a big eater. It was more the distance she was worried about; Cammie spent most of her time with her nose in a book, and didn't know if her legs were physically capable of carrying her the forty-five miles from Pride to Introvertia. She'd never slept outside before and didn't even own a sleeping bag. There weren't supposed to be wild animals in the Very Large Forest, the books said, but the books could be wrong...

But her father was talking about *war* if something didn't happen. Cammie could endure a few days of discomfort if it meant preventing a war. Now that she thought about it – she wasn't being a traitor at all, was she? She was *helping* Exclaimovia by saving them from a two-front invasion.

That made her feel a lot better, and also made her feel like this was something she *had* to do. If those people who'd talked to her father were among the highest Exclaimovians in the land, then maybe she didn't want to be Exclaimovian after all, anyway. Maybe Introvertia really *was* supposed to be her home.

Hopefully the Silent Ones weren't as quiet as the books – and that nickname – had made them seem. She could handle *alone*. She couldn't handle constant silence, not even if it meant coming back with stories that would make her famous.

An hour later, she'd stuffed a pack full of all the supplies she could think of, left a note for her parents in which she vaguely explained that she was going on a sixteenth-birthday trip, and started walking west.

Her mother might worry about her – especially since this was all so sudden and that note was the first they'd heard of any kind of trip – but she knew her father would trust her judgment.

The next two days were the most miserable Cammie could ever remember being. Her leg muscles had burned after the first hour, and her back had been sore after a night of trying and failing to sleep on the ground, and she had run out of songs to sing, and every time she got quiet, the silence of the forest seemed to press in on her until she felt like she had to push it back with a song or a monologue or randomly shouting the names of objects she happened to see. By her estimation, she'd gone almost half the distance by then...which meant there was no point in turning around, because it would be just as easy to continue as it would be to go home.

She was singing loudly to herself in the afternoon of her third day on the road when a voice suddenly said, "Hey!"

Cammie spasmed in surprise, but somehow kept from screaming. A boy was in front of her, about the same age as her, maybe an inch or two shorter. His hair was sandy brown and his clothes were green and gray, like he'd been meaning to blend into the forest on purpose.

Somewhere deep inside she knew it. She'd met an Introvertian. But she was also tired and sore and exasperated, so there was no telling what was going to come out of her mouth...

"You interrupted my song," she accused him.

SIX

The boy was stepping away from his tree, and a sudden panic filled Cammie. What if he wasn't friendly? What if he *looked* like an Introvertian, but was some kind of bandit? She sensed an odd heat in the palms of her hands, like nothing she'd ever felt before. The boy looked at her, but not looking her in the eyes, almost as if he was trying to make sense of her makeup. Then he looked down at her clothes – her very loud, very Exclaimovian clothes. "You're from the Kingdom of Yelling," he said at last.

"The *what*?" Cammie snapped – not meaning to, but she was so hungry and so scared that it just came out that way.

"The Kingdom of People Yelling and Having No Concept of Personal Space."

For some reason that was the funniest thing in the world to Cammie, and she *exploded* into laughter, holding her sides and doubling over. But something loud screamed next to her, and Cammie fell back in surprise as she saw a bright red dragon soaring up into a high tree branch.

"A DRAGON!" she shouted.

"Yep," said the boy. "And if she were a wild dragon,

you'd be extra crispy right now. Making loud noises around dragons isn't a great idea."

Cammie knew her mouth was hanging open in amazement. "IS IT YOURS?!"

The boy cringed at the shouting – oh, so *that* was why he'd made that joke about the Kingdom of Yelling – but answered the question. "Neemie's not an *it*. She's a dragon. And she's my father's."

"So you can REALLY TALK TO DRAGONS?!?"

"I would appreciate it if you could be quieter," the boy said with his jaw clenched. "I don't like shouting."

"WELL I DON'T LIKE SILENCE, AND I'VE BEEN STUCK IN IT FOR TWO DAYS!" Cammie bellowed. "Please talk to me! At least tell me your name. You're Introvertian, right? Is it true people there don't talk? I mean, you're talking to me, so that's probably not completely accurate, but...I guess I'm just really curious. I've always wondered whether –" Cammie knew she was babbling; it was like her mouth was a waterfall and words were just spewing over the edge all by themselves. The silence must have *really* taken its toll on her; if it was true that people in Introvertia didn't talk at all, then she was going to have to tell them about the dragons and get out as quickly as she could. Maybe she'd been a huge fool for thinking she was going to feel more at home there. All she wanted to do was keep talking...

The boy waited until Cammie had been finished for

several moments, as if he were being very careful not to interject or cut her off. "I'm Ezalen," he said. "I'm Introvertian. I already told you about Neemie. I'm supposed to get a dragon of my own someday soon, but..." He trailed off suddenly, like he'd decided that the thought was one he didn't want to finish.

"Hello, Ezalen the Introvertian. I'm Cammaina Ravenwood, from Exclaimovia. You can call me Cammie. So...what do you think about meeting your first Exclaimovian?"

"I've met a few before. I thought they were loud and rude, and so far you haven't done much to change my mind."

Cammie actually took a step backward in shock. "That –" she spluttered. "I thought you people were supposed to be *nice*! Why aren't you being nice to me?"

A look of absolute bewilderment crossed Ezalen's face. "You asked a question," he pointed out. "Introvertians are always honest. Wh –"

"You weren't *supposed* to answer honestly. You were supposed to make me feel welcome! I've been walking for two days to come visit your kingdom, and THIS is the greeting I get?"

"The greeting *you* get!" repeated Ezalen in amazement. "I was out minding my own business in the woods, and all of a sudden I was getting screamed at by an Exclaimovian, and when I asked her to please keep her voice down, she screamed even louder!"

For several seconds they just stared at each other.

"Oh," Cammie said at last. "Yeah. I, uh...I see where you got the whole *rude* bit from. That sort of thing is normal in Exclaimovia."

"Maybe it's best if you go back there, then," Ezalen told her quietly.

Cammie was going to argue with him, but just as she opened her mouth, she had an even better idea. "Okay," she said, turning around like she was going to take his advice. Just as she started to walk away, she added over her shoulder, "I just happen to know that your people are missing several hundred dragons, and I just happen to know where they are, but I guess I won't get a chance to tell you."

"WAIT!" Ezalen said – if it wasn't a yell, then it was *very* close. Still facing away from him, Cammie smirked. That had been *fun* – and she'd gotten an Introvertian to raise his voice! "What do you know about the dragons?" he asked, in a voice that was almost pleading. "Have they been stolen?"

"Um...yes," Cammie said, turning around in surprise. Had this entire trip been a waste? Had she come all the way to Introvertia just to tell them something they already knew? "How did you know that?" she asked weakly, disappointment stabbing at her heart.

"I didn't. I've suspected it for a few weeks, but –"

"Does anybody else know?" she cut in. He blinked in surprise the same way he had when she'd interrupted him the first time. That was fun. She might have to do more of it – if he didn't turn her away and send her home without even getting to see Introvertia at all.

Ezalen stared at her for so long that Cammie was wondering if he'd turned to ice. "Helloooooo," she said, waving her hands in front of his face. "I asked you a question!"

"Sorry. I think my ears are still bleeding from all that shouting earlier." His lips were *just barely* turned up in something that might have been a smile. "I, um...don't want to answer that question right now."

"Okay," she said. "Can you help me get into Introvertia so that I can tell your king and queen what I know?"

Again he didn't say anything right away, but his head tilted, like he was examining her. "Why would an Exclaimovian help us?" he asked.

Here it was. She could lie and say she just wanted to help Introvertia and do the right thing. But then – hadn't she left Exclaimovia because she was tired of pretending, tired of keeping secrets? "Sometimes I feel...out of place in Exclaimovia," Cammie confessed. "And I kind of wonder if I might be part Introvertian."

There. It was out.

Ezalen just stared.

And stared.

And stared.

Cammie turned around and looked behind her; maybe he'd seen some frightening animal and was trying to hold still so he didn't startle it. But...no. His eyes were creased at the edges and his forehead was tight. He was just...thinking.

Silently.

Then that red dragon came swooping off its high branch and settled onto Ezalen's shoulders. A few more seconds passed, and both Ezalen and the dragon looked at Cammie. She got the distinct impression that they were talking to each other about her.

"I'll help you," Ezalen said, determination in his voice. "I'll help sneak you into Tranquility. Let's go."

Cammie smiled triumphantly. She was going to see Introvertia!

It had taken every single ounce of Eza's self-control not to laugh out loud when Cammie had said she felt partly Introvertian.

She'd been looking expectantly at him after that, obviously eager for him to answer her. But there were *a thousand* thoughts running through Eza's head at that moment, and they were coming so fast that he couldn't even arrange his words into a response. The first thought was that if Cammie knew something about the dragons, then Eza *had* to get her into Tranquility...and the safest thing to do was probably to sneak her in.

Eza didn't like that. He didn't want to be sneaky; it felt too much like lying. But Cammie had asked who else knew about the dragons, and the honest answer, as far as he could tell, was *almost nobody*. If Eza showed up at the city gates with an Exclaimovian in bright red clothes and gaudy makeup, spinning some tale about missing dragons and how only this girl could help them, he and Cammie would be laughed right back out of the city.

Could he even trust her? What if she was a spy, telling a story about stolen dragons in order to get into Introvertia and learn everything she could about the kingdom? No one would question her if they thought she was there to help...

He had no reason to trust her. Then again he had no reason to *distrust* her, except that she was Exclaimovian.

At right about that point Neemie had decided to come join him, and she had settled the issue. Dragons could read body language and small facial gestures better than people could, and when Neemie had landed on his shoulders, Eza had immediately been overcome by a sensation of trust. Neemie, for whatever reason, had no doubts about Cammie's sincerity.

This isn't going to make me sound less crazy, Eza thought to himself, *if I tell the guards I'm bringing an Exclaimovian to Tranquility because my dragon likes her...*

They started walking back, and every single thought in his mind was consumed by how to convincingly sneak Cammie into Tranquility. Suddenly, though, after about twenty minutes, he noticed Cammie humming...*loudly.*

"Could you please stop making noise?" he asked politely.

"Why?" she said defensively. "I'll have you know that back in Exclaimovia, the host is expected to entertain the guest. You should be telling me stories, not letting me blunder along with only my thoughts..."

She trailed off, as if she'd been expecting him to interrupt her...which, Eza suddenly realized, she most likely *had* been. It was probably very rare in Exclaimovia that anyone made it all the way to the end of a sentence without someone else butting in. But Eza was just listening, the way Introvertians always did when another person was speaking; he was paying attention to her body language and her tone of voice, making sure he truly understood what she was saying before he even gave a single thought to replying.

"I do not like silence," she finished lamely.

"Are you asking me to make small talk?" Eza clarified.

Cammie looked delighted. "Yes! Small talk. Polite conversation."

"Introvertians don't do that. You're asking me to behave like one of you."

"I'm asking you to be accommodating to your guest,"

she answered, a hard edge in her voice. "Look, you don't even have to talk. I can tell you about myself. I'm an actress, and I've been in thirteen plays. I finished third place in a kingdom-wide essay writing contest last year. I love to read." Apparently Eza perked up just a little too much at that one, because Cammie quickly added, "Do you like to read, too? What are you reading?"

Eza sighed. He liked quiet, and he didn't like conversations that were about nothing. Cammie was going to come to Introvertia, tell the king and queen what she knew, and then probably go back home to Exclaimovia – what did it matter if Eza knew how many plays she'd been in? She was just talking for the sake of making noise. If Eza hadn't been there, she'd probably be telling it to the squirrels.

"*Collected Poems of Elzana Carrain,*" he said, hoping it would be the end of the conversation.

He really should have known better. "I like poetry!" Cammie said excitedly. "I just finished *Poems of Kartak the Proud*. See? I found something we can talk about!"

"We shouldn't be talking at all," Eza told her.

"Why not?" There was a flash of anger behind her split-colored eyes, one of them brown and one blue. "Because I'm Exclaimovian, and we're not supposed to be seen together, and..."

Again she trailed off, as if she'd been expecting to get interrupted, and again Eza waited until she was all the way finished before answering. "Did you wonder what I was doing in the woods all by myself so far from Introvertia?"

"Not really. I assumed you just enjoyed being alone. Maybe you were trying to become one with the forest or something."

"Well, that's...true," Eza admitted. "But I was there on assignment. I'm a student at the Dragon Academy in Tranquility –"

"The Dragon ACADEMY?!" Cammie blurted. "There's a SCHOOL where they teach you about dragons? I want to see it!"

Still reeling from being interrupted in the middle of his explanation, Eza paused to collect his thoughts. "Anyway, all the students in my class are doing a survival practicum in the Very Large Forest. Right now as we speak there are three hundred Introvertian cadets between us and Tranquility."

"Oh..."

"Yeah, *oh*. You may have found one Introvertian who's willing to help you sneak into our kingdom, but there might be a hundred more who'd rather toss you in the back of a wagon and point the horses eastward."

"Okay, listen," she said, rounding on him. "I get that small talk makes you uncomfortable. But silence makes me uncomfortable. I can't handle it. It makes me feel –" She cut herself off and took a breath. "I can't just walk in silence for the rest of the day."

"Would you rather be caught and found out and sent back to Exclaimovia?"

Cammie mumbled something unintelligible and scuffed the toe of her boot in the dirt.

"And since we're on the topic," Eza said, "anyone who sees you in *that* will know immediately where you're from, no matter how quiet you're being. You'll have to disguise yourself. I just happen to have a change of clothes with me." He started rummaging in his pack.

Cammie made a face of disgust. "Introvertian clothes? Introvertian *boy* clothes?"

"I'm not sure how else you'd try to sneak into Introvertia..."

Rolling her eyes and putting her hand on her hip again, she said, "And I guess you just happen to have a spare set of clothes on you right now?"

"That depends how you define *spare*," Eza hedged. "I told you I've been out here for a week, and I wore these clothes on Saturday, Sunday, and Monday, so I think the smell has –"

"Oh, no," Cammie said, backing up a few steps. "No, no, no. You want me to wear *used* Introvertian boy clothes?"

"If you're going to put it like that, then no, I don't *want* you wearing my clothes at all." Eza allowed himself a smile. "But unless you have a better idea..."

Cammie sighed loudly, shuffling her feet and crossing her arms as she glanced up into the trees. She looked like a child throwing a tantrum, Eza thought, and all at once he'd had enough of that attitude. "Look," he said, "I don't know why you're being so dramatic about this. You want to get into Introvertia because you want to see the place for yourself and find out if you belong there. I want you to get into Introvertia so you can tell what you know about the missing dragons. We both want the same thing. But we can't get you into the kingdom if everybody and his dragon knows you're an Exclaimovian. Right?"

Cammie cleared her throat and looked away.

"So it doesn't do you or me any good to complain about it. We know what has to be done, and that means we have to do it. Whether we like it or not doesn't matter. So take these clothes and go under that brush pile over there and come back when you're changed."

Sulking, Cammie took Eza's spare outfit into the brush pile, while Eza faced the opposite direction. A minute later he heard Cammie emerge, and he turned to see her slouching her way back to him, looking humiliated. "I'll have you know," she told him, wagging a finger, "that this is the greatest indignity to which I have ever been subjected. Look! Your pants are an inch too short for me."

"You look fine," he assured her. "Introvertians don't

95

judge by appearance, so no one will think twice."

"I hope you're convinced of my sincerity now."

Eza nodded. "I am. I can't think of anything in the world that would get me to wear Exclaimovian clothes. Now let's get moving. It's too late in the afternoon for us to get to Tranquility tonight, but I want to cover as much ground as I can before we make camp."

Cammie lasted about five minutes with her mouth closed before quietly blurting, "What's with the dragon, anyway?"

Eza tried very hard to keep his face under control as he turned toward her, but she was unapologetic. "What?" she asked. "I told you I don't like silence."

"Okay, but I already explained why we need to be quiet..."

"I'm not making small talk," she insisted. "I'm asking for clarification. You said you were a student at the Dragon Academy. Fine. What did you mean by that?" Eza hesitated, but didn't immediately scold her, so she surged ahead, emboldened. "I mean, if I'm supposed to pass as an Introvertian, I should know a thing or two about your culture, right?"

Eza scratched his head. Cammie was making a good point, and both of them knew it. "I'll make you a deal," he said at last. "If we can travel in silence, for safety, then tonight when we make camp I'll tell you a few things."

Cammie beamed with pride, obviously pleased with

herself.

Fifteen minutes later she was humming again, although quietly this time, and a warning glance from Eza made her stop. Maybe she really couldn't help it, Eza thought. She'd grown up her whole life around shouting, and now she was plunged into silence. What would happen to him if he was suddenly surrounded by loud noises, and someone got upset every time he tried to be quiet?

He didn't even want to think about that.

SEVEN

Eza selected a campsite near the Rapidly Flowing River. When he held up his end of the bargain and started talking to Cammie, the crashing water would mask the sound and make it so they couldn't be heard more than a few yards away. Cammie had certainly done her part in hauling some fallen pine branches to the site, where Eza had chopped them into shorter pieces with his hatchet. "You did a very good job," Eza said offhandedly. "Thanks for helping."

Even from across the clearing he could feel Cammie's body stiffen. His head snapped up in surprise, as did Neemie's, but Cammie said nothing.

"Is something wrong?" he asked.

"No," she said icily.

As far as Eza knew, he'd never been directly lied to once in his life. Even Captain Onanden hadn't said anything *false*; he just hadn't told Eza the whole truth. But Eza knew body language well enough to see that Cammie had just said the opposite of what she was really thinking.

He glanced at Neemie, who was radiating confusion so strongly that Eza could sense it from several feet away. These Exclaimovians were strange creatures, weren't they? Neemie was the one who had convinced Eza to trust Cammie...but even Neemie had no idea why Cammie had closed down so rapidly when Eza complimented her.

Eza decided that wasn't a problem he had to solve immediately, so he set about making the pine wood into a pyramid; the heavier logs went on top and the kindling on bottom, with space for air to move below the fire. Evergreen wood was not the best for a campfire; it popped and crackled loudly and tended to burn quickly unless the wood was still green, but they didn't need a fire for very long. When the pyramid looked perfect, he dug his flint and tinder out of his backpack, and in moments the fire was roaring.

"I don't have an extra blanket," Eza said apologetically, "but you can use mine if you don't mind that it smells like boy and campfire. The nights are really nice this time of year, at least on this side of the Impassable Mountains, so I'll be fine without one."

"Acceptable," Cammie said sullenly.

Eza heated up the last of his camp rations, glad that he had overprepared as he usually did by bringing a little extra. Cammie gave a sniff. "What is it?" she asked.

"Dried onala meat," he said. "It might be a little bland for your taste. And here's some flatbread."

"Thank you," she told him. "I'll take the bread. I don't like bland meat."

Eza gave her both portions of flatbread and kept the meat for himself. "Do you still want to know about the Dragon Academy?"

She looked up from her meal, her mouth already full. "Are you really –?" she asked, the words muffled by food; she quickly swallowed so she could finish the thought. "Are you really offering to make small talk with me like you promised?"

Eza smiled. "I'm offering to tell you about my culture."

That brought a smile out of Cammie, too. "I accept."

He told her how his family had been dragon-companions for hundreds of years, and how he'd started at the academy when he was twelve. When he got to the part about the vow of silence, though, her eyes got so wide Eza thought they might fall out of her head.

"You couldn't talk for *an entire year?*" she asked in shock.

Eza nodded.

"I don't believe it."

"If you want, I can be silent for the rest of our trip to Tranquility, to show you it's possible."

"No!" Cammie shouted, and Eza cringed, hoping no one had overheard her. "That...won't be necessary," she said, regaining her composure. "But...how did you do school? And what about your family?"

"The professors know which students are on their

Year of Silence, and they take that into account," Eza explained. "We're not called on to answer questions, or given assignments that require us to speak. The place it's actually hardest is on the ringball field." He saw Cammie's eyebrow furrow, and added quickly, "It's a sport we like to play. You pass a rubber ball with your hands or feet; foot passes can go any direction and hand passes can only go sideways or backward, and you try to kick the ball through the other team's goal. Normally when you're open, you call for the ball, or you shout the name of the play you want your teammates to run. When you're on your vow and you can't talk, you have to be a lot more aware of your surroundings, constantly scanning the field with your eyes, listening for the footsteps of people coming up behind you to take the ball. It really helps you be more focused."

He could tell Cammie was still very skeptical, so he kept going. "One thing we learned is that most people don't listen to understand. They listen in order to reply. When you hear what someone is saying, you're most likely thinking about what you're going to say back as soon as they finish talking, and that means you're not truly listening to them. You're not focusing on their words, their face, their body. When replying isn't an option, you have no choice but to empty your mind and receive what's being given to you. And that's the only way to hear a dragon's thoughts."

"So you really can talk to that?" Cammie asked, pointing at Neemie.

"Sort of. I can't exactly *talk* to her yet. I can understand feelings and vague impressions, and she can understand me a little. That by itself took a year and a half of work. It will be several more years before I can discern individual thoughts in her head and communicate specific things to her."

"And then what?"

"And then we keep Introvertia safe from its enemies," he said proudly.

"What if the enemies of Introvertia get their own dragons and come after you?"

"That'd be bad," Eza answered. "And that's why we're sneaking you into Tranquility."

"Hmm. Good point."

Eza paused a few moments and then smiled. "You're very inquisitive. I like that."

Immediately Cammie tensed up again. Was it the compliment? That didn't make any sense to Eza, but he could tell from Cammie's body language that this wasn't the right time to press her about it. He'd been trying to open a door to her, to tell her that he liked answering her questions – but if she was going to respond by slamming that door in his face, then fine. He was pretty sure he'd never understand Exclaimovians, and Cammie wasn't doing anything to convince him otherwise.

"Is there anything else I can get you before bed?" he asked, still determined to be a polite host.

Cammie shook her head.

"Okay," said Eza. "Sleep well."

He stayed alert until he was sure Cammie was asleep, then allowed himself to close his eyes.

Eza awoke right before dawn, the purple sky just beginning to wake up with stripes of orange light. He rolled over onto his stomach, pine needles sticking to his shirt, and placed his chin in his hands to watch the spectacle. The orange turned to yellow and then light blue, the darkness rolling back over Eza's head as the light chased it toward the western horizon. The forest began to wake up, birds chirping their good-morning songs and a cool breeze dancing along the ground as the river gushed excitedly off to Eza's right.

He sent Neemie up into the branches to scout. The three of them had gone a good distance last night and were on pace to enter Tranquility by noon. Neemie didn't see anything around them; it was Saturday, and the practicum had officially ended Friday, so they weren't likely to encounter any students except those who felt like spending some extra time in the woods. If there were any around, they were well hidden enough that Neemie couldn't see them.

Cammie woke up not long after that, and Eza greeted

her with breakfast. "There's not much left," he apologized, "but you're welcome to these biscuits if you'd like them. I'll treat you to a nice meal once we arrive in the city."

"Thanks."

"You'll have to wash that paint off your face before we get any closer to the gates."

"It's called makeup."

"It's called *not gonna be on your face anymore.*"

Cammie was not amused at the joke (and Eza had to admit it wasn't all that funny), but she made her way to the river and managed to avoid falling in as she washed her face. "You look nice," Eza told her as she approached the campsite again. A grimace of disgust flickered across her face, and he decided to press. "Did I say something wrong?" he asked.

"No. Come on. I'm ready to be done walking."

Eza was pretty sure she had lied right to his face again. He bit his tongue; this was another of those problems he didn't have to solve right away – or did he? Sneaking an Exclaimovian into Introvertia was one thing – sneaking in an Exclaimovian who was *lying to him repeatedly* seemed like a really, really bad idea...

They kept walking all morning. Eza knew he was setting a fast pace; Cammie was trailing a few steps behind him, and every so often he caught wind of humming. He decided not to make a big deal of that until they got very close to the city.

And so, just before noon, the brown walls of Tranquility emerged on the edge of Eza's vision. He pointed them out to Cammie. "All I see is forest," she said.

"Exactly," Eza agreed excitedly. "The whole city was made to be an extension of the forest, to blend in seamlessly." He got more serious. "Now it's time to focus, Cammie. So far you've just been getting annoyed when I tell you how differently we do things in Introvertia, but from here on, if you act like an Exclaimovian, you're going to be found out and both of us will be in huge trouble."

"I can do it," she insisted. "I'm an accomplished actress."

"Right. Well, now you're playing an Introvertian. You love silence and you hate small talk. You love open spaces, listening, and people living in harmony."

"What about kittens?" she asked sarcastically.

"Oh, that you get to choose," Eza answered, ignoring the sarcasm. "Some Introvertians like kittens and some don't."

"Delightful."

His heart kept pounding harder and harder as they approached the city. He'd never taken a risk this big before; there was no telling what the punishment might be for sneaking an Exclaimovian, of all people, into the capital city, but there was also no telling what the reward might be if it turned out she was telling the truth about the stolen dragons and the Introvertians were able to recover them. One of the biggest rewards would be that Eza would finally get his own dragon – and that was enough to make the whole venture worth it.

The city guards smiled at him as they always did, and that was it. They were in.

Cammie's eyes were wide as she took in the sights of Tranquility. It certainly lived up to the name. The forest seemed to have extended its reach into the city, with trees growing among houses on the city blocks, and pine needles underfoot soaking up the sound of boots on cobblestone. Cammie couldn't deny the beauty, but the whole place was as silent as a funeral.

Out of the corner of her eye she saw Eza wave at an older man. "I like your hat!"

"Thanks! That's a cute dragon you've got!"

"Thanks!"

Cammie cringed. She didn't know if the man was a friend of Eza's, but the exchange had put a smile on the boy's face, and he seemed to have a bounce in his step as they continued down the road.

"What was that?" she asked. "I thought Introvertians didn't talk to people. You're supposed to be all...quiet and stuff."

"We are, mostly. But there's never a bad time to say a kind word to someone. We're allowed to do that anytime we want."

Cammie felt bile rising in the back of her throat and had to swallow it hard. She was distantly aware of Eza saying, "There's Cappel's bookstore."

"Books," repeated Cammie, drawing to a sudden halt. The two-story building beckoned to her. "I don't have any of your money," she said, abruptly realizing.

"I'll buy you something," Eza reassured her. "As a gift. A souvenir. Not right now, though. I'm going to drop my stuff off at home and then we're going to go to the palace."

Cammie's eyebrow raised – the brow seemed lighter, she thought, without all the makeup on it – and she said, "What, we're just going to stroll into the palace, demand an audience with the king, and hope he believes us when we say we know where his missing dragons are?"

"Why wouldn't he believe us?" Eza asked, confusion on his face. "I'm a Dragon Academy student and a dragon-companion in the army. I have no reason to lie to him and he has no reason to disbelieve me."

"Apart from the fact that you've just snuck an Exclaimovian into the city."

Eza's head whipped around in terror. "Not so loud," he said, at a voice barely over a whisper.

Cammie had enjoyed getting that reaction out of him,

and had to stifle the smile that wanted to spread over her face. "Okay. Fine. Lead the way to your house."

So Eza did, narrating as he led Cammie through the Reading Square (acceptable, she thought, though far too quiet) and the Music Square, where she lingered as long as Eza would allow, grateful for the presence of constant noise. All this silence was an assault on her senses. Even as the thought occurred to her, she knew it was precisely backward, but that was how she felt.

"Why can't the rest of your kingdom be like this?" Cammie groused.

"We don't have a problem with noise," Eza pointed out, "as long as it's purposeful. We only talk when there's something to say. Games of ringball get pretty loud, but the shouting means something important. Nobody's going to get on to you for laughing too hard or anything like that."

Cammie raised both eyebrows.

"Uh...how loud do you laugh?" Eza asked.

"About this loud," said Cammie, taking a deep breath.

Eza choked off a cry of alarm and reached his hands for her mouth, but Cammie squirmed away and giggled. "It's so fun to tease you," she said.

"You were joking?" he asked in disbelief.

"Yes. Joking. Don't you have jokes here in Introvertia?"

"We do," Eza said, still composing himself. "But we

don't joke about loud noises. And we definitely don't joke about drawing attention to ourselves when we're smuggling strangers."

Cammie nodded. "Okay. That's fair. We can go to your house now."

Sadly she left the Music Square behind, following Eza down a smaller street and stopping outside a large two-story house. "This is it," Eza told her. "Wish me luck."

"What are you going to tell them?" Cammie asked, curious.

"Tell them?" he repeated quizzically.

"Yeah. Tell your parents. About me. What kind of story are you going to make up?"

Eza smiled slowly. "I get it. You're joking again. That's a good one."

Now it was Cammie's turn to be bewildered. "What do you mean? You're just going to tell them the truth, that I'm an Exclaimovian?" Eza's eyes shot frantically up and down the street, clearly hoping no one had overheard Cammie, but she persisted. "I thought the whole point of this thing was to get me in without anyone knowing!"

"We're heading to the castle right after this to tell them, aren't we?" Eza pointed out. "I'm not going to lie to my father. We're only hiding you because we don't know how people will react, and I think I know how he'll react."

"You think he'll just be fine with it?" Cammie mocked, her hand on her hip.

"I think he loves me and trust my judgment," Eza answered, looking wounded. "If your parents don't trust your judgment, I'm sorry."

Cammie had been expecting that sentence to end with "I don't blame them," because a casual insult was considered the perfect ending to a persuasive argument, a sort of verbal exclamation mark. When he didn't take that approach, she blinked at him a few times. "Okay," was all she could manage.

The inside of the house was too plain for an Exclaimovian cattle stall, in Cammie's opinion. There was only one piece of art on the wall, two simple couches, and an understated wood pattern on the floor. "Are you poor?" she blurted.

Eza seemed to be getting used to her sudden outbursts, and didn't overreact to this one. "No. Dragon-companion families are well paid. We're pretty rich by Introvertian standards."

"Then why isn't your house more..."

"More Exclaimovian?" he asked, turning to face her.

That was exactly what Cammie had meant, but coming from Eza's mouth, she could hear how insensitive it sounded.

"All you've done since we met," Eza said, frustration evident in his voice, "is compare me and my kingdom to the way you do things back home. Every single time I've told you we do things differently here, you've complained or gotten sarcastic. But you told me you're here because you don't fit in back home. So you're going to need to pick a side and stop griping. Is Exclaimovia the greatest nation ever and we're backward peasants for not doing things your way, or is Exclaimovia a place where you feel uncomfortable and you came here because you wanted a change?"

Cammie furiously chewed the inside of her lip. He had a point. She *hated* that he had a point. "Both?" she asked, trying to save face.

Yet it was – *true*, wasn't it? Exclaimovia wasn't perfect, but it was *home*. She didn't like the unwritten rules, all the mind games, all the expectations and social pressure...but at least she knew how to handle all of that. It was comfortable, even if it wasn't good. This, though, was all new, and Cammie didn't know what to do with it...

Eza was clearly unsatisfied with that answer, but didn't have a chance to push, because someone walked around the corner from another room. "Good afternoon, Eza! What's all this about Exclaimovia?"

"Dad, this is Cammaina Ravenwood. She's from Exclaimovia and she knows what's happened to our dragons. Cammie, this is my dad, Ezarra."

"Pleased to meet you, Mr. Ezarra," Cammie said with

a little curtsy. Inside, though, her brain was screaming. Eza had really just told his dad the truth, with no games and no dancing around, with no worrying about how it would sound or how it would make him look. *That* would take some getting used to – but something inside Cammie was *longing* for that kind of openness, that kind of freedom from what anyone else was going to think. She'd *never* had that in Exclaimovia, not in her entire life. There was not a single person there who she could speak to without a mental filter the way Eza had just spoken to his dad. A kind of bitter jealousy filled Cammie, and she felt horrible for thinking that way about her home kingdom. Exclaimovia was a nice place...

Except for all the things about it that I hate, she added.

Abruptly she noticed that Eza had not said anything about his mother. When she'd asked what story he was going to tell his parents, plural, he'd only mentioned his dad. That didn't sound like a good situation.

"I'm pleased to meet you, too, Miss Ravenwood." Ezarra nodded welcomingly at her – of course he wouldn't hug or shake hands, she suddenly realized, without knowing whether she wanted to be touched. "How did the two of you meet?"

"It's a long story," said Cammie, at the same time Eza said, "On my survival practicum."

Ezarra smiled, and Cammie could see Eza in his face when he did. "I was just preparing lunch. You're probably hungry."

Very suddenly Cammie realized that she was. She almost yelled "I can't wait!" in proper Exclaimovian style, but remembered her surroundings. "That would be lovely," she said instead.

EIGHT

Eza's heart pounded as he led Cammie through the wide iron front doors of the palace and into the cool front hall. The guards had smiled and allowed him to pass as soon as he'd said he was there to see Captain Onanden, but getting past the guards was the easy part. The hard stuff was still to come.

He glanced over at Cammie to see if she was as nervous as he was. Both of them had a lot to lose from this. If things went sour, Cammie would be ejected from the city, either alone or taken under guard back to the city of Pride. She would doubtless face shame and punishment for attempting to sneak away and join the enemy – she would technically be a traitor, Eza realized as they shuffled down the long hallway to Captain Onanden's office. She could face the death penalty, although he hoped even the Exclaimovians, angry and violent as they could be, wouldn't execute someone as young as Cammie...

Abruptly he realized he didn't know exactly how old she was other than that she looked about his age. It hadn't come up. Perhaps she was right about him not being a very gracious host.

Then they were standing in Captain Onanden's office.

The officer looked mildly surprised to see both of them, although he was nothing but courteous, as always. "Please, Cadet Skywing. Have a seat. Who is your friend?"

"Cammie Ravenwood," she said, answering the question that had been directed at Eza and stepping forward to shake the officer's hand.

Eza closed his eyes. If the captain hadn't guessed that she was an Exclaimovian, he now knew.

"I see," Onanden said as his eyes narrowed. "Correct me if I'm wrong, Miss Ravenwood, but you are not from our kingdom?"

"Correct!" she said excitedly, at a volume a few notches too loud for the small room. "I'm from Pride, in the Kingdom of Exclaimovia, and I know what happened to your dragons."

Onanden's face was frozen in a smile that looked to Eza like he was hiding something. "What do you mean by that?" the captain asked, and Eza thought the politeness in his voice was a little bit forced.

"My father," Cammie began in a very formal tone, "is General Barin Ravenwood. Perhaps you've heard of him. He led the armies of Exclaimovia when we were invaded and nearly defeated by the kingdom of Ironhand. He's a national hero, and a man of character and integrity." She stopped suddenly then, as if the thought of her father had made her homesick.

115

"A few days ago," she continued when she'd regained her composure, "I overheard some of our leaders asking him to rejoin the army, because they had stolen dragons from Introvertia, which they intend to turn into an army like yours. I – I don't know exactly where those dragons are being kept. But my people have them. If I can help you get them back...I'd like to."

Eza had never seen a face quite like the one Captain Onanden was making. Introvertians were typically very honest people; they would tell you exactly what they were thinking, as long as they were sure you wanted to know. But Onanden looked like he planned on saying something completely different than what was really in his head. "I thank you for bringing this to my attention," the officer said at last. "I'm sure you understand the difficulty of asking me to accept such a story on nothing more than your word. Not that I, even in the slightest, doubt your word," he added hastily to Eza. "Your service record at the Academy has been exemplary the last two years and your family has a long and proud history of service to the crown. However, think logically about what you're saying. You, Cadet Skywing, know better than anyone the difficult and rigorous training that must be undertaken by anyone who wants to be a dragon-companion. Do you truly believe any Exclaimovian could empty his – or her – head enough to receive a dragon's thoughts?"

Eza had to admit he did not find that very likely, but he said nothing.

Onanden continued. "I will notify the king of your story immediately, and I'm sure he will devote his full care to ascertaining the truth of whether there are any Introvertian dragons in hostile hands." His eyes locked on Eza's. "However, you must get her out of the city. I understand you thought you were doing the right thing, but you know our policy, and it exists for a reason. She may remain until tomorrow morning, as my personal favor to you, Cadet. If I didn't trust your judgment, I wouldn't be making this choice. Understood?"

Eza nodded mutely.

"And you must speak of this to no one. That's an order, Ranger. Am I understood?"

Eza drew himself up to his full height. "Clearly, sir!"

He and Cammie were hustled back down the long hallway and deposited outside the palace. Eza's head was spinning from the whole thing. He had expected Captain Onanden to take them a little more seriously, to write some notes about what they'd said, perhaps even to call the king and queen themselves in to hear the story –

"That was odd," he murmured, half to Cammie and half to himself.

"Are you *blind and deaf?*" Cammie shrieked, drawing hundreds of shocked eyes to her from all over the

117

Reading Square. Eza wanted to melt into the cobblestones, but Cammie's tirade continued: "He was *lying right through his teeth*! This is *not* how Introvertians are supposed to act!"

One of the palace guards had taken a few steps forward from in front of the iron door. "Are you unwell, ma'am?"

"I've just been lied to by an Introvertian!" she informed him so loudly it felt like the trees were leaning away from her.

"She's unwell," Eza said hastily, putting an arm around her back and trying to steer her toward his house. "I'm sorry for the disturbance."

The other Introvertians in the square, upon hearing that she was unwell, nodded in sympathy and went back about their business. *What did I just do?* Eza asked himself. *Now I'm the one lying, and to protect an Exclaimovian, too! This is why our ancestors left...*

Cammie was very obviously not done ranting, but repeated coaxing from Eza convinced her to keep a lid on things until they had walked back through the front door of Eza's house. *"For the love of everything good in the world!"* she screamed so shrilly that the plates in the kitchen rattled. "I have *never* in all my life been treated with such disrespect by someone I was trying to help!"

Eza's father had come running around the corner at the first yelp, holding a hammer in one hand and a hatchet in the other, apparently assuming that someone was being violently murdered. When he saw Cammie and Eza, his shoulders dropped. "What in Mazaren's name is going on in here?" he asked in shock.

Eza opened his mouth, but it was obvious that this was Cammie's story to tell. "That man in the castle," she roared, "*ignored* us! This is the single worst thing to happen to Introvertia in *decades if not centuries* and he rushed us out of his office without so much as a hard candy for the trip home! And then he told me I had to leave the city! The one who's trying to help the *nation of her sworn enemies!*" She threw up her hands in disgust, howled wordlessly at the ceiling, and sank into one of the sofas.

Father and son stared at each other with wide eyes. It seemed the tantrum had left Cammie deflated, and she just sat on the couch shaking her head in disbelief and muttering. "He told Cammie she had to leave within twenty-four hours," Eza added.

His father looked as stunned as Eza felt. "I'm sorry," Ezarra said at last. "I truly thought you'd be taken seriously."

"It's okay," Eza said.

"Now that I know no one's dying," Ezarra concluded, "I have to go back into the garden. You should spend some time with Neemie later, Eza. She misses you."

"Okay," he answered obediently, his eyes drifting

back to Cammie. For the first time he felt really bad for the girl. She'd left everything behind to come to the place where she thought she'd be at home, only to be disappointed by how out of place she felt. She'd come trying to help, but she'd been soundly rejected – first by Eza, although he was trying his hardest to be charitable, and now by Captain Onanden, the only person who could have believed her story and helped her. She'd put everything on the line and gotten absolutely nothing. That wasn't right. Somehow, Eza knew, he had to do something to help her.

But what?

Cammie still looked devastated. Eza sat down next to her and laid a comforting hand on her shoulder, trying to think of the right words to reassure her.

She flinched so hard that Eza's hand came loose, and glared at him like he'd been trying to steal her purse. For a few moments the two of them just looked at each other, anger still on Cammie's face and disbelieving confusion on Eza's. "I was trying to help you feel better," he heard himself saying. She hadn't minded when he'd used his hands to steer her out of the Reading Square a few minutes before...so what was this?

"Thank you," Cammie replied, her body stiff.

Introvertians didn't typically regard silence as awkward, but even Eza could tell that this silence was. Clearly Cammie hadn't received his comforting touch in the way he'd wanted. He stood in frustration, not just at that but at everything that had happened, at people not listening to him and at strangers thinking they deserved to be in his town and at being lectured on kindness by an Exclaimovian and at not even knowing how to reassure someone from such a different culture. He blew out a long breath and headed for the kitchen to calm down the best way he knew how – alone.

"What are you doing?" Cammie asked a little too loudly, fear in her voice.

Eza stopped by the oven, closing his eyes and sighing. Of *course*. Being left alone would only frighten her more; that was probably something Exclaimovians did for punishment. He turned back to face her. "I don't know what I'm doing," he said honestly. "About anything. I'm scared and I'm frustrated and I don't know what to do. I haven't been a good friend to you and my commanding officer doesn't believe me and..." he trailed off, shaking his head. "I don't like feeling this way."

Cammie stared at Eza, pushing her glasses up on her face. Why was he being so open about his emotions? No one in Pride would *ever* have admitted that kind of vulnerability, not willingly. Even the look on his face betrayed his pain and confusion; he either wasn't trying to conceal his emotions or didn't even know how. Whichever it was, Cammie felt a little uncomfortable to know his true feelings so plainly. In Exclaimovia...

Actually, Cammie didn't know *how* that sentence was supposed to end. There were times back home when people bellowed their opinions at the tops of their lungs, and there were other times they carefully guarded their faces in order to keep people from knowing what they were thinking. You never knew whether you were going to get brutal maximum-volume honesty or subtlety and deception. There was something...*charming* about Eza's straightforwardness. These Introvertians would take an awful lot of getting used to, but Cammie could definitely see herself enjoying a society in which she wasn't constantly trying to guess who was lying to her and who wasn't.

Or rather, she *could have seen* herself enjoying it. By this time tomorrow she'd be on the way back to Exclaimovia to face whatever was waiting for her there. Maybe that wouldn't be such a bad thing; she could really use a huge hug from her dad right about now, not that little shoulder thing Eza had attempted. Even being tickled to death by Aed would be an improvement over sitting here in *stupid* Introvertia on this *hideous* couch and being *lied to by the government*...

At that moment Eza's dragon – no, his father's dragon, Cammie corrected herself – appeared at the back door, which was hanging slightly open. She wondered, not for the first time, how exactly her people intended to transform these runty little things into an army. The dragon barely came up to Cammie's waist and Eza had said it couldn't even breathe fire. On top of that, you couldn't communicate with a dragon unless you'd spent a year in silence. How was that supposed to work?

The dragon hopped up onto Eza like it belonged there, and sat perched over him, one clawed foot on each of his shoulders. Eza got a distant look in his eyes, like he was present in the room physically but not mentally. After several moments he looked up at the dragon, who stared back down at him. "Are you sure, Neemie?" Eza asked out loud. Apparently satisfied by the answer he got, he looked back to Cammie. "Neemie is scared."

"Of what?" Cammie snapped in annoyance, not seeing how that was relevant. "Pigeons?"

"She believes your story and she's scared for those stolen dragons."

"Oh."

"And," said Eza, as if he could scarcely believe the words that were about to come out of his mouth, "she wants us to do something about it."

"Do...some..." Cammie repeated.

"What if," Eza continued, "we went to Exclaimovia and tried to find the dragons for ourselves?"

It took Cammie a few seconds to realize what he was saying, and then a huge smile leaped to her face. "You want to see my home?"

"I don't *want* to," Eza confessed. "But I have to do something. I can't just go back to class in two weeks like everything is normal, pretending I don't know exactly what happened to the dragons. What would I tell my classmates when they started speculating why the army ran out of dragons to give us? Lie and I say I don't have a clue?"

Cammie knew she was only half-listening to Eza. She had never given a stranger a tour of her city before, and the idea of letting this quiet Introvertian have a proper taste of Exclaimovia excited her *very much indeed.* "LET'S DO IT!" she shouted, making Eza cringe. "Sorry," she added quickly. "Forgot where I was. Let's do it. I'd love to show you Pride. I think you'll find it...stimulating."

"That's what I'm afraid of."

Cammie was already thinking of her family, and at the thought of her dad, something occurred to her. "But...what will your father think?"

"I'm fifteen," Eza said matter-of-factly. "I'm an adult. But even if I weren't, I think he'd let me go anyway. He told me something last week, that he'd made a lot of sacrifices so I could follow my dreams and have a better life than the one he had. I think this sort of adventure is exactly what he was talking about. He might even let me take Neemie with me." As far as Cammie could tell, the dragon was very pleased at this idea. "He'll completely understand, too. He taught me everything I know about duty. If no one else is doing the right thing, then somebody has to, and that somebody is us."

Cammie felt herself bouncing from giddiness. "You're right," she said quickly. "You're exactly right. That's exactly what we should do."

"I'll be right back," Eza promised. "I'm going to tell my dad."

He disappeared out the door, and this time Cammie truly didn't mind being alone. She hummed to herself and clapped her hands together. This was going to be a proper adventure, the kind she'd read about in books – and at the end of it she'd be back at home, with her family and with Alair. She'd hoped Introvertia would be comfortable, would make her feel like she'd always belonged there...but it was just as uncomfortable as Exclaimovia, although for different reasons. If she was going to feel out of place no matter where she went, then she might as well stay in the place where she had family and friends.

The thought of Alair made her feel just a little bit guilty. She hoped he was doing okay, and she hoped he hadn't failed any tests without her being around to help him study. That thought, in turn, suddenly made her realize all the things she'd left behind. What if she failed her classes because she'd been gone for too long? She'd made an impulsive decision, which wasn't at all unusual for an Exclaimovian, but going back home meant she'd have to face the consequences...

But then again, people might not mind if she brought back an *actual Introvertian* for them to examine. Kalek talked to foreigners all the time, but Cammie was fairly sure the rest of her family had never met an Introvertian. Considering how her people loved stories and tales, bringing Eza and letting him tell tales of Introvertia would surely make everything okay...

Wouldn't it?

Eza came skipping back through the door, looking as excited as Cammie felt. "Dad said it's okay. We can leave tomorrow morning and take Neemie with us."

"Yes!" shouted Cammie, jumping up and punching the air, and this time Eza just smiled.

"If we're going to be on the road for a few weeks," he said thoughtfully, "we should probably have some reading material."

As soon as she walked in the door, Cappel's bookstore was already Cammie's second-favorite spot in all of Tranquility, behind only the Music Square. She took a deep breath, looking around her at books of every size and color, wonder on her face. It was easy to see why Eza loved the place so much. Cammie found a biography of a famous Introvertian king and began thumbing through it out of curiosity.

The bookkeeper himself struck Cammie as a very

friendly person; he had a wide and easy smile, and with his white hair, he looked like someone's kind grandfather. "It's been a long time since I last had an Exclaimovian in my shop," he said by way of greeting.

Cammie dropped her book in shock. "How did you – "

Mr. Cappel laughed, obviously enjoying the reaction. "Perceptive people notice things, my friend. And sometimes they notice things they didn't know they were supposed to be looking for."

Cammie didn't know exactly what that meant, but she kept a polite face on anyway as she tried to change the subject. "You make it sound like you've met Exclaimovians before."

"Of course," he said. "Not all Introvertians are Introvertians, if you take my meaning, and not all Exclaimovians are Exclaimovian. Very nearly all, mind you, but not all. Even those Introvertians who have Exclaimovian tendencies are conditioned by culture and by the way we're raised. I'm guessing you're probably here because you wondered if you might feel more at home in Introvertia, but you've found that you were brought up with certain habits and cultural practices that have put you in conflict with Ezalen more often than you might want."

"That's...exactly true," she answered in surprise.

"Becoming an Introvertian is not as simple as putting

your belongings in your backpack and moving to Tranquility," Mr. Cappel continued. "We all need to be aware of that cultural baggage we've accumulated. We need to examine that baggage and find out what feels comfortable to us simply because that's what we know and are familiar with, against what feels comfortable to us because it matches who we truly are inside."

This was *way* more philosophy than Cammie had expected inside a bookstore, of all places. "Ezalen and I are going on a trip together," she said. "Do you have any good books for us to read on the road?"

But that was the proof that Mr. Cappel was right, wasn't it? Cammie had changed the topic twice now because she was uncomfortable, just like Exclaimovians always did. Was that *her*, or was that how she'd been taught to react, like a verbal martial artist trained to parry an opponent's punch or kick?

"I want a history book," Eza said, having just wandered over from the opposite end of the store. "Something that tells the true story of Introvertia and Exclaimovia. I don't want it from one side or the other. I want to know what really happened."

"What really happened," repeated Mr. Cappel, his eyes bright. "I have just the thing. There's a book which is hated in Introvertia and Exclaimovia both. What does that tell you?"

Cammie interjected. "It says bad things about both of

them and therefore it's probably true?"

"Exactly," Mr. Cappel said, jabbing a finger excitedly at Cammie. "Here. *The Dawn Song.* I wouldn't be recommending this to just anyone, you understand. But I think the two of you can handle it."

"I don't have any money," Cammie said.

"My treat," said Eza. "I hope it'll give you at least one good memory of Introvertia."

"Thank you."

Eza beamed. "It's my pleasure."

They ended up leaving with four books, two that Eza had bought for Cammie, one for himself, and one that Mr. Cappel had insisted on giving them. Reading material in hand, they made their way back through the wide cobblestone streets. It was late afternoon now, the sun setting in front of them and lighting the clouds orange against a deep blue sky. The wind was blowing from the south, and as they passed into the Reading Square, they could hear the rush of water from the Rapidly Flowing River. Eza held out a hand and Cammie stopped next to him. "Just look," Eza told her. "Listen."

Cammie took a deep breath, allowing herself to be captivated by the beauty she saw and heard. Something about the way the sun caught the buildings took her breath away, and she looked up at the sky, then over at Eza, whose face was also golden as the fading sunlight shone directly into their faces. His eyes looked greener than she'd ever seen them, and the smile on his face was real and pure. In that moment, *she got it*. Whatever magic the Introvertians had that let them get lost in silence, it had just fallen on her.

And then it was gone; the sun sank a little lower and the clouds weren't orange anymore and the wind shifted so they couldn't hear the river. The spell was broken, and Cammie blinked as if waking up from a dream. "That was incredible," she murmured.

"It's there all the time," Eza said, starting back to his house, "for anyone who wants to be amazed."

That was it: her first real taste of what it would be like if she were an Introvertian. "The book was nice," she told Eza as they walked, "but *that* was a good memory of Introvertia."

Back at Eza's home, he began stuffing things into his backpack. Cammie sat there feeling useless, and thought about asking if she could help, but he was moving with such efficiency that she felt like she'd just be in the way. She hummed to herself softly, hoping it wasn't loud enough for Eza to hear, because she didn't want to annoy him.

Into the pack went survival tools, rope, a knife, some other things Cammie didn't see...and then food. Strip after strip of jerky, seemingly endless cakes of flatbread, paper envelopes of spices and seasonings, dried shavings of fruits and vegetables, some wrapped cheeses, and more. Cammie's mouth was actually watering. "Do we have to wait till tomorrow?" she asked jokingly. "I could do with some of that now."

"I think my father made stew," Eza answered, not looking up. "I smell something on the fire, anyway."

"Good enough."

The books went in last, and then Eza was finished, standing and testing the weight of his backpack with a face that made Cammie laugh. "Maybe we don't need to take all four books," she suggested.

"Urgh," said Eza, setting the pack down and removing two of them. "I'm taking *Legends of the Artomancers* for sure. If we can only take one other, is it okay if it's *The Dawn Song*?"

"That's perfect."

There was indeed stew on the fire, and after dinner, Eza stood up. "I can show you to our guest bedroom now, if you'd like."

Cammie didn't move. "I know you don't like hearing about the way things are done in Exclaimovia," she said apologetically, "but when we have a meal together, it's always nice to sing songs afterward. Would you mind?"

She truly didn't know how Eza was going to react, and when he left the room momentarily, she wondered if he'd overreacted and gone straight to bed. He reappeared a moment later, though, carrying a six-stringed instrument. "This is called a ballaina," he told her, strumming the strings. "My mother taught me to play before she died. This is one of the songs she used to sing to me."

There's beauty all around you, son
In the trees and in the hills
So much joy to dance inside
For the taking, if you will

There's magic all around you, son
In the land and in the air
Love and peace are free to all
For the taking if you dare

So when the summer thunders come
The howling rains will pound
Never stop the wonder, son
There's goodness all around

When the summer thunders come
And you can't see the sun
Just take a breath of life, my love
You've only just begun.

Eza played through the final verse again without singing any words, then let the final chord ring without resolving. "I think she wrote it herself," he said. "But I never asked her, and dad doesn't like to talk about it, so..."

That word hung in the air like the last chord of the song, unresolved. Cammie was busy trying to swallow the lump in her throat. "I don't know how to play your instrument," she said by way of apology, "but that song reminds me of one my father always used to sing to me. I'm pretty sure he didn't write it, but I don't know where he got it from."

If I could reach inside your heart
To show you just how beautiful you are
I would, I would

If I could make your dreams come true
So each day you saw the wonder all anew
I would, I would

Cause you are a princess
Your kingdom awaits
So reach for your crown
And stand up straight

You are a treasure
With beauty inside
So hold out your arms
The world's open wide

133

And it's waiting for you
The world's open wide
And it's waiting for you

She trailed off, tears in the corners of her eyes. "There's more to it," she said, wiping her face, "but I think that's enough for now. It reminds me of my family, and..." More tears came. She really didn't want to be crying in front of this boy she barely knew, so she forced herself to hold it together. "And I miss them," she finished, meeting Eza's eyes with a forced smile.

"They must be amazing people," he said.

"They are," she agreed.

Eza stood, stretching. "We'd better get to bed, though. Tomorrow's going to be a long day, and so will the day after that, and the day after that...I think you get the idea."

Cammie smiled. "Thank you for the hospitality, Ezalen Skywing. I appreciate you going out of your way to make sure that my time in Introvertia was as happy as it could be."

Eza pretended he was tipping his hat to Cammie. "Thank you for your kindness and patience, Cammaina Ravenwood."

Cammie went up to the bedroom Eza showed her, still humming the song she'd sung. Eza was right. It had, despite how it had begun, turned into a truly great day.

NINE

The spring morning air was crisp and a little bit cool as Eza, with Neemie on his shoulders, led Cammie toward the northeastern part of Tranquility, where Carnazon Fortress sat. That northeast gate out of Tranquility was rarely used; Eza had memorized all the stories about the battles fought at Carnazon back in the ancient days of Introvertia, but the kingdoms that used to menace the northeast border were long destroyed or collapsed. The kingdom of Telravia, far to the north, and Claira, in the distant northeast, were out there somewhere – well, and also Exclaimovia far off to the east, south of the mountains. But there were countless miles of plains between Introvertia and their nearest neighbors, dotted by independent farming villages and trading outposts.

There were two ways to get to Exclaimovia. One was the road through the Very Large Forest, which Eza knew well. But the Forest was a popular place, and he didn't enjoy the thought of explaining to people – Introvertian or Exclaimovian – why he was traveling. He didn't want to tell the truth and he didn't want to lie.

That left only one possibility: to the north, skirting the edge of the Impassable Mountains, a longer route which would take them near those ruined kingdoms and across battlefields Eza had read about in *Heroes of Introvertia*. He should have done this trip with his father a long time ago just for the history, he thought. Suddenly he wondered if he'd see the same battlefield where Mazaren and Arjera had fought the sorcerer, and a thrill ran through him.

They couldn't have asked for a nicer day to get on the road. A few white wisps of cloud drifted far overhead, and the rising sun hadn't warmed up the day very much. Eza smiled at the gate guards, who smiled back.

"Good morning, Ranger," one of them greeted Eza, who was wearing his Dragon Academy traveling cloak over his gray cotton shirt and pants. "Where are we headed today?"

"Out for reconnaissance," Eza said, which was entirely the truth – he was just headed out to Exclaimovia rather than out to the wilderness beyond the gate.

"Take care," the guard answered. "We've had some reports of blizzards and landslides at higher altitudes. Try to avoid the mountains if you can; they won't be safe until about the time summer starts."

"We'll do our best," Eza promised, and with that they were out the gates, Tranquility and Introvertia at their backs, and the whole wide world at their faces. For Cammie, she was heading home, albeit the long way; for Eza, he was about to go further from home than he'd ever been.

Even Cammie seemed content to simply take in the landscape for the moment rather than pester Eza for small talk. Off to their left stretched seemingly endless plains; about sixty miles off in that direction was the kingdom of Claira, who hadn't fought with Introvertia in nearly a thousand years but had been at war with their closer neighbors almost constantly since then. To the right were foothills which quickly climbed into steep peaks – the Impassable Mountains, which had earned their name fairly, as there was no known pass from one side to the other. Eza had heard rumors of strange creatures, perhaps even magical ones, living far up in the caves and crags where no one had ever gone. Maybe one day he'd get up there to see for himself.

"So," Cammie said, following closely behind Eza for safety as her nose was buried in a map, "it looks like we basically skirt the edge of the mountains until we reach Some Son of a Lake in about...forty miles."

"There is no such place as Some Son of a Lake."

"Is too," she said indignantly. "It's right there."

"Give me the map." Eza held it open in front of himself. "It's Some *Sort* of a Lake, you goof."

"Whoever drew this map has terrible handwriting, then."

"Hey! I drew this map!"

"Clearly they don't teach penmanship in Introvertia,"

Cammie sniffed.

Eza couldn't even tell if she was teasing him or being serious, so he opted to tease right back. "Maybe not, but we do teach talking to dragons, so I think we win."

There was a thud behind him and the sound of hysterical laughter. Eza whipped around, nearly sending Neemie flying. Cammie was on the ground, doubled over. "I can't...breathe," she wheezed. "The dragon...stuck out her tongue at me!"

"Attagirl, Neemie," Eza said out loud, radiating pride for the dragon to feel. "See? Neemie knows the winner."

"Well," Cammie replied, standing up and wiping the dust off her borrowed Introvertian clothes, "it's too late now. The lake has been dubbed. It is officially Some Son of a Lake."

"Fine," agreed Eza, trying and failing to hide his smile.

"Why in the sun's name did you call it Some Sort of a Lake to begin with?"

Eza chuckled to himself. "I don't know the real name. I've never actually been out this way. I found a map that looked a little like that one at the beginning of one of the history books I read, and I copied it down. Whenever I read a book that described a location, if I was pretty sure I knew where it was, I added it to the map."

"So you don't...know for a fact that any of these places are out here," Cammie clarified, horror creeping into her voice.

"It's not like they sell maps of the northern wilderness in the market," said Eza defensively.

Cammie blew out a long sigh, *both* hands on her hips this time.

"Well, that's fine," Eza said philosophically. "I'll just have to tell all the people in Pride that Cammie Ravenwood doesn't like adventures. She doesn't want to come back with good stories to share."

"NO!" Cammie shrieked, jumping toward Eza like she was going to cover his mouth. He laughed and danced away from her, and she gave up the chase quickly. "Don't do that," she said, adjusting her glasses, which had gone askew. "Don't even joke about that. Gathering around to tell stories is one of the most important things that happens in Exclaimovia. It's who we are."

"Does anyone ever get through an entire story without being interrupted?" Eza asked, only half-joking.

"It is...rare," conceded Cammie. "And stories have a funny way of changing the more times they're told. But it's not about the stories, Eza. It's about the togetherness."

It's about talking just for the sake of talking, Eza thought, but didn't say it out loud. What was the point of telling a story at all if someone was going to butt in before you got a chance to share the ending? Who was so arrogant as to think that the sound of their own voice was more important than letting you finish what you were saying? Apparently his face gave away exactly what he was thinking, because Cammie coughed. "We should get going."

As if to declare victory, she began loudly humming to herself, periodically breaking into words and singing through the choruses of songs Eza had never heard before. The songs weren't bad, and he truly did try to enjoy them, but the constant noise began to grate on him after a while. He couldn't hear the sounds of the forest, couldn't tell if there were footsteps or animals sneaking up on them. It made him uneasy. Neemie spent a lot of time in the treetops; she was supposedly scouting, but Eza suspected she just wanted to be as far away from the racket as possible.

At lunchtime they brokered a deal. Since Cammie had made noise all morning, Eza would get to enjoy silence for a few hours, after which they would talk about something interesting to both of them. The plan held up, much to Eza's surprise; when it was time for their conversation, he found himself asking a lot of questions about Cammie's school and her friends back in Exclaimovia. He didn't actually tell her very much of anything about his own life, because he'd found that she would happily monologue for as long as he would let her, and on the rare occasions she ran out of things to say, a well-placed follow-up question would send her

141

spinning off in a whole new direction. It was not wholly objectionable to Eza. Cammie was interesting and well spoken, and (although Eza was sure she would never admit it) she seemed absolutely delighted that she actually had the chance to tell an entire story clear through to the end without someone interrupting with a "better" one.

She had been going for several hours when Eza took a sudden right turn and led them up into the foothills a bit, off the road and behind a few outcroppings of rock to a place that would be hidden from prying eyes. A stream ran down through it, which delighted Cammie for some reason Eza couldn't place. As far as he knew, she'd spent her whole life in the city; there had been lots of stories about books and school and things she'd learned, but nothing about spending time outdoors. That was fine. Not everyone was a Ranger. If she wanted to be excited about some flowing water, that was her prerogative.

Eza sat down to eat some bread and dried meat, watching in mild surprise as Cammie tore off her boots and socks and stuck her feet in the water. Eza knew it had to be freezing, this early in the spring, and sure enough Cammie had yanked her feet free in moments, squealing. "It's so cold!" she shouted. "You try it, Eza!"

"I'm eating," he said, trying to stop a smile from spreading across his face. Something about her enthusiasm was infectious; he enjoyed watching her enjoy herself.

Again she plunged herself in water up to her ankles, writhing around and laughing and screaming at the cold before bursting out of the water a few moments later. "I counted to seven!" she declared gleefully. "That's a new record! I'm the freezing-river record holder!"

Oh no, thought Eza. She had found his weakness: competition. Before he even knew what he was doing, his fingers were yanking his boots off and he was padding barefoot to the bank of the stream. "Whoever pulls out first loses," he announced. "Ready?"

"Ready!"

Eza stuck his feet in the water and *immediately* regretted it. He hadn't realized the water would be *that* cold, had thought Cammie was exaggerating or being dramatic as usual. A strangled groan escaped his lips as he rolled back and forth – making sure his feet stayed in the water.

Cammie howled and slapped the ground, then arched her back and shrieked. Eza was fairly sure the cold was somehow entering his feet and being transported directly to his brain; all he could feel was ice. At long last – he had no idea how long it might have been, and "forever" did not seem nearly long enough – Cammie screamed in agony and rolled out of the water. "I can't do it," she gasped, her chest heaving. "Too...cold..."

Eza looked her in the eyes and deliberately kept his

feet in the water for several more seconds, dying inside the entire time, then casually stood. That was a mistake; his toes wouldn't bend, and he lost his balance and nearly fell in the stream. Cammie guffawed at him, pointing and laughing, and Eza had to laugh at himself too.

"Okay," Cammie said at last. "You win. Best two out of three?"

"You lost," Eza protested, smiling in disbelief. "Fair and square!"

"Yeah, but I had my feet in the water before you did."

"That just means you were already used to it!"

"No one is ever going to get used to that water," objected Cammie. "Best two out of three, come on!"

The competitive fire lit up in Eza, and he kneeled down and massaged some feeling back into his feet. "Fine. But this is it. No three out of five."

"Deal," Cammie promised.

Then their feet were in the water again and the clearing echoed with agonized groans and wails. Eza had thought he was doing a pretty good job controlling himself, but all of a sudden he was being pushed; Cammie was trying to dislodge him and make him squirm out of the stream!

"What are you doing?" he asked, his mind still exploding from the cold.

"Winning!"

He tried to swipe her away, roll her onto her own back so she would bend her knees and pull out, but he had raised his arm and one of her flailing hands found his armpit. His arms and legs spasmed uncontrollably, but he was pretty sure both feet had stayed in the water.

"HA!" Cammie shouted in triumph, still lying on the ground, her head sideways to look in his eyes. "I win!"

"You do not! I'm still in!"

"You pulled out!"

"I never did," Eza said, pointing. "And even if I did, it's only because you cheated!"

"Nobody ever said it was against the rules to use physical force," she said, straightening her glasses.

"The challenge was for feet! Not for wrestling or – or tickling!"

Cammie gave a loud "AAAAARGH" and rolled up and out of the stream, lying on her back and kicking her feet up in the air to dry them off. "Fine," she said, sticking her tongue out. "You win this round, Introvertian."

"I'm going to win every round," Eza said, his feet still in the water and his teeth beginning to chatter. At last he crawled back to his sleeping bag, wishing he'd brought an extra towel or something to dry his feet faster. He didn't like being barefoot under any circumstances, didn't like the thought of being unable to run away from a dangerous situation or kick an assailant or wander away from his campsite during the night to use the bathroom without fear of stepping on something pointy. He felt vulnerable, and Cammie obviously didn't feel the same way, because she seemed to enjoy it.

"You're really fun to be around," Eza told her. "I mean yeah, sometimes you drive me nuts, but I think you're really interesting and I'm glad we're out here together."

Oh, yeah. *That reaction* was why he'd stopped giving her compliments. Instantly she was sitting up, her legs drawn up tightly under her, her body language closed off. "Listen," she said, a hard edge in her voice. "I don't know what you're trying to get from me. Maybe you think that since we're out here all by ourselves, you can act however you want and there'll be nobody to hear me. But that's not going to happen. I don't care how strong you are and I don't care if you have a sword and a dragon. It's not going to happen."

Eza stared at her, mouth open, shock on his face. Was she playing some kind of prank? If so, it wasn't funny. "What is *wrong* with you?" he demanded, louder than he could ever remember saying anything. "Are you *completely insane*? Have you literally never heard a compliment before in your life? Is your country so *stupid*, so backward, so primitive and emotionally stunted that you've never heard of SAYING A KIND WORD TO SOMEONE?"

That outburst seemed to have stunned Cammie even more than hers had stunned Eza. A slow look of comprehension finally dawned across her face, as if she were just realizing something that she should have figured out a long time ago. "No," she said at last. "No, Eza. We don't give compliments in Exclaimovia."

"What kind of ridicul–"

But Cammie held up a hand and Eza's objection died in his throat. "There are rules," she said quietly, almost tentatively. "Rigid...social boundaries, about who can say what to whom. You can't compliment people older than you, or people of a higher social status, because it's rude to make them feel emotionally vulnerable. You can't compliment a boy if you're a girl, or a girl if you're a boy, because people will think you're...you know, together." Even in the gathering dusk, Eza could see that she was turning red. "That happened to me more than a few times with my friend Alair."

"I'm sorry," Eza said, not knowing what else to say.

"The other thing," Cammie said, as if she were collecting her thoughts, "is that most times people will only compliment you when they want something out of you. It's a form of manipulation."

Eza wanted to make sure he understood. "So when I say something nice to you, it comes off like I'm manipulating you or like I'm trying to declare my love to you."

"When you say it out loud, it sounds kind of silly, but yeah, Eza. That's how it would work in Exclaimovia."

"Then it's a good thing we're not in Exclaimovia right now."

"We're not in Introvertia, either."

They looked at each other. "Well then," Eza said, "I guess that means we get to make our own rules. And if compliments make you uncomfortable, then I won't give them anymore."

Cammie looked as if that were not at all the outcome she was expecting from the conversation, but recovered herself quickly. "Okay."

"Okay," Eza echoed.

It was now almost entirely dark out, and Eza dug in his backpack. "Here," he said. "I brought reading candles. Do you want to start on *The Dawn Song* together?"

That brought a smile to Cammie's face. "Of course."

Trying not to step on the dirt with her wet feet, she shuffled her sleeping bag over next to Eza's so they could huddle together around the book. Cammie was reading out loud, and Eza followed along; it was a very well written book and Eza could immediately see why Mr. Cappel liked it. However, Eza's mind was drifting. He was thinking about touch.

The night before, he'd seen Cammie upset and his first instinct had been to put an arm on her shoulder, and just now he hadn't minded when she tried to shove him out of the water (except, of course, that she was trying to make him lose the game). He hadn't recoiled in horror from unauthorized touch like he had when he'd met those other Exclaimovians in the Very Large Forest. It appeared some part of Eza considered Cammie a friend. That was interesting by itself; was it possible for someone to get on your nerves that badly and still be your friend?

Eza didn't know why, but the thought of Cammie as his friend was okay with him, and he smiled, trying to focus back on her words.

The two of them took turns reading until it was very late indeed, and probably would have kept going except that the candle had burned nearly to the bottom and was starting to flicker. The air had also turned cold, and Eza was glad for his thick sleeping bag as he wriggled down inside it and pulled it up around his neck. He hadn't realized how exhausted he was from the stress and excitement of the past few days, and he was asleep nearly as soon as his head hit his pillow roll.

TEN

It was the chill that woke Cammie up in the morning. She'd kicked and thrashed and worked her way mostly out of the sleeping bag during the night, and she wriggled her way back in after waking up, but couldn't fall back asleep. Counting her trip to Introvertia, she'd slept outside four times now, and she concluded that it was overrated.

She had to admit the morning was pretty, though. A few puffy, dark-purple clouds hung down around the horizon to the north and west, golden on the bottom from where they were catching the rising sun's rays. Dawn had always been one of her favorite times of the day, when the world was quiet before everyone else woke up...

Cammie put her hands on the back of her neck, staring up at the sky. She didn't know what to do with herself. Sometimes she'd think things like that and wonder if she was more Introvertian than Exclaimovian. But then sometimes she'd annoy Eza to death because she hated the sound of silence. Who was she? Old Mr. Cappel had really gotten in her head with his words about personality and culture. Who was the real Cammie Ravenwood? Was she an Introvertian at heart who was only uncomfortable there because she'd been raised by Exclaimovian parents? Or was she a true Exclaimovian, but a quieter one than normal? Was she some sort of half-introvert, half-extrovert – an ambivert? Was that even an actual thing?

Then the silence got to her and she crawled out of her sleeping bag to wake up Eza.

"Hey," she said very quietly, and instantly Eza's eyes popped open and his scana appeared in his hand. Cammie scrambled back, hands in the air. "Whoa! It's just me!"

Eza blinked hard, his eyes seeming as if they didn't want to focus. "Sorry. I meant to wake up before you. You just startled me."

"I can see that."

Eza slid out of his sleeping bag, rolling it up quickly with practiced motions that told Cammie he'd done it thousands of times, then strapped his bag to the top of his backpack and Cammie's to the bottom. "Ready to walk?"

So they did, eating breakfast as they went. Cammie was lost in thought, and she was startled when Eza said, "Are you okay? You're awfully quiet."

"Are you making small talk?" she blustered, trying to hide that Eza had seen right through her.

Eza frowned in confusion. "Small talk is meaningless chatter about things that don't really matter. Asking if someone's okay is literally the exact opposite of that. It's one of the most important questions you can ask." He paused. "As long as you wait around to hear the answer, that is."

Cammie ignored the jab at her people. She wasn't sure she wanted to be this open with Eza yet. Playing with him by the stream was one thing, but this kind of talk – deep conversation about hopes and fears – that was a whole different level of friendship. Even in Exclaimovia there weren't many people who she'd allow in so close.

But it seemed her only choices were that or silence, so she shrugged and went for it.

"Have you known anyone in Introvertia who...didn't really seem Introvertian?"

The question seemed to amuse Eza. "What, you think we're all alike?"

"Uh...it did kind of seem that way to me."

"The only thing all Introvertians have in common, personality-wise at least, is that we feel..." Eza hunted for a word. "Refreshed, I guess, from being alone or with a small number of friends, and we feel drained from being around too many people. Our laws protect that by making sure people can't be forced into social settings. We're not all the same, though. Some of us are shy and quiet all the time. Some are only shy until you get to know them and then they won't shut up."

Cammie perked up. "Really?"

"Really. Some of us are lighthearted and adventurous; some are more serious, like my friend Razan. We're all different, honestly. There's no such thing as only one type of Introvertian." Eza looked over at her. "Why do you ask? Does this have to do with what you said about not feeling at home in Exclaimovia?"

"It does," she said, a bit annoyed that he'd figured it out but also glad that she could talk about it. "I've never told anyone this before, not before I told you in the forest that day. I don't feel like I can say something like that in Exclaimovia. I think people would just make fun of me and tell me to be louder."

"Based on what little I've seen, I think you're probably right."

"So," Cammie finished, "I don't know where I belong. Part of me is comfortable with the way they do things in Exclaimovia, but that's not truly me. I enjoyed certain things about Introvertia, like the honesty and sincerity, and I want more of that, but you saw. I don't fit in well there either. I don't enjoy silence that much. It's like I'm half and half. But if neither place is perfect for me...then where is home?"

She was right; there was *no way* she could have said something like that in Exclaimovia. Fifty different people would have interrupted her before the end to explain why she was wrong, or argue with her, or try and fix her problem. Eza had just listened. Finally he cleared his throat. "I really don't know what to say," he told her. "But I'm glad you shared it with me. Thank you. You can talk to me about something like that anytime you want to."

Incredibly, even though Eza hadn't given her any useful advice, Cammie actually did feel better. Maybe just being heard was good enough. "Thank you for listening," she said. "Now can we have a meaningless chat?"

Eza laughed. "That seems like a fair compromise. We talked about something worth discussing, so now we can talk about something silly. What's your favorite flower?"

"Amaryllis," she said immediately. "Yours?"

"I like lilies. I saw purple ones once, and they were gorgeous."

"Why do you have a favorite flower?" Cammie asked in amusement. "I'm not sure most boys your age in Exclaimovia would bother to notice."

"It's the Ranger thing. I've memorized basically every tree, plant, and flower out here. Have to know what's poisonous, what's good to eat in a pinch, what wood makes the best campfires, all that sort of stuff."

Cammie was impressed. "Very interesting."

Just then Eza's head cocked and he held out a hand, motioning for Cammie to stop. All she could hear was the whisper of wind through tree branches and the sound of her own breathing. But Eza seemed on edge, and silently pulled his scana out of its sheath. Neemie took up a position in a spruce tree, the thick branches mostly hiding her brilliant red scales. Now Cammie could hear humming from in front of and below them; there was a little ledge, and in moments she saw hands at the top. Then a man with sandy-brown hair like Eza's pulled himself up, stood straight, and dusted off his brown pants. He noticed Cammie and Eza and smiled.

"Good morning, Ranger," the man said easily. He looked like he was in his early twenties. "What brings you two up into the mountains?"

"That's an odd way to start a conversation," Cammie said before Eza could open his mouth. "I think most people would introduce themselves before demanding answers from someone they've just met."

A hard look crossed the man's face for just a moment and then the smile came back. "You'll forgive me, I hope. It's not often I find people your age wandering around the mountains, and in a Dragon Academy uniform, no less. My curiosity overwhelmed my manners. I'm Azanna, and this is my dragon."

Cammie hadn't seen the dragon until Azanna had pointed to it, but there it was, peeking over the ledge that Azanna had climbed a few moments before. It spread its wings and leaped up, and Cammie's jaw fell. It was *huge*, at least two feet taller than Neemie, easily coming up to

Azanna's chin. "Big," she blurted.

Azanna laughed. "Yes, Keena here is much larger than Introvertian dragons."

Eza's brow furrowed. "She's...not one of ours? But your name is Introvertian."

"Very good," Azanna said. "I was in the companion program about ten years ago, but the further I went, the more I felt like army life wasn't for me. I tried to withdraw, and they took my dragon away. So I left Introvertia and never went back. I found Keena here in the mountains and bonded with her, and we've been partners ever since. We live in a village to the north, kind of halfway between Claira and Introvertia."

"You *found* a dragon in the mountains?" Eza repeated, sounding shocked.

"That's right. Where do you think your government gets them from? Sure, they breed most of them, but some of them come from the wild."

"Wild dragons," Eza murmured. Cammie recognized the dreamy, faraway look on his face. She had a few friends who were obsessed with planning their own weddings, even though they weren't engaged, and that was the look they got when they started going on about dresses and flowers and shoes. He wanted to find a wild dragon, and he wanted to do it *now*. "But how did you get her so big?" Eza added.

"Oh, you know," Azanna said vaguely. "I just took

good care of her and she did the rest. Now, I believe I've done my part. I've told you who I am and where I'm from. What brings you here?"

"I'm helping him," Cammie said, pointing at Eza. "With his survivalship practicum. He has to gather samples of five different plants and five different trees to take back to the Academy." She met Eza's eyes, silently willing him to go along. She didn't like this man and his wild dragon, and somehow she knew he was lying to them thanks to her sixteen years of dealing with Exclaimovians and their bluster. Eza would never have thought to lie; he was way too honest for that, and she just hoped that he would either follow her lead or else keep his mouth shut.

"That sounds exciting," Azanna said. It was his smile that bothered her, Cammie decided. It didn't reach his eyes. She's seen that kind of false enthusiasm more times than she could count. "What are your names? Can I help you with your collecting?"

"This is Ezalen. I'm Cammie. Thank you for the offer, but I think Ezalen should be the one who does the work. It is his practicum, after all."

"Of course. Though I must say I know this area of the mountains quite well. If there's anything in particular you're looking for, perhaps you can tell me and I'll help you find it."

"Nothing in particular," Cammie said. "He just has to

find any five plants and trees. Look, there's a plant right there." She reached down and plucked a leaf. "What's this one, Ezalen?"

"Boulder raspberry. They're just starting to flower now, but they won't bear fruit for another six weeks or so."

"See?" Cammie said. "Nothing to it. So thank you, but we're fine."

"Suit yourselves," Azanna told her. "Pleasure to meet you, Ranger. Be careful out here." He paused. "Do you have your dragon with you?"

"Do you see a dragon?" Cammie snapped, gesturing around with her hands.

Azanna smiled again, and again it was with his mouth and not his eyes. "No, of course not. Silly me." He and Keena disappeared back down the ledge, and Cammie listened as they began to move away to the north.

Cammie and Eza stared at each other for a few moments. "Do I have to explain myself?" Cammie asked.

"No," Eza said. "Something about him made me uncomfortable, too. Especially the way he asked if we had a dragon with us."

"Yeah. I wonder what would have happened if we'd said yes."

"It sounded like he went north. I was hoping to head that way myself, since the ground is really broken here.

We'd make faster progress if we went to a lower elevation. But I definitely don't want to risk running into him again, so we'll have to cut through the rough stuff."

"Okay," said Cammie. She'd already walked more in the last couple of days than she had in her life, and part of her wondered if her legs would ever stop being sore, but the extra effort was worth not coming across Azanna a second time.

"That also means we should probably be quiet. We don't want him deciding to follow us by the sound of our voices." Eza looked over at the tree where Neemie was. "Neemie will have to stay low, too."

"If they saw her, they might just think she was a wild dragon."

"Maybe, but let's not take the chance." Eza shook his head. "I really wish I knew how he'd gotten his so huge."

They set off as quickly as they could, descending the same ledge Azanna had (Cammie got all the way down with Eza's help, which made her very proud) and began heading east. Eza wasn't joking when he'd said the ground was broken. They scrambled up boulders and down through ravines with rock walls rising up on both sides of them. Every time they ended up exposed, with an open view to the northern plains, Eza would lead them higher up into the hills. After a few hours, there was a ridge blocking their view, meaning no one – including Azanna – could have seen them if he had continued on his way north.

It was punishing work, though, and before long Cammie's palms and knees were bruised, with little rocks embedded in them. Despite the discomfort, she had to admit it was a stunning hike. Trees sprang up from tiny cracks in the stone, and mountain peaks soared majestically to the south, some of them looking like they were nearly vertical. Small specks were moving way up on those peaks, and Cammie squinted for a better look. "Mountain goats," Eza said softly when he caught her staring.

"How do they stay up there without falling?"

"I've watched them do it and I still have no idea."

Eza eventually felt confident enough to let Neemie fly up and do some scouting. He and Cammie stopped in a glade of yellow and white flowers, with a sheer mountainside on their right and some large boulders to the left. It was midafternoon now, and Cammie finally forced herself to eat. "Do you think we're safe now?"

"You're not."

The voice came from behind them, and Cammie whirled. Eza was already pushing his way in front of her, scana in hand, shielding her with his own body. Somehow, impossibly, Azanna was right behind them at the edge of the glade, blocking the way they'd come from. Over his shoulder, his dragon loomed menacingly.

"You said you didn't have a dragon," Azanna said

accusingly.

"I never did," objected Cammie. "I asked if you saw one."

"Well, now I do. And I see something else. I see some valuable hostages. I imagine the Introvertian king will pay handsomely to have one of his soldiers and one of his dragons returned alive."

That gave Cammie a strange kind of hope: at least he wasn't going to kill them. Fear still grabbed her by the throat, though, and her breath started coming in ragged gasps.

Eza didn't seem to like the sound of Azanna's plan, though. He hurled himself at the older man, who had barely enough time to unsheath his own scana and parry. Cammie watched, stunned; she'd never seen Eza fight, and what she saw were movements that were calm but explosive, fast but controlled. There was no hint of fear in the way he whipped his body back and forth, but every time he thrust or slashed, Azanna's sword was there.

"Use your head, boy," Azanna said through gritted teeth as Eza tried to gain an advantage. "I went to the Academy. I know the same moves you do. Every attack you use, I know the defense."

Neemie came hurtling in from the east, smashing into Azanna's head and knocking him off balance. Eza leaped in, swinging hard at Azanna's stomach. Azanna almost lunged out of the way in time, but Eza's sword grazed the top of his thigh, drawing blood as the older man staggered back to his feet.

But Neemie's attack had gotten Keena's attention, and the larger dragon screamed fiercely, winging herself into the brilliant blue sky and belching a long stream of fire at Neemie, who was climbing as rapidly as she could. Cammie felt the blast of flame all the way down on the ground, and she cringed, feeling exceptionally useless. But she was no fighter; the only violence she'd ever committed was the one time she'd summoned enough courage to kill a spider, or possibly trying to fight off Aed when he was coming after her tickle spots. If she tried to help Eza, the best that could happen is that she wouldn't be helpful; the worst was that she might get in Eza's way and he could be hurt or killed. So she watched in horror from the side, willing Eza to win.

The only hope was that Azanna wanted them alive – for now.

Azanna was struggling, blood from his wounded thigh soaking his pants and beginning to drip onto the ground. Eza, on the other hand – Cammie had never imagined seeing him like that, with his back straight and intense concentration on his face as he circled. He looked like he'd been swordfighting for his entire life, and didn't seem overmatched even against someone several years older and three inches taller.

Just then, though, Keena tucked in her wings and hurtled straight toward Eza. "LOOK OUT, EZA!" Cammie shouted.

There was no hesitation as Eza shoulder-rolled to the right and Keena surged past right where his head had been. The hit would surely have knocked him out. Eza popped back to his feet with fury on his face, launching into a ferocious string of attacks that Azanna parried only with great difficulty. It looked like their would-be captor was tiring, either from the exertion or from blood loss.

Cammie was scared, more scared than she could ever remember being. The fear mingled with anger, rage at her own powerlessness. She felt something bubbling up in her, something hot and fierce, like lava that wanted to erupt out of her. What was happening to her –

Keena landed in front of her, facing Eza, and then Cammie was howling, extending her hands toward the dragon. She watched in horror as her hands burst into flame – but the flame didn't burn her – it screamed out from her hands and enveloped Keena, who shrieked and writhed as the intense heat baked her scales and melted her wings. In seconds the dragon's corpse lay crumpled in the glade, scorched flowers all around it.

The lava inside Cammie was gone, and an incredible gnawing had replaced it, as if her stomach were trying to eat itself. She stumbled and sat down, feeling weak and sick all over. She was dimly aware of Eza running over to help her, and caught a brief glance of Azanna fleeing in the opposite direction as fast as his wounded leg would take him.

"What was *that?*" Eza asked, trying to help her to her feet.

"I can't...I need to rest..."

"We can't rest here," Eza said urgently. "We have to go. Even if it's not far. We have to find someplace safer."

Her legs wobbled from weakness and she leaned heavily on Eza. Her vision was going black around the edges, and it was all she could do to keep just putting one foot in front of the other.

"Eza, I'm scared..."

"We'll be okay," he told her. "We'll make it together."

ELEVEN

Eza could hardly sleep at all that night. Cammie had complained about being ravenously hungry and sick to her stomach at the same time, and had fallen asleep – almost literally *fallen*, not merely *going* to sleep like normal people do when they lie down and close their eyes, but sitting cross-legged on her sleeping bag one moment and horizontal with arms and legs splayed all over the ground the next moment. Eza had covered her with his own sleeping bag, like a blanket, before lying back on the ground and staring up at the sky full of stars that hung above him. Neemie was asleep on the other side of Cammie, snoring contentedly.

So many questions danced around Eza's head. Would Azanna come back – with friends? What had given Cammie that *incredible* power all of a sudden, and could she use it again when she wanted? Could Eza use it too?

He sighed. It was no use; he was never going to be able to sleep, and besides, he should probably be awake in case danger returned. Out came one of his reading candles, out came his flint and tinder, and shortly after he was engrossed in *Legends of the Artomancers*.

Eza knew his people used to be extremely magical. *Heroes of Introvertia* was full of of the tales, sorcerers good

165

and bad. Why had all that gone away?

In a matter of minutes *Artomancers* had completely captivated him. The narrative picked up roughly two thousand years ago, right when the Introvertians had just rebelled against Exclaimovia and journeyed fifty miles westward through the Very Large Forest to establish their new capital city of Tranquility. That rebellion had been started and led by powerful sorcerers, each with unique powers: the Artomancers used visual creativity to shape reality; physical mages could move heavy objects with ease; elemental mages reached inside themselves to manifest fire, water, and air. For the first fifty years or so, Introvertia had been peaceful; the spellcasters had been respected and formed a sort of upper class in society, freely passing along their knowledge to any who would study under them.

Then the dream ended and the nightmare began. For the next thousand years, evil sorcerers began popping up more and more frequently. Most spellcasters were still good, but the evil ones did so much harm that people began to fear magic. Around eight hundred years ago, in an event the book called the Great Reckoning, the remaining mages were given an ultimatum: cease using their powers or leave the kingdom. Almost all of them loved Introvertia so much that they chose to give up magic and stay in their homes. A small number chose to leave, some to other kingdoms and some to a life of seclusion in the wilderness. A dozen or so were kept on as instructors at Carnazon, teaching the young dragon-companions how to use magic in battle, until even that practice was abandoned five hundred years ago.

At this point, Eza suddenly realized how sore he was; he'd been lying on his stomach, leaning on his forearms, for (based on how far the moon had traveled across the sky) about seven hours now, and his shoulders were killing him. He rolled over onto his back, watching the moon and the stars, his brain spinning. Magic was gone because that's what his people had wanted. Cammie could do it and Eza couldn't because a few idiots a thousand years ago had ruined things for everybody, and a bunch of people had overreacted...

Eza knew he wasn't thinking straight; it was three in the morning, and nobody thought straight at three in the morning. But he also knew he wasn't done reading. He'd gotten one of the answers he wanted, but surely that couldn't be the end of the story. Could he learn magic? Was there anyone left alive who could teach him?

He forced himself to finish *Artomancers* – it wasn't the first time he'd read an entire book in one night when he should have been sleeping – and was shocked near the end to find that it contained a fairly detailed description of where one of the Artomancers, or possibly a handful of them, had fled upon leaving Tranquility. Dawn was approaching by this point, which was good because Eza's second reading candle of the night was already a misshapen blob of wax, and as the sky began to turn orange and then blue, he squinted at the pages. The book referred to a trail that went south from a large lake, past a certain landmark in the foothills of the mountains, and to a village where the Artomancers had settled. There was no more detail than that.

Breathlessly Eza grabbed the map that Cammie had made fun of a few days before. Some Son of a Lake was the only large body of water on the map, and Eza had drawn the eastern edge of the Impassable Mountains below it. That was one of the first things he'd added to the landscape, back when he was reading *The Northern Wars* and trying to keep track of the movement of armies and spies. Around a dozen sites were marked nearby, most of them battlefields. If the map was accurate – which was a large *if*, but Eza knew he had been very careful – the ancient Artomancers' village would be right about...*there*.

Eza rocked back on his heels. The sun was trying to dominate the sky, but wouldn't crest the highest peaks of the mountains for a few hours yet. There in the clearing it was still shadow. Eza suddenly became aware that dew had fallen during the night; the whole clearing was damp, including his and Cammie's sleeping bags.

There was no way the Artomancers still lived in that same settlement, of course. He knew in his head it was improbable, maybe even impossible. Surely they would have been found by now, or would have moved in search of better ground – a defensible castle, perhaps, or another kingdom far away where spellcasters were appreciated rather than scorned.

Lost in all of this was the very first thought that had occurred to Eza when he and Cammie had first met Azanna – this meant there were *actual wild dragons* here in the mountains, untamed and belonging to no one. What would happen if he could find one and bond with it? Was that even possible, or was Eza not a strong enough companion to make that happen? After all, he still couldn't share specific thoughts with Neemie, a dragon he knew well and had been working with for a year and a half. How could he ever possibly hope to get through to a wild dragon who had never seen people and was probably skeptical of them? Could he even get close enough without being turned into Roast Introvertian, Extra Well Done? And how, just how, had Azanna grown his dragon so *massively huge?*

Eza couldn't explain why, but it seemed like those two thoughts – wild dragons and wild magicians – were intertwined in his head, connected somehow in a way his thoughts couldn't express yet.

Cammie was just beginning to stir, and Eza slid over next to her, being careful not to touch her. Suddenly her eyes snapped wide and she grabbed his hand, as if trying to convince herself he was real. The frightened look in her eyes scared him too, and he forced a gentle smile. "Hey," he said. "It's okay. I'm here."

"Where are we?" She didn't have her glasses on, so Eza handed them to her, and she squinted as she looked around the clearing.

"We're safe. I found a protected place for us after you, you know..." He waved his hands vaguely. "Whatever it was you did."

"Hm. Yeah. That." Her eyes swam for a moment, and then she fixed her gaze on Eza. "I'm really hungry."

"Okay. I have some –"

"You don't understand," she interrupted, with an intensity that surprised Eza. "I'm *really* hungry."

She was not exaggerating. Eza watched in alarm as she devoured what should have been three or four days worth of supplies – bread, meat (even the onala meat she had refused when they'd first met), dried fruits, and more. Where was she putting it all? At last, just when Eza was beginning to wonder if they'd have to call off the whole trip and head back to Tranquility for more food, Cammie sat back, satisfied.

Eza knew it was rude to pry, especially considering how Cammie had been close to tears the night before. But he had to know more. If this was something they could use, it was important for them to learn how – maybe the Artomancers could even teach them. What was more, and what made Eza's blood really run cold, is that if Cammie did have some kind of rare magical gift, that might make people want to capture her for their own purposes. Either way he needed answers.

"So...do you know what happened last night?"

Cammie shook her head.

"Okay," Eza said. "I was just trying to find out if –"

"I don't KNOW, okay?" Cammie shouted, instantly on her feet. "I already told you I don't know! I don't know what happened and I don't know where it came from and I don't know if it's going to happen again and...
"

She had yelled at Eza before, but for some reason this one really hurt. They were out here all by themselves, and he was only trying to help her, but she was lashing out at him like he was the one who caused the problem. His bottom lip started to shake and he bit it, hard.

But Cammie had run out of energy, and looked down at Eza, who was staring at her, still trying to hold himself together. "What's wrong with your FACE?" she bellowed.

"Do you feel better now?"

"Of course I don't FEEL BETTER you –"

Eza held up a hand, and Cammie trailed off. "I know you'd happily rant all day if I let you," he said. "But now isn't the time. We have to get moving. Azanna might come back for us, and if you keep eating like you did for breakfast, we'll be out of food before we reach Exclaimovia."

"Yeah, being that hungry was weird," Cammie said casually, as if her previous outburst hadn't happened. "I felt...like all the energy had been sucked out of me."

"Maybe it had," Eza mused. "Maybe that fire was made up of heat and energy from your body, and you had to eat food to put it all back."

"Possible."

"If that's true, you'd better keep eating a lot. That thing may happen to you again, and we might not have time or a safe place to let you rest for..." Eza checked the sky, guessing how close to the mountain peaks the sun might be. "Fourteen hours afterward."

Cammie looked like the thought of another magical outburst hadn't occurred to her. Neemie was thoroughly roused by this time, and came hopping over to the two of them. Eza was surprised by the thoughts radiating from her; she seemed very curious about Cammie. Neemie wanted something, too, and cocked her head at Eza as if willing him to understand.

"Her?" Eza asked, pointing at Cammie.

The dragon affirmed this.

Eza looked at Cammie for a few moments, wondering how she was going to react. "The dragon wants to sit on your shoulders."

"Oh, why not," Cammie said. "It won't be the

weirdest thing to happen in the last week."

Eza was surprised at the feeling of satisfaction wafting off of Neemie – not that the feeling was there, but the strength of it. Neemie seemed to be happier than she'd been in the entire time Eza had known her. That was peculiar, and a little offensive; Eza was peeved that she would prefer the company of this Exclaimovian over that of Eza himself, or even his father, who had been Neemie's companion for decades.

Cammie giggled. "This is fun. I see why you like having her up there."

In a few minutes Eza had cleaned up the campsite and left it as if they'd never been there. He covered the imprints of their bodies and sleeping bags with loose dirt, then sent Cammie to the far edge of the clearing and scuffed out their boot marks. If anything at all was out of place, Eza couldn't find it, even with all his Ranger training.

The sun had just peeked over the tops of the Impassable Mountains when they got on the road, winding a back-and-forth route through the foothills rather than moving down onto the open terrain where they could potentially be seen from miles away. Eza could indeed spot the main road roughly ten miles to the north, so far away that it might not have been visible from ground level. A few scattered towns dotted the path, home to people who chose to live outside the borders of any of the known kingdoms so they could scrap out an independent living. Eza wondered if the towns ever feuded with each other the way kingdoms did, in battles of a dozen or so people on each side rather than twenty thousand.

The good thing about the high ground was that, even if he and Cammie were visible from the road, so was anyone coming their direction, which would give them a chance to find a hiding spot or pick up their pace. The thought of danger coming from the mountains never occurred to Eza.

It was another gorgeous spring morning, and the light, bouncy melody Cammie hummed to herself seemed to add to the beauty, rather than take away from it. If she was still on edge about what had happened the day before, she wasn't showing it. Neemie was still on her shoulders, apparently overjoyed to be there. That meant they didn't have a dragon in the sky scouting for them, which put Eza a little on edge, but he wasn't about to ask Neemie to move.

He should have. It was just after three o'clock when Eza hopped a narrow ravine and then rounded a bend to see a pack of twenty wild mountain goats in front of him. Goats would not have been on most people's list of things they were scared to see in the mountains; as animals go, plenty of people kept them as farm animals, and Eza had even heard of children riding around on them like miniature horses.

But wild goats, especially mountain goats with the huge curved-back horns, were extremely aggressive and extremely territorial. Being surprised by them was very bad, because it almost always meant you were already inside their territory. Even as Eza stopped short and began backing up, forty goat eyes turned to face him. Less than a second later, most of them were charging at him.

"Neemie!" he shouted, willing the dragon to attack from the top and distract some of the goats. Instantly Neemie left Cammie's shoulders, soaring twenty feet into the air with a screech and winging herself into a nearly straight-down dive, taking enormous chunks out of one goat's back before climbing up into the sky.

But most of the animals were still charging straight for Eza and Cammie. "Get up!" Eza shouted, locking his fingers together next to Cammie and praying she understood what he meant. Somehow she did, planting one foot in his palms and leaping upward as he thrust his hands to the sky. The movement gave her enough height to grab on to a low-hanging birch branch next to them, and with difficulty she wrapped her legs around the branch and climbed on top of it. Unless the goats managed to head-butt the tree down – which was possible – she was safe.

Eza, on the other hand, was not. Saving Cammie had

left him exposed to the thundering herd of animals, and he shoulder-rolled to his left, behind the tree trunk, just in time to dodge the first one. Goats were not the most nimble animals when charging, and their momentum carried them well past him; he pulled his scana free of its sheath and swung at the nearest goat, opening a long and deep cut on its side and spilling its insides onto the soil. The animal fell with a heavy thud.

This gave Eza another huge advantage: a barricade. Now here was at least one angle from which he couldn't be charged, so he kept a hand on the dead goat, watching the others circle around. Neemie was still in the air overhead, breathing fire as best she could – was it just Eza's imagination or did the fire seem stronger than usual? – while Cammie desperately clutched the tree.

Eza picked up the thudding of footsteps behind him almost too late, leaping on top of the dead goat and then again to an empty patch of ground. He'd been charged from the rear, hadn't been watching his back. That wasn't good enough. Something reminded him of the ravine he'd crossed right before seeing the goats, and he sprinted back around the bend...

Yes, there it was, a ravine just narrow enough for the goats to fall into, if he could somehow coax them into it. But if they didn't follow his lead, or even if some of them didn't, then he'd be on one side and Cammie would be stranded on the other side without him. There was no time to think. He had to act. Scana in hand, he sprinted toward the ravine, spinning around just as he got to it.

"Hey, you stupid goats!" he shouted at the top of his lungs, feeling very Exclaimovian. "I ate your mother last week!"

The goats almost certainly did not understand him (although, Eza thought, it was a possibility), but they seemed to grasp his intent, and a chorus of angry brays echoed off the granite hillsides. Seven goats had come around the bend and were pawing at the ground. In the next second they were charging him, and Eza was turning, leaping –

The goats screamed as they fell, a horrible sound that faded and then ended with a wet splat. That was a total of eight dead, seven in the ravine and one by Eza's sword, but the remaining twelve were clustered on the far side of the ravine, angrily bleating at Eza, as if daring him to come and get some.

Another shape rounded the bend behind them, and for just a moment, Eza was terrified, wondering if it was some kind of king goat – was there such a thing? – before recognizing Cammie. She howled in fury, a sound Eza recognized only too well, and then fire exploded from her body, searing all twelve goats in a single flash. Neemie barely escaped, launching upward as fast as her wings could carry her while the goats on the ground rushed around in terrified circles, their wool on fire, head-butting each other. Several ran headlong into the ravine, while others merely slumped where they were, scorch marks all over them. In moments it was over, and silence descended over the ravine.

Cammie collapsed.

His heart still pounding, Eza leaped the ravine one more time, rolling Cammie over onto her back and checking for signs of life. She was breathing, but unconscious. He kicked himself for not forcing her to eat more throughout the day. If she'd been full of food, if she'd had energy to spare, maybe she could have used the magic without it completely ruining her –

But of course he didn't know that, didn't know how any of this actually worked. All he knew was that he was forty miles from home, most of the way to Exclaimovia, with no proof the stolen dragons were there at all and no plan for what to do once he arrived. A thousand thoughts careened around his brain, whispering to him that his quest was doomed. He shook all of that off. Those were problems for tomorrow; his only job now was to rescue Cammie and get out of the goats' territory in case there were any more left.

That thought made him pause, and he tried to slow his breathing long enough to listen to the forest. There were no sounds except the wind through the birch trees and the trickle of water somewhere far off at the bottom of the ravine. He spent a few moments thinking about which direction the water would be flowing, not wanting to drink from a stream that had been flowing through goat carcasses. If there were any other animals around, he couldn't hear them, but he knew that any wolves or bears in the vicinity would be attracted by the smell of barbecued goat. There wasn't much time.

Deftly he used his scana to slice free several pounds of fire-roasted goat steaks, stuffing the meat into his backpack and hoping it didn't make everything else smell. But that, again, was a problem for the future. The bigger issue was Cammie.

She wasn't going to like this, if she happened to wake up during it, but there was no choice. Eza lifted her arms and upper body, draping half of her over himself and using his thighs to hoist her into the air. He was shocked at how light she was. He'd done a lot of physical training at the Dragon Academy, but it seemed hardly any effort at all for him to carry her. Maybe that was just his nerves; maybe he would get her a mile up the road and then collapse from stress.

But he made up his mind not to stop, and so he didn't. The sun was behind him; he tried turning around once to see how low it had gone only to have Cammie's weight nearly knock him off his feet, so he kept facing east, guessing at the height of the sun based on what the eastern sky looked like. It was nearly dusk before he finally found a secluded campsite, a stand of trees hemmed in by rocks on three sides and with only one path in. Exhausted, he eased Cammie to the ground underneath a huge cedar, his shoulders and knees and back suddenly screaming at him. If his guess was right, he'd been carrying her for nearly three hours, and all at once he felt the strain of every step. Completely spent, he flopped to the ground.

After lying there for ten or fifteen minutes, staring at the navy blue sky as it faded to purple and then to star-speckled black, he rolled over toward his backpack, extracting some goat meat. One thing was for sure: if anything attacked them in the night, or if Azanna somehow found them again, they were done for, with Cammie unconscious from the magic and Eza in no condition to fight. When the scream of pain in his thighs had dropped to a dull shriek, he laid out Cammie's sleeping bag on the ground and rolled her over on top of it, then spread his own over her to keep her warm. Either they had fled higher into the mountains while running from the goats or else it was an uncommonly cold night, because Eza was chilled to the bone, but he didn't dare risk a fire. A reading candle should have been safe, especially if Eza used it under the cover of that rock overhang a few feet away. For some reason, though, he didn't feel right about it. He just lay there in the dark, listening for the sound of anything moving. All he could hear was Cammie's deep, regular breathing, and Neemie snoring.

TWELVE

Cammie's first thought upon waking up was that she was dead; the herd of goats must have trampled her. That was clearly impossible because she was in far too much pain to be dead. She let out a groan as she rolled over, every joint in her body desperately achy. Her mouth was dry. "Water," she croaked, and Eza brought her one of the canteens, which she promptly drained without pausing for breath. Only then did she actually glance at Eza...who looked as awful as she felt.

"What's wrong with your face?" she blurted.

"My face is exhausted from carrying your face for most of the afternoon yesterday."

"You *carried* me?" Cammie asked in shock.

"I know you really pulled back when I touched you the night before we left. You're almost Introvertian like that." Eza smiled. "But I didn't have a choice. We were still in the goats' territory and we had to get out. I'm sorry."

"No," Cammie said. "I'm actually...really impressed. You don't look strong enough."

"Please," Eza answered, laughing now. "I've carried books heavier than you."

"Hey!"

"If you have any muscles on your body larger than my pinky finger, then I'm a badger."

Cammie stuck out her tongue. "I pushed you out of that river, mister!"

"You did not! I kept one foot in the water the entire time!"

"Mmmmhmmm," Cammie said skeptically, raising an eyebrow.

Eza stood to his feet, looking like he immediately regretted it. "Right. Sometime when we're not both half dead, we're going to have a rematch."

"Speaking of half dead, I'm really hungry. Again."

"I told you," Eza scolded, passing her some of the roasted goat. "You have to keep eating all day long. I think the magic does take energy directly out of you, like you said yesterday. The more you've eaten, the more of an energy reserve you have. You can run a mile after a good meal a lot easier than you could run it on an empty stomach. Though I'm not sure *you* could run a mile at all."

"*HEY!*"

But there was a mischievous gleam in his eyes, and she knew he'd only been teasing. "Did you just say something unkind to make a joke, Ezalen Skywing?" she asked in mock horror.

Eza suddenly seemed to realize that he had done exactly that, and the look on his face made Cammie double over, laughing so hard that she flew into a coughing fit. "I'm rubbing off on you," she needled him.

"Well rub back off," he said, wiping his sleeve off on her shoulder with a suppressed grin.

"NOPE! I'm a part of you now." She took a bite of the goat. "This is disgustingly bland. I thought you were a good cook."

"I didn't cook it," Eza said. In response to her blank stare, he added, "You did."

"Oh..."

That made Eza laugh, and he dug into his backpack for some spices. "There's bound to be something loud and unruly in here to suit your taste buds."

Cammie picked the reddest spice she could find and rubbed half the jar into the goat meat, making an enormous mess of her face as she devoured the whole thing, and then a second piece, and then some flatbread. "So where are we now, and where are we going?"

"I think we've gone a total of fifty miles, but not all in a straight line," Eza said, unfolding his map. "My best guess is that we're...here. If we are, then that lake –"

"Some Son of a Lake," Cammie corrected.

"Yes, that lake, will be north-northeast of us. We should be able to see it once we get down out of the mountains a bit. If I'm right, then we could reach the Artomancer settlement by the end of the day today. We'll have to hustle, but I think we can do it."

"Are you up for hustling?" she asked.

"Cammaina Ravenwood, is that concern I detect in your voice?"

"Not in the slightest," she said loudly, turning red. "I'm just doubting you."

Eza laughed again, shaking his head. "Doubt no more. It takes a lot more than some sore legs to stop a Dragon Academy Ranger."

"Well well, Mister Ranger," Cammie said with a mock salute, "lead on!"

Neemie settled back on to her shoulders, and the two of them set off through the mountains. Eza seemed to be leading them back down into the foothills, like he'd mentioned; every time they had the opportunity to descend, he chose that, and by mid-morning – about the time Cammie's tummy was grumbling for a snack – they had made it almost down to ground level. There, off to the left, was Some Son of a Lake, exactly where Eza said it was supposed to be.

Maybe his silly homemade map wasn't worthless after all.

The lake itself stretched out toward the northern horizon, huge and flat like a giant sheet of glass. Cammie thought she could see a city on the far shore, reflected in the still water – it had to be forty miles away, and if the morning hadn't been exceptionally clear and cool, she was sure it wouldn't have been visible. "What is that?"

she asked Eza, pointing.

"Mistal," Eza answered. "The capital of Esteria."

Cammie stared in amazement. "Not *the* Mistal? I've heard they ride magical dogs there."

"I've heard the same thing," Eza agreed. "But I don't know for sure. From what I've read they're even less friendly to outsiders than Introvertia is. They probably have good reasons for keeping their secrets, though, just like we do."

Suddenly Neemie, still atop Cammie's shoulders, spun so hard that she knocked Cammie off-balance and into the dust. "What'd you do that for?" Cammie brayed loudly as Neemie winged herself high into the sky.

Eza looked nearly overwhelmed at the sensations he was picking up from Neemie. "She's giving off recognition. She sees something familiar, but not familiar, like looking in a smudged mirror..." Eza's head snapped up. "I think she sees a wild dragon!"

Neemie went tearing off to the north, up toward the higher peaks of the mountains, with Eza rushing headlong behind. Cammie wasn't as athletic as Eza, no matter how much she had tried to tease him earlier, and in seconds she was red-faced and wheezing, lagging far behind them. "Eza!" she shouted. There was no sound around her except for Eza's rapidly disappearing footsteps. "Eza!" she cried again in desperation.

This time there was only silence.

Eza was barely breathing hard when he saw Neemie pinwheel out of the sky. Boulders and thorn bushes blocked his way, but he heaved himself over them, a few briers sticking in his Ranger cloak. He was at the bottom of a narrow crevasse, with vertical rock walls sticking up on both sides of him and a path barely wide enough for Eza to pass through. He hesitated, unsure, but he could sense Neemie somewhere ahead, so he turned sideways and crept through the narrow squeeze.

After a hundred yards the squeeze opened into a slightly wider area, a bowl-shaped glade ringed by the same high rock walls, which were nearly forty feet tall. A few scattered pines, wispy and thin, reached for the sky. Neemie was near the middle of the glade, and on the far side...

Eza's breath disappeared from his chest. It was a dragon, coming up to Eza's mid-chest, much taller than Neemie, who only came up to his waist. Whereas Neemie was red, this dragon was silver-gray, and as it spotted Eza, it spread its wings to their full width and gave a shriek.

Eza's hand immediately strayed toward his scana, recognizing even as he did so that if this dragon wanted him dead, there was probably not much he could do except for die. But the dragon's wings furled back in. Neemie was radiating many, many different things; Eza could only assume she was communicating with the other dragon somehow, perhaps with the same thought-talk dragons used with their human companions. Whatever Neemie was doing, it seemed to be working, and the wild dragon looked hard at Eza.

He was shocked to realize he could sense thoughts coming off it, too. They were much more vague than what he could pick up from Neemie, but it was something. There was curiosity and – wonder, maybe? Perhaps it had never seen a dragon partnered with a human before. Eza reached out with his own thoughts, trying to tell the dragon it could trust him...

There was an intense wave of confusion now. Eza assumed the dragon was unprepared for a human to speak in a way that it could understand. But already the confusion was subsiding, giving way toward a curiosity and a desire to know more. Eza's heart was pounding so hard it actually hurt. If he could get close enough to the dragon to put his hand on its snout, he could link with it, and they would be bonded.

But would it let him?

Eza felt like he had to try. Slowly he began edging his way toward the dragon, both hands out in front of him, wearing what he hoped was a disarming smile. The dragon tilted its head, watching him come. He tried to open his mind completely to the dragon, show it he wasn't hiding anything or plotting anything. If it so much as sneezed, he'd be extra crispy before he knew what had happened.

Whatever Neemie was telling the dragon seemed to be working, though. One trembling foot in front of the other, Eza moved to within an arm's reach of the dragon. There he paused, listening to its breathing. Slowly he raised his left hand and looked the dragon in the eyes. It took a half-step forward until its snout was touching his hand. Eza gently placed his hand on its forehead and closed his eyes. He had heard about this part but didn't know what it was supposed to feel like –

For just a moment it felt like he was seeing himself through the dragon's eyes, just the way Mazaren had seen through Arjera's eyes. He was looking at himself, left hand out, hair matted with dirt and a few twigs – *Cammie must be laughing her head off every time she looks at me*, Eza thought – with an expression of awe and amazement on his face that made the real Eza giggle. Just like that the connection was gone, but something had remained behind – like this wild dragon was occupying a part of his brain, like he could sense its thoughts more clearly than he had ever sensed Neemie's. So this was what it was like to be bonded. He had to admit it was pretty incredible.

He ran his fingers down the dragon's snout, reaching out to it again, wanting to know more. It was a girl, and she would need a name. "What do you think about

Aleiza?" he asked. "It was – my mother's name. I think she'd be happy to know she shared it with a dragon."

The dragon may not have understood all of that, but she seemed to understand that the name Aleiza was now associated with her, "EZALEN SKYWING!" came a ferocious bellow from behind Eza, and instantly Aleiza was in the air, wondering what sort of human trickery had just been uncorked on her.

"That's Cammie," he said out loud. "She's my friend."

Aleiza looked him dead in the eyes and gave him a thought that, roughly translated into human language, was: *Is she always that loud?*

All the nervous tension of the past ten minutes bubbled to the surface and Eza found himself laughing uncontrollably, collapsing to the ground and struggling to breathe. "You deserve to choke for leaving me back there by myself!" bawled Cammie, and she had a point, but Eza had a *dragon*, and that mattered way more.

Several minutes later, when he had finally composed himself and wiped the laughter-tears from his eyes (and Eza had to admit that he was very impressed with Cammie's dedication, the way she stood there with her hands on her hips and tapping her foot the entire time it took Eza to stop laughing), he said, "Cammie, I want you to meet Aleiza, my dragon. Aleiza, this is my friend Cammie."

"Your...dragon?" Cammie repeated in shock, sizing up

the silver animal. "How? Wh – *how?*"

Eza explained to her what had happened while Aleiza looked on, obviously still unconvinced about this noisy human. At the end Cammie furrowed her brow, pushed her glasses up, and cleared her throat. "So is she actually *your* dragon now? Like she has to do whatever you say, and all of that?"

"Well, no," Eza said. "There's a reason we're called dragon-companions and not dragon tamers or trainers or anything like that. We have a mutual friendship with our dragons."

"So she may get bored and fly away in ten minutes and you'd never see her again."

"If that's what she wants to do, sure. From what I've been told, though, she has a connection to me now; even if she were to fly away, she'd still be in my head and I'd still be in hers, and she'd know where to find me if she wanted to again." Eza smiled at Aleiza, putting his hand on her head. "But I don't think she'd do that. She's very intrigued by the idea of Neemie and me being friends, and she seems to be very excited about me being her companion."

"What are you going to do with her?"

"I guess she's going to follow us to Exclaimovia and help us get the others back."

Cammie considered this, then asked the one question Eza had been wondering himself. "Why is she so much bigger than Neemie?"

"I don't know," Eza admitted. "Maybe they grow bigger in the wild, or maybe this one is a different breed of dragon, like how some kinds of horses are taller than others."

"What if it shrinks?"

Eza stared at her, boggled by the question. "I think you're jealous," he said at last.

"*Jealous?!*" Cammie repeated at maximum volume, making Aleiza flinch. "Why, the nerve of you, to think that I would be..."

She trailed off, as if waiting for Eza to jump in and argue his point, but they both knew by now that he wasn't going to.

"You know what, *fine*," she said at last. "I guess I am a little jealous. I want a pet dragon."

"Aleiza isn't –"

"You know what I meant."

"Okay," Eza said, feeling bad that she actually was jealous. "But you can shoot fire and that's pretty neat too."

Aleiza overheard the word "fire" and obligingly launched a ten-foot-long stream into the air. The heat wave made Eza close his eyes and turn away, but he could tell Aleiza was very proud of herself, and he let her know he was proud of her too.

"Yes, I can shoot fire and then collapse and sleep for

half a day," Cammie said bitterly. "Some magic."

"Well, listen. We should be at the Artomancer settlement by the end of the day –"

"If it's there and if we can find it," Cammie butted in.

"Yes, you optimistic ray of sunshine, if it's there and if we can find it. But maybe they can teach you how to use your magic better."

"You really think so?"

"I think it's as good a chance as any. Come on, though. We were already cutting it close if we wanted to be there by sundown, and now we're half an hour behind."

Then Eza turned to Aleiza. He really, really hoped she would want to come along. If she decided she didn't want to, or if it turned out she had baby dragonets to take care of or something, Eza would have to say goodbye to her so soon after making friends. He reached out with his mind only to find that she was already listening to Neemie, who was passionately explaining the plight of the stolen Introvertian dragons. Of course that made sense – after all, Neemie was the one who had suggested that Eza and Cammie set off by themselves when Captain Onanden wouldn't help them. Whatever Neemie had said, it seemed to be working. Aleiza was furious, determined to do whatever it took to help her captured...well, *family* wasn't exactly the right word, because Aleiza almost certainly was not related to them by blood, but it seemed to Eza like dragons all regarded each other as family. That was the only explanation for why Neemie took it so personally that dragons she'd never even met were being mistreated.

Cammie loudly cleared her throat behind Eza, and he suddenly realized how disorienting it must be for her. He and the two dragons were all communicating without words, and the one person who hated silence must have felt very awkward. "Neemie is convincing Aleiza to come along," Eza said. "And it sounds like Aleiza is all for it."

Cammie nodded thoughtfully. "If one dragon is good, two must be better, right?"

"That's what I'm thinking. Hey, be sure you're eating constantly too. You need your energy in case you have to use that magic again. The Artomancers may want to see what you can do."

"Good point. Can you pass the goat?"

THIRTEEN

Cammie's feet and legs had been in utter agony for the entire afternoon. Eza, who was already in better shape than her, had been moving even faster than normal, either wanting to get to the Artomancer village before nightfall or else really, really excited about having his own dragon. Cammie felt like she was dying, but she didn't want to ask him to wait up for her, didn't want to seem weak.

The exhaustion was making her homesick. She missed her mom and dad, and Aed, and Alair and Keiko and all the others. She missed hot food and songs after dinner (Eza had sung a few for her after lunch, but it wasn't the same) and cuddling with her family on rainy days. She missed the Shouting Square and her school. The only thing that kept her going was the thought that every step she took brought her one step closer to Exclaimovia.

And then what? She'd found out about a secret plot to steal Introvertian dragons and turn them into an army for Exclaimovia, and she was bringing an Introvertian with her to steal them back and return them to Introvertia. Her father might be brought to ruin. She might be discovered and charged as a traitor – or worse.

195

And all because *stupid* Cammie Ravenwood had been *stupid* enough to think she fit in better with Introvertians...

But some other part of her mind, perhaps the part that still sort-of felt Introvertian, was reminding her that she'd done the right thing. If dragons were being stolen and abused, it was wrong even if her own people were the ones doing it. Her allegiance to good, to the truth, mattered more than whatever kingdom she'd happened to be born into. And if something went horribly wrong and Exclaimovia banished her forever...

Maybe, just maybe, she'd be able to adapt to life in Introvertia.

"I was thinking," she said to nobody in particular, but hoping Eza was close enough to be listening, "about what Mr. Cappel said that night. About how there are things we think are part of our true personality, but they're really just habits we formed based on the way we were brought up."

"Yeah, that was really interesting," Eza replied.

Cammie brightened. Was he making small talk with her? "So...if we had been raised in the same place, do you think we'd be more alike? Maybe even friends?"

Eza smiled widely. "Would you really want to see loud Eza?"

"YES!" Cammie shouted, drawing a glare from Aleiza, who was circling twenty feet in the air above them. "I would LOVE to see loud Eza. And besides, I'm going to anyway, because once we get to Exclaimovia you're going to have to blend in, just like I did in Tranquility."

"Like you tried to," Eza corrected, still smiling. "I hope I do a better job than you did."

"I cannot *wait*. My friends will love to meet you. I think you and Alair will get along really well."

"Oh, yeah. He's the one who everyone thinks you're dating."

"Yes." Cammie was fairly sure she was turning red and tried to hide behind a coughing fit.

Eza seemed to discern that Cammie was unsettled about something, though, and he kept his green eyes on her. His smile had faded, but the earnest care on his face set Cammie at ease.

"It's just," she continued, "the whole stolen dragons thing. I know what my people are doing is wrong. It's more than just wrong; it's an act of war. If your captain had taken us more seriously, there could be armies marching toward each other right now. We might be the only people in the five kingdoms who could stop that war."

Eza nodded, impressed. "That's..."

"That's what?" Cammie prodded.

"I'm sorry. I was about to compliment you, and I know you don't like that."

Cammie stared at him.

"Well," she said at last, "maybe I can learn to tolerate them."

"In that case, I was going to say that was a really smart way of thinking about things, and I'm very impressed with you."

Now Cammie was *sure* she was blushing. "Thank you, Eza."

"Thank you for receiving the compliment, Cammie."

"What I was going to say before I distracted myself is that I'm...scared. My father is involved somehow in the whole stolen dragon thing. Helping you might bring dishonor to him, or might even end his career if it's discovered that I'm involved. I could be banished from my kingdom as a traitor." Suddenly there was a lump in her throat, and she swallowed hard, staring at Eza with her jaw clenched to keep from crying. "If that happens," she said at last, "and I'm not welcome in Exclaimovia, and I don't fit in back in Introvertia...then you might be the only person who cares what happens to me."

"I'm sure your friends and family won't abandon you," Eza said gently.

"What are they going to do, come with me to Introvertia?" Cammie asked, more harshly than she intended.

"If we succeed in getting our dragons back, I'm sure King Jazan and Queen Annaya will find a way to reward you. They'll take care of you, and they'll take care of the people who matter to you."

Cammie couldn't help picturing her family living in a house off the Reading Square, with sounds of shouting and tickle fights coming from the open windows and irritating everyone who was trying to focus on a book. The thought made her laugh in spite of herself, and Eza tilted his head, looking confused. "Sorry," she said. "I just imagined my family living in Tranquility."

A brief look of horror crossed Eza's face before he recovered. "That would...certainly be something," he managed in the end.

"Can we take a little break, though? I know you want to get where we're going tonight, but my feet are *killing me*."

Eza checked the sun, then looked up at Aleiza and Neemie as if asking them what they thought. "Sure," he said. "There's a hill with a flat top a little distance that way. The brush on top will keep us hidden, but we'll have a great view of the plains in case anyone tries to sneak up on us."

"Will we be able to see the Artomancer village from there?"

"Hard to say. We'll be able to see the place where it's supposed to be, absolutely. But it could be tucked into the mountains, or it could be hidden by magic. It could have moved sometime in the past eight hundred years, or it could have been destroyed by an enemy army."

Cammie smiled dryly. "Who's the ray of sunshine now?"

"I really hope we find it, but if we don't, that's not the end of the world. We came this way before we even knew there might be spellcasters out here. If we don't find them, we've lost nothing." Eza chuckled. "That's what optimism looks like."

They made it to the hilltop twenty minutes later, and Cammie barely let her sleeping bag settle to the ground before landing on top of it with a heave, staring up at the few wispy clouds moving through the clear sky. The sun was about halfway toward the horizon, and Eza made his way to the southeastern edge of the hill to scout their surroundings. Some Son of a Lake was still to their north, although Cammie could tell they had come a significant distance to the east, because it was now to their left and a little bit behind rather than directly to their left. Esteria wasn't visible on the far shore anymore, probably due to the midafternoon haze.

"Exclaimovia is that way," Eza said, pointing.

"You can see it?" asked Cammie. She sprang to her feet and instantly wished she hadn't as she sat back down heavily, her feet and thighs screaming at her.

"No. The mountains are in the way, but the border is about twenty miles that direction, and Pride is another ten. Today is..." Eza did some quick math in his head.

"Wednesday, and we can be there by midday Friday if we hurry." He looked back over at her. "You look really rough. Is there anything I can do to help you?"

"Not unless you want to rub my feet."

Cammie had only intended it as sarcasm, but realized as she said it that the thought of letting Eza touch her wouldn't even have occurred to her unless some part of her brain was okay with it. She was expecting Eza to hear the tone of her voice and react accordingly, but his head did that tilting thing again and she could tell he'd made the connection. "You'd be okay with that?" he asked.

"Ezalen Skywing," she said in mock surprise, "did you just read between the lines? There may be hope for you yet."

"Don't get used to it," he said, trying and failing to hide his smile.

"I really am rubbing off on you."

Eza just raised an eyebrow as he pulled off her boots.

Cammie's question about being able to see the Artomancer village had really gotten inside Eza's head. Not the question itself, but his answer to it. Of *course* it would be there; the book said so. But it could have been destroyed or moved in the meantime, or – Eza had thought of this part much later – the people there might be unwilling to help an Introvertian. He didn't know how long Artomancers held grudges, after all. Yes, it was true that he and Cammie had come via this northern route for a reason that still made sense, which was to avoid the Very Large Forest, and it was true that they hadn't even known the Artomancers were out here until a few nights ago. But Eza had gotten his hopes up. In his head – with that wild Introvertian imagination of his – he'd already reenacted several meetings with them, dramatic apologies for the unjust way his kingdom had treated them centuries before, surprise and delight as they trained him in their ancient ways of magic.

Cammie's "little break" had turned into the entire afternoon. The closer they got to Exclaimovia, the more she wanted to tell stories about good times with her family and friends. Eza had gotten to where he really enjoyed her stories. At first he had tolerated them out of politeness, but he couldn't lie to himself – he'd gotten *excited* when she had started telling the first story that afternoon. And Cammie still seemed in disbelief that he listened all the way to the end rather than butting in. Eza got the impression she had begun each of these stories dozens of times before but had never made it to the end of any of them. Even when she repeated a few she'd told before, he didn't stop her. The story had been good the first time and it was just as good the second time.

After that they'd spent a while reading *The Dawn Song* together and then singing, but quietly, so that the sound didn't carry to the plains. Eza had kept Aleiza and

Neemie on the ground, not wanting to risk them being seen. Aleiza still seemed excited about the whole adventure, and anytime Eza wasn't talking to her, Neemie was filling her head with...well, whatever they were talking about.

Cammie had fallen asleep nearly as soon as the sun dipped all the way below the horizon, while the western sky was still on fire with yellow and orange. Eza watched as dark blue advanced from east to west, like a blanket being pulled over the earth as its bedtime approached, and then the stars came out. Before long both dragons were snoring (so it wasn't just a Neemie thing, Eza thought), and Eza let himself fall asleep too.

The next morning was bright and clear like the past few had been; the weather wouldn't turn properly rainy until the summer. Cammie looked fully refreshed when she woke up, and worked herself through a very loud routine of stretching before she stood up, putting her arms into the air, then her legs, then spreading out her fingers and toes, then shaking like a dog that was trying to dry off. At last she stood, smiling at Eza. "I feel amazing!"

"I hope you feel like breakfast. Today's the day we meet the Artomancers."

"Hopefully."

Eza smiled. "Whatever you say, sunshine."

Cammie froze, one sock halfway on her foot, staring

at Eza. "That is not about to become my nickname."

"That's up to you," Eza said with a shrug.

"Okay, FINE. I'll be the most optimistic person you've ever met, then."

"You should try it. Be an optimist for twenty-four hours. If you get to see loud Eza, I want to see hopeful Cammie."

"No, no. I get to see loud Eza because you already got to see quiet Cammie."

Eza exploded into laughter. "When was that? When you were shouting at me outside the palace? When you refused to leave the Music Square? When you interrupted me inside Cappel's Bookstore?"

"OKAY, EZA..."

"OKAY, CAMMIE," he said, so loudly that he startled Aleiza, who was just waking up.

Cammie gaped at him, then laughed so hard she rocked back onto the ground. "Loud Eza!" she said gleefully in between howls of laughter. "I love it!"

Eza couldn't help smiling at just how entertained she was, although he worried that the noise might carry. "Alright, alright," he said. "Settle down. Let's get going."

He spent the next fifteen minutes trying to convince Aleiza that he had just been playing a joke on Cammie and that his people generally never shouted except in emergencies. The dragon might as well have been an Introvertian herself, Eza thought. At least she would like the place when they finally made it home together. Every step made Eza just a little more excited, and in a few hours they had covered seven miles. If his map was accurate, there was only one mile to go. But there was also a problem.

Aleiza had spotted riders moving in this direction, nine of them. This could have been a coincidence; they could have been travelers heading to Exclaimovia, or miners coming into the mountains to look for gemstones. They might even have been Artomancers on their way back home.

Eza's first instinct was to hide and let them pass, but something made him go for a second look. The riders were pretty distant, still about eight miles off, but Eza dug out his spyglass anyway and pressed it to his eye. Even magnified, they were still pretty small, but...

His breath caught in his throat. "I think that's Azanna," he said softly to Cammie.

"Are you sure?"

Eza wasn't, not from this distance, but he'd played a lot of ringball, which had made him pretty good at recognizing people by the shape and movements of their bodies. It helped him when, out of the corner of his eye, he could see a teammate sprinting toward the goal and he knew, without looking up, who it was and how they liked to receive their passes. There was very little doubt in his mind that this was Azanna: the shape of the shoulders, the way he held his arms, the profile of his nose when he turned sideways to talk to one of the other riders...

"Do you think he knows we're here?" Cammie asked.

"I don't know, but from his body language, it sure seems like he's looking for something."

"Maybe another dragon," Cammie said, but Eza could tell that even she was doubtful. "We're not that far from where you found Aleiza, after all."

"Could be." Eza paused, still watching, but becoming increasingly convinced that he had to make a decision, and fast. "I think he's looking for us."

"For us?" Cammie repeated in alarm. "Wh – how? Why?"

"Revenge, maybe, or to keep us as hostages. He knows I'm a Ranger, and you heard him say he thinks he can get a ransom for me. We need to make it to the Artomancer village."

"The one that we don't even know is there?"

"It's a safer bet than trying to hide and being outnumbered if they find us."

"Okay," Cammie said. "I trust you. Let's go."

They took off at a sprint across the rolling ground. Eza chanced a single look behind him and saw that all the riders were tearing across the plains at them. The horses would slow once they reached the broken terrain where Eza and Cammie were, but until then, the riders were winning the race.

Cammie started to fall behind. Eza wanted to scream at her to hurry, but she was probably doing the best she could. Aleiza, who had been circling above, suddenly swooped down and hooked her claws gently around Cammie's upper arms. Cammie struggled for half a moment, then realized what was happening, and let the dragon support her. She ambled in a kind of run-hop over the hills, and in less than a minute had caught back up to Eza.

Half a mile ahead was a large semicircle of rock that looked deliberately built. Maybe it was the Artomancer village, or the entrance to it, or something. Eza's feet pounded on the ground and he looked behind him one more time. The riders were almost on top of them. Azanna was unquestionably at the front.

Eza heard the unmistakable sound of "Capture them alive!" float toward him on the wind.

FOURTEEN

The fear that slithered through his mind must have gotten Aleiza's attention, because she deposited Cammie back on the ground and then soared thirty feet into the air. Neemie had been hanging right behind Eza, but she swooped up behind Aleiza, and the two of them together launched toward the ground in some kind of dragon attack pattern.

Fire exploded from Aleiza's mouth, real proper fire a hundred times beyond what Neemie had ever done in her wildest dreams. Instantly three riders at the back were incinerated, their horses somehow escaping the worst of it but wheeling in terror and sprinting off, empty-saddled, back toward the north. That made Eza's heart quicken even more; people were *dead* now. Of course, he was training to be a soldier, and he knew in some distant way that he might have to kill a person someday, maybe even with his own weapon – but he had never...

But suddenly purple energy erupted from Azanna's hand toward Aleiza, and Eza's mouth fell open. It was just the way he had imagined the battle between Mazaren and Arjera and the evil sorcerer in *Heroes of Introvertia* – except this was in real life. So that kind of magic was real! And Azanna knew how to do it!

Aleiza had rolled over hard in order to get out of the way of Azanna's attack, and seemed suddenly reluctant to get any closer. Another purple lance pierced the clear spring air, and Eza forced himself to keep running toward the semicircle he had seen. Neemie had snuck in from behind, knocking one rider off his horse and headfirst into a tree; it was now five riders against Cammie, Eza, and the two dragons.

But arrows and crossbow bolts had joined Azanna's magical attacks, and Aleiza and Neemie were forced to back off as the riders kept bearing down on Cammie and Eza, who were rounding a corner into –

Tall, polished walls formed a perfect half-circle around a bare dirt patch of ground. This was definitely man-made, Eza thought, whatever it was. It was exactly where the Artomancer village was supposed to be, down to the last detail. But there were no doors, no houses, no way in...

"What's this?" Cammie asked in a panic. "Are we stuck? Are we lost?"

Eza looked all around him, thinking hard. There was a small shelf over there, with something underneath it...a box...

"They're coming!" Cammie said, peeking around the edges. "They're almost here!"

There was a stick of chalk in the box. He picked it up,

looking at it. Maybe it was a magic wand. He tried pointing it at the wall and saying, "Door!"

Nothing happened.

"Aleiza got another one," Cammie said excitedly. "There's just four of them now!"

Artomancer. Art magic.

Eza took the chalk and began to draw on the polished stone.

"What are you doing?" demanded Cammie.

Eza squatted to the ground and drew a large, irregular, door-shaped object. As soon as he was done, it began to shimmer as if with magical energy. Excited, he pushed on it, but it wouldn't budge. Cammie was next to him, holding on tight; he glanced back and saw the dragons whirling in the air, magic and arrows all around them –

Of course. He hadn't drawn a doorknob.

He did, and it shimmered too, and then became solid in his hand. He turned the knob and opened the magical door, beyond which was a dark staircase down into the earth. With his mind he was already reaching out to Aleiza and Neemie, and in the next instant they were shooting toward the door, and then they were through it, and angry faces appeared at the rim of the semicircle –

Eza, still holding the chalk, slammed the magical door behind him, and the wall was solid again.

Cammie, Eza, and the two dragons stood there,

peering down the stairs. Every few feet, a part of the wall was glowing. They were magic lights, Eza realized abruptly. It looked like he was in the right place. There was an odd buzzing sensation in his ears, a tingling energy throughout his whole body. He didn't know what that meant, but it certainly felt magical.

"Are we stuck down here?" Cammie asked, a hint of panic in her voice.

"Probably not." Eza smiled at her. "Let's be sunshine, okay?"

But Cammie's fingers closed around his upper arm and she clung to him as they started making their way down the steps. They had gone down about fifty steps when the staircase opened onto a large room – no, a large *city* –

The room they were in was a cavern, with a ceiling several stories tall and passageways leading off it in every imaginable direction. A giant round crystal in the center cast beams of rainbow light all over the room, and the walls glowed brightly in alternating hues of yellow, red, green, blue, and purple. Shops and carts ringed the room's edge, as if the place were some sort of central market hub, but the whole thing looked deserted. On one side, a slab of shining rock seemed to be showing an image of the place where Eza and Cammie had entered through the magic door; Azanna and his three lackeys were still hunting around, searching for whatever button

Eza had pushed to open the trapdoor or trying to figure out what trick he had pulled to disappear into solid rock. Eza paused, fascinated. This was *real* magic.

"There you are."

The voice startled Eza and his hand was on his scana before he realized what he was doing. Aleiza and Neemie were immediately on edge as well, rearing up to their full height in case the speaker was hostile. But the tall, muscled man who emerged from behind a stone chair didn't seem hostile. His blue eyes were bright with interest, and he was looking at Eza the way Introvertian children looked at their pile of gifts on the Day of Lights.

"You," said the man, reaching his hands to Eza's face in wonder. "You're finally here."

"I am?" Eza asked. "I mean, yes, I am, but..."

"The prophecies foretold of your arrival," the man said, looking deeply into Eza's eyes as if searching for confirmation. "A young man your age, with hair of brown and eyes of green, would unlock the secret and arrive here on this exact date."

This was *incredible*. Eza knew there must have been a reason he was able to locate the Artomancer village so easily, and he had figured out exactly how to get in. He looked excitedly at Cammie, who was positively bubbly.

"My boy," continued the man. "I may be premature, but I believe you may be the *chosen one*."

"The chosen one?" Eza repeated, nearly beside

himself with excitement. "Really?"

The man kept staring at him for a few moments and then exploded into laughter so fierce that Aleiza screamed and flapped her wings. "Of course not," the man said in between gasps. "Chosen one. Honestly. The whole prophecy-chosen-one thing is *soooooo* overdone. Oh me." He wiped tears from his eyes. "Oh, that was too much fun. I totally had you, too."

Eza was stuck somewhere between disappointment, annoyance, and appreciation for what really had been a good practical joke. "Who are you, then?"

"I'm Gar. I'm the Keeper of the City for this spring."

"Are you an Artomancer?" Now that Eza's head was clearing, he sized the man up; Gar didn't look much older than Eza's own father, with dark brown hair, and wrinkles at the corners of his eyes that showed he laughed hard and often.

"I am," Gar said. "There are around thirty thousand of us. We don't all live here in the Prismatic City anymore. Actually, none of us really *live* here in the way that you live in – what, Introvertia, is it?" He turned to look at Cammie. "And you're from Exclaimovia? Oh, *this* is going to be a good story. I like good stories."

"Why don't your people live here?" Eza asked, his eyes wandering around the room. "It seems...really nice."

"Oh, it's very nice. But think about it, Introvertian –"

"Ezalen."

"Think about it, Ezalen. Imagine you're an Artomancer. You use drawing and painting and sculpture to manipulate the very nature of reality itself. You use beauty to change the world and make other people's lives better. How much of your own life do you want to spend cooped up in an underground city?"

"Er...that's a good point," Eza said, looking to Cammie, who nodded in agreement.

"So we're everywhere," Gar said with a dismissive hand wave. "Some of us live in Exclaimovia and some of us live in Introvertia – yes, we really do, Ezalen, don't look so surprised – and some of us live in Esteria, or Claira, or even Telravia. Some of us just kind of wander around."

"But you said you're Keeper of the City," Eza pressed. "If nobody lives here anymore, why is this place so important?"

"Come and see," Gar offered, extending a hand to one of the passages.

Eza looked over at Neemie and Aleiza, who didn't seem concerned. With Cammie right behind him, so close he could almost feel her breath on his neck, Eza followed Gar down the wide tunnel, and down, and around. The passageway bent and curved and snaked, and after about two minutes of walking, just when Eza was beginning to have second thoughts about the whole thing, Gar led them into a room so stunning that Eza's legs failed him and he had to sit down.

The room was shaped like a massive dome; the top must have been eighty feet above him, and at the very peak was a huge clear section like a glass window. Something about it, though, made Eza sure it was actually magic. Sunlight shone down through it (*that* was how he knew it was magic, Eza thought – the light was coming from directly above even though it was still only mid-morning), reflecting off some gently rippling water at the center of the room and casting a million rainbows all over the walls. The rainbows gleamed and danced, colored light bending and weaving as if alive. Maybe it *was* alive, Eza thought. He didn't know anything about how this art magic worked.

Besides the rainbows, the walls were decorated almost from floor to ceiling with drawings, sketches, diagrams, graphs, charts, and carvings. Eza could sense energy emanating from the artwork, and he knew there was great magic power in them. "Are these your spells?" he asked Gar.

The Artomancer nodded. "This, Ezalen, is why we can't leave the Prismatic City. The collected knowledge of thousands of years of Artomancers is here on these walls. This is every spell an Artomancer has ever discovered or invented. It would take fifty lifetimes for someone to learn all of them."

"And the Keeper of the City has to guard all of this?

But...have you ever been attacked? What if a hostile army came to, you know, attack it?"

"Why? There's nothing here of value to them. These spells are only useful to Artomancers. I suppose someone might want to destroy all this knowledge, but the only way in is the one you found – well, and one particular spell called the rainbow door that can only be performed by Artomancers. If anyone got in who I didn't want in here, I'd draw a hole to swallow them up, or make a new doorway that just led somewhere else, or something. Art magic is not combat-oriented, of course, but a creative enough spellcaster can find the right tool."

"Can you teach me Artomancy?" Eza asked excitedly.

"That depends, I guess," Gar said with an easy smile. "You still haven't told me why an Introvertian, an Exclaimovian, and two dragons have stumbled into the Prismatic City. Quite frankly, it sounds like the setup to a joke with a horrible punchline."

"We're on the way to visit Exclaimovia," Cammie said smoothly. Eza was impressed; the time he'd been talking to Gar might have been the longest he'd ever heard her stay silent. "Eza took me to visit his home in Introvertia, and now we're going to see my family. He read about this place in a book, figured out where it was, and wanted to stop by on our way through."

"That's a good story," agreed Gar. "It doesn't explain that angry spellcaster attacking you on the way in, or why you have two dragons with you, but I'll take it for now. It would be pretty stupid of you to tell everything to someone you just met and barely know, after all." He turned back to Eza. "As for whether I can teach you Artomancy, first I have to know one thing: what other magic do you know?"

"None," Eza confessed.

"That's the right answer," said Gar, looking satisfied. "It means you don't already belong to a school of magic. There are about eight different schools of magic in the world, and once you study one, it opens itself up to you – words are imprecise here, you understand; use your imagination – and the others close themselves off. Some people can, with great difficulty, begin to learn a second school, but they never attain anything remotely close to mastery. Your kingdom's prohibition on magic has benefited you in that way; you haven't been claimed by a school yet." Then Gar paused. "Have you given thought to the fact that learning magic means you will, in fact, no longer be welcome in your society?"

"You said there were others already living there," Eza pointed out. He was determined by this point; he could keep a secret if he had to. *Whoa. I really sound like an Exclaimovian now*, he thought. "I'll do what it takes to learn."

"Not smart, in my opinion, but I've never said no to a willing student. How long do you have?"

217

"Uh, well, today is Thursday. I have to get to Exclaimovia and be home in nine days, so...like two days?"

"Two days!" Gar howled in hysterical laughter. "He wants to learn Artomancy in two days! Ezalen, I can barely get you started in two days."

"Then I'll barely get started, then," Eza said, not liking to be laughed at.

"You should cancel your sightseeing trip to Exclaimovia and at least give me the whole nine days. You still won't have a clue what you're doing, but you'll at least be somewhat closer to having a clue."

"I can't do that."

"Ah. So there's something important happening in Exclaimovia that requires your presence. Maybe you're asking the girl here to marry you, but you need her father's approval and you want to impress him with some spells." Gar exploded laughing again at the look on both of their faces. "Okay, so definitely not that. That's fine. I don't need to know what. I'm just telling you the truth. There's not much I can do for you in two days."

"But there's something?" Eza asked doggedly.

Gar stared at him for what seemed like an entire minute. "Yeah," Gar said. "Something. I guess we're about to find out if I'm as good as I think. What about her?"

"She, ah, can already do some kind of magic."

Gar fixed his gaze on Cammie. "Alright. Out with it."

Cammie fidgeted. "I, ah..."

"You can only manifest fire when you're angry or otherwise emotionally volatile," Gar said, sounding bored. "Like I haven't heard that one a thousand times."

"Excuse me?" Cammie asked shrilly, hand flying to her hip.

"Untrained elemental magic. You can't do it now because you're not upset. What's the best you've done, light some paper on fire? Accidentally singe the couch when you were arguing with your mom?"

"I char-broiled a dragon and then roasted a dozen goats in one shot."

Gar's eyes widened in surprise and he looked to Eza for confirmation. Eza nodded. "Okay," said Gar, "that's actually quite something. I've never heard of someone who had that much power before training. When you can, you should absolutely seek out someone who can teach you more. I can't help, because like I just said, schools of magic. I don't do elemental."

"Okay," said Cammie, looking very disappointed. "So I can't learn Artomancy?"

"You can try. My guess the elemental magic has claimed you too strongly; you'll most likely find that Artomancy is a language you simply can't learn. But I'll try if you will."

"Let's do it!" Eza declared triumphantly.

FIFTEEN

Cammie could not in her entire life remember being so bored. Eza and Gar had been in the center of the color dome for over a day straight, not sleeping and only pausing for a brief snack twice. Cammie had read the entire rest of *The Dawn Song* even though she was supposed to be reading it with Eza, and had borrowed his copy of *Legends of the Artomancers* before getting annoyed that she couldn't learn Artomancy and quitting partway through. She and Neemie had explored as much of the Prismatic City as she could; with Neemie's sense of direction and Cammie's perfect recall, they were able to go wherever they wanted without fear of getting lost.

She'd taken two naps, eaten one of each kind of food in Eza's backpack just to see what it tasted like, and tried to imagine what each of her friends in Exclaimovia was up to right now. She pictured Alair in the Shouting Square, but that just made her homesick, so she stopped. Then she got as close as she dared to Eza and Gar and began singing loudly, hoping Eza would get distracted and pay attention to her for a few minutes. Gar had merely doodled in the air with his finger and a thick white curtain appeared in front of Cammie, masking the sound of Gar's instruction and Eza's answers to the questions Gar was asking. Great. Now she couldn't even hear them.

Cammie was so desperate for amusement that she attempted to befriend Aleiza, but the dragon seemed to have made up her mind about Cammie already and wanted nothing to do with her. Neemie, at least, was friendly. But speaking of Neemie...

"Come here," Cammie said to Neemie, beckoning with her hand in case the dragon didn't understand her words. Neemie came hopping over, and Cammie stood up straight directly in front of her. "It's not my imagination. You're *at least* two inches taller than when we first met. I remember you barely reached up to my waist the first time we got close, and now you're to my belly button. That's strange, isn't it?"

Neemie was looking at her with an expression that might have been interest or might have been bewilderment. Cammie tried reaching out with her mind, the way Eza had described to her, but there were *way* too many thoughts of her own up there and all she could hear at the moment was a craving for her father's two-day-marinated pork barbecue. "What a weird thing to be craving," she told Neemie. "Anyway, do dragons get growth spurts like people? Even if they do, two inches in a week is a *lot*, isn't it?"

Neemie responded by hopping up onto Cammie's shoulders, a position she had occupied quite frequently since the day Cammie had first used her fire magic. Cammie hand-fed her some roasted goat, then looked back at the white curtain. "I'm sorry!" she called. "I won't do it again!"

There was no answer, so Cammie made herself eat yet again just in case Azanna was still waiting for them outside. She wanted to be able to do magic if she could. "So I'm an elemental mage," Cammie said to Neemie, who peered down at her. "That's nifty. I wonder if there's somewhere I could go to learn how to do it more. Maybe my mom and dad know some magic. But then why did they never tell me I might be a sorceress too?"

Neemie didn't have answers, but the presence of a shoulder-dragon made Cammie feel better anyway. Interesting sensation, that. "Why do you like me and that other one doesn't?" she asked.

In the absence of anything else to do, she had laid out her own sleeping bag on the stone ground and put Eza's over the top of her, the way he had done the two nights she had been incapacitated from using her magic, and somehow managed to fall asleep yet again.

She awoke to find Neemie nestled next to her, Cammie's own arm over the dragon like an overgrown scaly stuffed bear. "You sure do know how to snore," she said by way of greeting. Neemie didn't wake up; she just rolled over the other way and kept snoring. On the other side, Aleiza was tucked against Cammie, too. That was *extremely* surprising. Why would Aleiza do something like that?

Eza was appearing from behind the curtain, looking absolutely exhausted but happier than Cammie had ever seen him. "It's about time you showed up," she scolded him. "I was so bored that..."

Eza tossed Cammie a small seed, which she fumbled before her fingers closed around it. In the next instant the seed had erupted into a bouquet of white amaryllis flowers, and Cammie nearly dropped it in surprise. "You remembered," she said in surprise. "But red is my favorite."

Eza looked at Gar, who gave a slight nod, and then Eza's fingers were moving again. The flowers erupted into a deep crimson. "They're perfect," she murmured.

"Yes, well, I'm sure that a well placed bouquet of flowers will solve whatever problem you're about to face in Exclaimovia," Gar said. "Although I must say I'm very impressed with how much I was able to teach Ezalen over the last thirty hours. I knew I was good, but I didn't know just how good."

"Speaking of problems in Exclaimovia," Eza said, "I want you to come."

"To come..." Gar hedged.

"Exclaimovia has stolen a lot of Introvertian dragons. If my people find out, there will probably be a war. We're going to steal them back so that doesn't happen."

"Uh, nope. No. Nuh-uh, hard pass. I don't get involved in political stuff. Zero percent chance. You Introvertians and Exclaimovians can go play with fire, for all I care. That's no business of mine. Artomancy is life-giving magic; it adds beauty to the world and makes people feel good. If you want to use it for that whole kingdom-versus-kingdom business, that's on you. But I don't like that game. None of us do."

Eza spread his hands in confusion. "What's more life-giving than preventing a war and keeping people from killing each other?"

"Yeah, that's not how any of this works, my guy. You have no idea what's going to happen if you try to steal dragons back from Exclaimovia. You might accidentally cause a war ten times worse than the one you thought you were preventing." Gar put his hands on top of his head. "You can't just..."

He trailed off as footsteps came down the long winding passageway that led from the entry hall to the great dome. Momentarily a figure rounded the corner and entered the great dome, stopping as if surprised to see so many people there. "Hello, Gar," the man said. "And...company."

"Hello, Saranna," Gar replied. "This is Ezalen, and his two dragons, and some random Exclaimovian whose name he hasn't been polite enough to give me."

"Cammie," she and Eza said at the same time.

"Anyway," Gar continued, seeming not to care about her name, "Ezalen here wanted to learn Artomancy. I got him through sixth term in thirty hours."

"You did not either," Saranna said in disbelief. "Prove it."

"Ezalen, show him the summer sun."

Cammie watched as Eza waved both arms in opposite directions, his right up and his left down, and suddenly sunlight was exploding from the roof of the dome, so bright it blinded Cammie. When her vision cleared a few moments later, she saw grass and flowers blooming up from the patch of floor that the sunlight fell on, a brilliant nature-scape of green and gold and blue, and then suddenly the ground on one side washed over the colors like a wave, swallowing them back up into the stone. The blinding sunlight faded, leaving only the normal light of the artificial window at the peak of the dome. Eza smiled. "I'm hungry."

"There's no way the boy did that," Saranna protested. "You did it for him somehow."

"I did not either," Gar said, mockingly repeating Saranna's own words.

"He did not learn six entire terms worth of magic in thirty hours."

"Yeah, so," interjected Cammie. "If these boys are only interested in arguing about who's the best, and they don't plan on coming with us, what do you say we hit the road, Eza?"

"I'm all for it," he agreed, despite looking like he was going to fall asleep on the spot. "Thanks for everything, Gar. I hope to be back to learn more someday."

"Fine. Saranna may be the one here when you return; he's also a Keeper of the City, and I wasn't expecting him for another couple of weeks. Regardless of who's here, when they find out I taught you six terms in a day and a half, they're going to get their dander up and want to do better. Either way, you're on the fast track to mastery, thanks to me. So you're welcome, Ezalen. You're very welcome."

"And you have bragging rights for the next thousand years, we get it," Cammie snapped. "Come on, Eza. I want to go home."

She stomped off up the winding passage Saranna had just come from, the skittering of dragon feet and the thump of Eza's boots behind her. In spite of herself, she smiled. The actress in her loved that she'd made such a grand and dramatic exit.

Up and up they circled, to the entry hall, and then up the long staircase that led them to the magic door they'd first entered. Only then did Cammie hesitate. "Uh, Eza, do you think Azanna and his friends are still waiting for us out there?"

"Let's see," he said, using his hands to paint something invisible on the flat wall.

Suddenly there was an oval doorway, bright and glowing and rippling with every imaginable color, like when spray off a waterfall made a rainbow in midair. Through it Cammie could see the semicircular clearing where they'd first entered the Prismatic City. One of the riders was camped out there...but only one. Azanna was nowhere to be found.

"That's the rainbow door spell Gar mentioned," Eza said, sounding very proud of himself.

"Why isn't there anyone else around?" Cammie wondered out loud. "Does Azanna think a single rider can handle us? Or is that one a sentry with orders to flee and report in if he sees us?"

"I don't know," Eza said. "But let's give him something to report, shall we? Hop in!"

Fighting skepticism, Cammie followed Eza through the glowing doorway, with both dragons right behind her, and then they were standing in the clearing, face to face with a very surprised rider. Even after the magical daylight of the dome room, Cammie's eyes hurt from the bright glow of the afternoon sun. She just managed to see the rider hurling some kind of throwing dagger at Eza, and Eza drawing another glowing door in front of him, with the exit behind. The dagger seemed to pass right through him, clattering against the stone wall at their backs and falling to the ground. Fear rose inside Cammie, and she felt her magic trying to get out, She'd snacked for the whole past day and a half – but had she eaten enough for a full-on magic battle, or was she going to be wrecked by fatigue again?

Eza drew in the air again, and another glowing rainbow hole opened underneath the rider, swallowing him but not his horse. A faint scream echoed out just before the hole closed up and normal ground reappeared. The horse whinnied and bolted, thundering off as fast as it could. Cammie stared at Eza. "Where'd he go?"

"The dome room, I think," Eza said. "I'm going to let Gar and Saranna deal with him." He closed one eye and kneeled with a grimace. "That rainbow door is about the most complicated thing I know how to do, though. I really need to eat, and fast. Sending both of us through the rainbow door was a *lot* harder than the times I went through one by myself and I don't know why."

"We should go, though," Cammie pointed out. "We don't want to be here if Azanna comes back with even more buddies."

Eza nodded. "You're right. Come on, Aleiza. Come on, Neemie."

The two dragons took to the air as Cammie and Eza began picking their way through the thick trees, heading southeast toward Exclaimovia. "How far did you say we were from home?" Cammie asked.

Eza had been stuffing his face with flatbread, and he

looked at Cammie with crumbs hanging off his lips. "I believe the border is about fifteen miles and Pride is another ten past that. It's Friday afternoon at the moment, so we won't be able to make it before nightfall, but if we really hurry we could be having dinner at your house tomorrow."

That thought brightened Cammie's face. "I'll push myself as hard as I can," she promised. "But I might need another foot rub."

"It's yours if you want it."

"And I also want to see the rest of your art magic. Even if I am really jealous that you have two dragons and now magic and I just have a fire thing that only works when I'm mad."

The trees were thinning again, and Cammie could spot the dragons turning lazy circles overhead. "You heard Gar," Eza reminded her. "There are people who can teach you how to use your magic."

"Yeah, but who? Where? I want magic, too." Cammie knew she was pouting, but she didn't care if Eza was judging her.

"We'll find out together," Eza assured her.

The gentleness of his answer surprised her; she was expecting a lecture about how important it was to stay focused and not complain. "Thank you," she said, surprised to find that she believed him. "That means a lot."

Eza smiled back, and they walked in silence for a few moments. "You know," Cammie said, "if we're going to be in Exclaimovia tomorrow, you're going to have to dress like a local, and I don't have any spare clothes."

"I made sure Gar taught me how to blend in. Watch this."

He stopped for a moment, looking like he was concentrating hard, and then whipped his hand upward into the air. An explosion of color blew off of him, as if someone had tossed a bucket of glittering sand into the air, and then his clothes were different. The cut was more flamboyant and the colors were richer, the pants a light gray and the shirt a deep purple that made his green eyes stand out. His Ranger cloak hadn't changed, though; apparently there were some lines Eza was still unwilling to cross.

"That looks *nice*," Cammie said, admiring the outfit. "Who told you that purple and gray go together?"

Eza laughed. "What, you think I have no fashion sense just because I'm Introvertian?"

"That's EXACTLY what I think!" Cammie shouted.

"The gray is me making a statement," he said, unclasping his cloak and stuffing it into his backpack. Cammie noticed the pack had also changed color and was now a light plum. "Gray goes with purple, but it's an Introvertian color. I'm representing my people even while I'm dressing like yours."

"That's...actually really brilliant," Cammie told him. Immediately she realized what she'd said and covered her mouth in shock.

"Cammaina Ravenwood, did you just compliment me?" An enormous smile appeared on Eza's face, and he broke out into a spontaneous happy-dance. "I'm rubbing off on youuuuu!" he announced in a singsong voice.

"YOU ARE NOT!" Cammie protested fiercely. "I spoke without thinking. I do that all the time. I'm Exclaimovian, after all."

"Yes, but *why* was a compliment the first thing you blurted?" Eza needled her.

Cammie stared at him, then grudgingly smiled. "Fiiiiine. You win this round." Something suddenly occurred to her. "What are you going to do with your dragons when we go into Exclaimovia?"

"I've thought about that," Eza said. "I guess they'll just need to find a place to hide and wait to hear back from me. I don't know how far my mind link with them can reach."

Cammie could see that Eza was really upset about having to abandon them. "I'm sorry," she said. "I had to leave friends behind when I came to Introvertia, and now I get to see them again. I'm sure you'll feel the same way when you reunite with your dragons."

Eza smiled. "That was really kind of you. Thanks."

They talked and laughed together as the miles passed

under their feet. They were still staying close to the foothills, but the scenery had changed. The tall evergreens and rocky prairies of the Introvertian side of the Impassable Mountains were gone, giving way to prairies of shoulder-high switchgrass, which danced in the breeze all the way to the eastern horizon. Even up in the mountains, pine trees had been replaced by aspens and alders. Something about it just felt *right* to Cammie. Even though the border was still several miles ahead, this was *home*.

Eza stopped sharply a short distance before the Exclaimovian border, tilting his head as if hearing something far away. "Aleiza spotted a cave," he said. "She's going to take Neemie there to hide until we get back. If we're not back in a week, they're going to go to my father and tell him where I am."

Yet Eza didn't move at the end of the sentence, as if he were hoping that Cammie or one of the dragons could convince him it didn't have to be this way. He watched the two dragons soaring together off toward the mountains, and Cammie felt bad for him. "It's a good thing you found Aleiza so that Neemie has a wild dragon to help her out," she offered.

"Yeah," Eza said, brightening. "That's a really good point. Thank you." He glanced at the sun, which was winding toward the horizon. "I don't know if the border here is guarded. Do you?"

"No. I've never been up this direction."

"Then I think we should wait here till nightfall. It's only a few more hours. We can sit in the grass and read *The Dawn Song* together if you want."

Cammie scuffed at the ground with the toe of her boot. "I kind of finished it."

"Then maybe you can tell me stories."

That brought a wide smile to Cammie's face. "I'd love to."

"Keep the volume down, but I don't think we have to worry about a border patrol sneaking up on us. Something tells me Exclaimovians probably don't patrol by themselves, and if they're in groups, it's most likely not quiet."

Cammie giggled. "I think you know us pretty well."

"Just one of you. But I think I know her well enough."

The next few hours were the most fun Cammie had ever had telling stories. Yes, Eza had been a good listener from the first moment she'd met him, but now the dragons were gone and it was just the two of them. They laughed together, muffling the sound with their sleeping bags when the noise got too loud, and then Eza would always shush them so he could listen for movement nearby. Every time, when he was satisfied that nobody was near, he would encourage Cammie to start again.

At last when dusk had fallen, Eza led the two of them stealthily southward. Pride was just five miles away, the pinnacles of its highest buildings now clearly visible on the horizon. They would be to the outlying farms and settlements in half an hour, and then inside of Pride another hour and a half later.

Cammie was almost home, and Eza was further from his than he'd ever been.

SIXTEEN

Cammie was buzzing with excitement. She hadn't realized how much she missed her home until she was setting foot back in it. A million different thoughts and emotions swirled in her head. Alair! Mom and dad! Music and stories! Family meals, dresses and shopping, and singing and laughter! She was suddenly overcome with the urge to cry and laugh at the same time. What would her family say when they found out about Eza?

Cammie chuckled to herself, growing red at the thought of even more teasing when she got home, glad no one could see her blush in the fading daylight. After so long away, the thought of home almost didn't seem real, but each step took her closer. Passing through the farms and small settlements was easy enough; Eza didn't need to act too much, other than straightening his posture and learning to wave with his whole arm rather than the wrist or, even worse, his head. What was the point of just nodding at someone? That was so rude.

Cammie caught herself mid-thought and amended it. That wasn't rude; it was just how Introvertians did things...for some reason.

They stopped just outside of Pride as stars began appearing overhead, nervousness clawing at Cammie.

She could fit in fine, but if Eza managed to give them away, she didn't know what she would do.

"Pride is beyond this gate, following the main road." Cammie explained. "My home is to the left when we reach the split..." She trailed off, needing to prepare herself to step through the gate. "This is when you really need to try and act like you belong," she continued, shifting her weight from one foot to the other and fidgeting with the hem of her shirt.

"It's not just smiling and being theatrical," she continued. "The way you walk, when and how you speak, who you speak to...and no compliments to people older or younger than you. If you're not sure then just say nothing. But don't say *too* much nothing, because people will wonder why you're not talking." Cammie cleared her throat and straightened her posture. She closed her eyes for a moment, reminding herself of the customs of her people. At last she took a breath and opened her eyes, lifting her chin and pulling her hair up into an intricate braid with quick motions.

For some reason she found herself remembering the times she had colored her hair just for fun. She looked down at her clothes and grimaced. "Do you still have my dress?" she asked, looking up to Eza. "The one from when we first met."

She watched as Eza dug through his pack and yanked out the brightly colored dress, which was now slightly wrinkled from being shoved down to the bottom of his bag.

Cammie sighed and pulled the dress on over her Introvertian clothes, smoothing the wrinkles as much as possible. She couldn't wait any longer. "Let's go. We can't dawdle out here the whole night." In truth, it was Cammie whose nerves were shot with anxiety like she'd been struck by lightning. Eza didn't say anything, however; he just smiled at her and stepped back to let Cammie lead the way.

She took a breath, held her head high and her shoulders back, and passed through the gate, Eza following her in the best imitation he could muster. Ahead she could see the tall apartments and gaudy spires of Pride – that was odd, she thought; she'd never considered the spires gaudy before visiting Tranquility – and her heart started pounding even harder than it already was.

"I'm going to take you on the grand scenic tour of Pride," she told Eza excitedly. "First stop: the Shouting Square!"

"The...what?" Eza asked in horror.

"The Shouting Square," Cammie answered, hopping in excitement. "Come on!"

She put her hand inside his arm like she had done with Alair all those days ago, and Eza's gaze snapped down to her fingers. "Won't people think we're..." he hedged.

"Together? No, no. It's a normal way for two friends to walk."

"So we can lock elbows, but I can't say something kind about you?"

Cammie thought about that. "It does sound kind of strange, when you put it that way."

Eza's eyes were wandering toward the buildings. Cammie had always seen the city through the eyes of someone who lived there, but now she was trying to imagine what Eza was thinking as he saw the place for the first time. The houses in this quarter of the city were smaller, but painted with bright patterns in each family's colors. Conversations echoed back and forth across the street; sometimes people stood in doorways on opposite sides of the road hollering at each other. "Just...why," Eza murmured, almost to himself.

"Make small talk with me," Cammie told him.

"About what?"

"About nothing. That's the point of small talk. In Exclaimovia, whenever a man and a woman are together, it's the man's job to host. That means you steer the conversation and make sure it keeps going."

The new look of shock that crossed his face made her giggle, and she wrinkled her nose at him the way she always used to at Alair. Being back home was bringing out her playful side more than usual.

"Erm...nice weather we're having?"

Cammie howled with laughter, squeezing Eza's arm. "The weather! Really?"

A nervous smile crossed his face. "I think you just like seeing me squirm."

"Try again. Dig deep."

"Okay." Eza chewed on his lip for a moment. "What's the architectural history of this city? How old is it and how has the building style changed over time?"

Cammie pulled his arm closer, rubbing her shoulder playfully against his. "That's not *small talk*, you goof."

"For the love of loud noises..."

"It's okay. We're almost at the Shouting Square anyway."

Eza's jaw was clenched. "Yeah. I can already hear it."

He was right, Cammie realized. Her ears were used the cacophony, and she could pick out half a dozen different songs being loudly bellowed by crowds of people, a snippet from a famous Exclaimovian speech that someone was reciting, and loud conversations about nothing in particular. To Eza's it probably just sounded like a wall of noise.

"You look overwhelmed," she whispered to him. "Relax. Try to seem like you're enjoying it."

She pulled him through the crowds of people, and by the end he was nearly sagging against her. "Please tell me the next place we're going is quieter."

"You didn't like the Shouting Square?" she teased.

"About as much as you liked the Reading Square in Tranquility, I bet."

"Okay. I want to show you Declamation Square, and then the palace complex, and then I'll take you home."

"Lead the way. And while we're walking...what's your favorite kind of gemstone?"

Cammie clapped excitedly, which wasn't easy with one of her arms intertwined with Eza's. "Small talk! I'm proud of you!" Instantly she clapped her hands over her mouth, looking around in shock to make sure no one had overheard her giving him a compliment. "Wow. I didn't think a week away was enough to make me forget how to hold my tongue."

"Sounds to me like you never enjoyed that particular rule anyway," Eza mused.

That made Cammie slow her stride and look over at Eza. "What do you mean?"

"All the things you can and can't say. All the unwritten rules about how you have to act or else people will make wild assumptions about you. You don't enjoy any of that, and you wish you could live somewhere that people didn't play those kinds of games."

"Is there such a place?" she asked softly.

"Introvertia."

"But I'm not comfortable there either. I'm loud and I blurt things out and I don't like silence."

"Is that the real you or is that just who you've been trained to be?"

Cammie snorted a laugh. "Why hello, Mr. Cappel!"

With a smile, Eza shrugged. "Just asking the question."

"That's very kind of you. Thank you for caring about me."

One of Eza's eyebrows drifted skyward. "Is that another compliment?"

Cammie whacked him on the shoulder with her free hand. "It's an observation. Come on. I'm hungry. We can save Declamation Park for another time; let's just go home."

Truth be told, Cammie didn't know *what* the reaction would be when she waltzed in the front door of her house like she hadn't just been gone for a week – and with an Introvertian hiding behind her. She'd been telling herself all along that they'd be delighted that she'd come back with such an incredible story, and that was probably true...but she also knew her mother had probably been worried, and she was just hoping that her father would be able to defuse the situation.

She slammed the front door open and leaped theatrically into the living room. "I'M HOME!" she bellowed. Eza followed hesitantly, easing the door closed behind him.

"CAMMIE!" Barin's deep voice came from the kitchen, and he came running in to wrap her up in his arms. "Your note said you were going to the Trading Circle to see if you could meet an Introvertian. I see you were...successful."

"Father, this is Ezalen Skywing," Cammie said formally. "Eza, this is my father, General Barin Ravenwood."

Eza stepped forward, extending his hand. Oh, this was *not* going to end well, Cammie thought. "Pleased to meet you, Gener*UUUURRRKKKKKK* –"

Barin had wrapped him up in such an enormous hug that Eza was struggling to breathe. "Welcome to the greatest kingdom on earth, my boy," Barin said, ruffling Eza's hair the way he always did to Cammie.

"I have a secret for you, daddy," Cammie said, putting some extra excitement into her voice. She hadn't known it until that moment, but she was going to tell him the full story of what she had done – well, not *why* she had done it, not the whole feeling-out-of-place thing, not the whole traitor-to-Exclaimovia thing, and *DEFINITELY* not the part about helping Eza steal those dragons back, but at least the part about sneaking into Introvertia.

"CAMMIE!" her mother shouted, rushing into the living room and giving her a hug nearly as big as the one Barin had given Eza. "I missed you."

"Huh," Cammie said, rubbing her mother's back. "I was expecting you to say you'd been worried sick."

"Worried about you? By the sun, no. You're the smartest girl I know. Kalek is as dumb as a wagon of bricks; if he can make it to the Trading Circle and back safely, I had no doubt that you could."

"Yeah, well...I went a *little* further than the Trading Circle."

Barin led everyone to the kitchen table, where Cammie spent the next hour telling about all the things she and Eza had done together. Every two or three minutes Barin would give her a questioning eyebrow and Cammie would have to swear on the sun that she wasn't exaggerating or making things up. Even so, if it hadn't been for Eza next to her, quietly nodding along with her words, she was pretty sure her parents wouldn't have believed her.

At last Barin turned his gaze on Eza. "And what made you agree to accompany Cammie back to Exclaimovia?"

Eza's eyes went wide. Cammie hoped with everything inside her that he didn't decide to lie – he was so inexperienced at it that Barin would know *instantly*. But – he couldn't tell the truth either –

"I wanted to...see...what was here," Eza stammered, as if thinking about each word before saying it.

It took all of Cammie's self-control not to explode in

laughter. Well, he'd done it. He hadn't lied.

"He's an awkward one, isn't he?" Barin asked Cammie, pointing his thumb at Eza.

"You have *noooooo idea*," Cammie said, forcing an enormous smile. "He never takes his shoes off! Not even at home!"

"Well, that's...not too strange," Barin answered.

"UGH! You two can go be awkward together, then!" shouted Cammie playfully.

Barin held up his hands, wriggling his tickle fingers. "Watch it, firebug."

"DADDY!" Cammie shouted, shoving her chair back from the table and backing up against the wall.

Just then the door slammed open again. "Hey everyone!" shouted Aed from the living room.

"Ah!" Barin declared triumphantly. "Reinforcements! Come in here, Aed!"

"NO!" Cammie protested, already laughing, as Aed came sprinting into the living room and saw what Barin was up to. Her father and brother started coming around opposite sides of the table, and Cammie waited until they were almost to her before sprinting forward and sliding underneath the table, grabbing Eza and nearly leaping up on top of him. "SAVE ME, EZA!"

"Buh..." was Eza's only reply.

"Oh," Aed said, noticing Eza for the first time. "Hi. I'm Aed."

"Eza."

"Nice to meet you. You're, uh, defending my sister. Mind if I..."

"DON'T DO IT, EZA!" Cammie screeched in Eza's ear.

Barin moved forward. "Well, if he won't move, I guess we'll just have to tickle him too."

Instantly – Cammie swore she didn't even see him move – Eza was on the other side of the room, knees bent in a ready position, looking like he was about to whip out his scana. But Barin and Aed ignored him now that Cammie was defenseless, and in moments she was writhing on the ground, screaming in laughter as Barin held her arms over her head and Aed mercilessly tickled her ribs and armpits.

At last they stopped, and Cammie stuck out her tongue at them, her chest still heaving. "If I...knew that was the...welcome I would get...I'd have...stayed in Introvertia."

Barin's face went hard. "Don't joke about that, firebug. Please."

Just like that, it was as if all the humor was sucked out of the room. Barin stared at the ground and Aileen pretended to be busy putting away some clean dishes. It must have been something with the dragons, Cammie decided. Maybe Introvertia had found out – was there going to be a war? Cammie's heart started hammering.

"Daddy?" she asked. "Why not?"

"It's just – not safe right now," he said evasively. "Visiting Introvertia is one thing, but to joke about moving there...anything that might sound like you're taking the wrong side..."

What did he mean by *side*?

Cammie stood, looking across the room at her father. "Is Eza in danger here?"

"No. But – don't go shouting to the world that you have an Introvertian in town."

"Okay," Cammie said, not liking the sensation that she had in the bottom of her stomach, as if a rock had taken up residence and was starting to move the furniture around.

"Let me worry about that, though," Barin said briskly. "Let's have some food, and then some songs!"

That's exactly what they did. Cammie had forgotten how much she missed the nearly deafening sound of the kitchen at dinnertime...even if she often did need to retreat to her bedroom for some quiet time afterward.

Taking the wrong side...

That sure made it seem like her father was expecting a war, and *that* just made Cammie even more determined to help return those stolen dragons to Introvertia. It wasn't just that thousands of lives might be saved – it was that one of those lives may be her father. Cammie felt that the phrase should probably have been the other way around – "not just my father, but thousands of other people too" – but she'd meant it exactly how she'd thought it.

"Alair's been here nearly every day while you've been gone," Barin said conversationally as the meal was wrapping up. "You should go say hi to him tomorrow."

Cammie turned red and snuck a glance at Eza. "I will. I want to introduce him to Eza. He's never met an Introvertian before."

Barin rose from the table. "Well, Ezalen, it would be an honor if you allowed us to host you for the night in our guest room. May I show you to it?"

Eza nodded wordlessly, as if hearing another sound would cause him to burst, and followed Barin to the guest room. "I like you," she could hear Barin booming as he led Eza away. "You're a good listener."

He is definitely that, Cammie giggled to herself.

She waited several minutes, making fun of Aed in the meantime and helping her mother clean the kitchen, and then went to Eza's room, closing the door behind her as she entered.

"So that's my family," she said brightly, knowing how overwhelmed he must be feeling.

Again Eza nodded. "They're very gracious hosts. I can see that they love you very much."

Cammie took three steps to the bed, and she and Eza sat down on it, next to each other. "We have to move quickly," she said. "You heard what my father said. We may not have much time left before our kingdoms start fighting."

Eza closed one eye and started rubbing his temples. "Tomorrow. I have an enormous headache."

"Want me to massage your head for you?"

That made him blink several times in confusion. "Won't they think we're..."

"Nah. They know I like Alair. I mean, Aed is going to mess with me no matter what happens. He's probably waiting outside the door right now to tease me for being in here with you." She reached up and started massaging Eza's scalp. "But you gave me those foot rubs when I was sore, so I figure I owe you a favor back. And if my family decides to make assumptions..." Cammie grinned. "Let them."

SEVENTEEN

Eza was awake before any of the Ravenwoods. As he lay on his back staring at the ornate patterns on the guest bedroom ceiling, he desperately tried to cling to the peace and solitude of that moment. If only he could put this quiet calm in a jar and let a little bit out when the day got loud and he started feeling overwhelmed again, that would be perfect. Then again, it wasn't even *that* calm; Barin and Aed were snoring like they were in a competition to see who could be louder. Eza thought Barin was winning, but it was close.

Opening the curtains wide to let the early sunlight in, Eza laid out his clothes on the floor. He'd have to change the color, and maybe even the cut. These Exclaimovians were real admirers of fashion, and if Eza wore the same outfit twice, they'd be on to him in a heartbeat. That wouldn't do. Eza had really liked the purple and gray, especially since it had let him smuggle in a neutral Introvertian color. Hmm...what about red?

He'd seen quite a few people in red and black the day before, and it struck him as a strong combination. Eza's hands moved over the shirt and the blue washed out of it as it brightened from purple to a boisterous crimson. His pants, in turn, faded from gray to black. Eza sat back, satisfied at the change. He could live with this. Slithering out of his pajamas, he put on the new outfit, beaming with satisfaction.

Outside the window, Pride was beginning to wake up. The narrow street was alive with milkmen loudly shouting greetings to the street sweepers, who were hollering at the people pushing the garbage carts. The yards here were large, but further up Eza could see tall buildings on both sides of the road that blocked the sunlight from actually reaching the cobblestones.

Abruptly he realized how hard he was breathing. It was like the whole city made him panic. All this noise and chaos drowning out the sounds of nature, all the Exclaimovian perfume overwhelming the scent of the trees and the flowers. Was this how Cammie had felt in Tranquility? Was this what silence did to her?

Soon he heard bustle from the living room; Cammie was screeching at something and Aed was guffawing at her. Eza stepped out of his bedroom, feeling satisfied, ready to show Cammie his outfit. She whirled around with a smile on her face, and Eza had to admit she looked radiant in a magenta shirt with brilliant blue accents and matching blue pants. As soon as she saw Eza, her smile immediately faded. "Oh, child, no," she declared. "That outfit..."

"What about it?" he asked, confused and hurt at the same time. He'd thought it looked good and had been expecting a compliment – well, of course he wasn't going to get a compliment from Cammie, not when she was around her family, but he'd at least been expecting acceptance, an acknowledgment that the outfit looked nice on him. "I saw lots of people wearing red and black yesterday," he added feebly.

"It's not a bad combination," she rushed to assure him. "It's just not right for you. Fashion isn't only knowing colors; it's knowing what works for your skin tone and hair color and eye color."

Aed was over at the breakfast table snickering, and he looked very sharp himself in a long-sleeved sky blue shirt with gold pants and a matching gold vest. Feeling overwhelmed, Eza turned to go back into his bedroom. He didn't like this feeling of cluelessness, and there was a lump in his throat that he couldn't explain. There was no reason for him to be this upset, but he was, and if he didn't get away from the situation *right now...*

Immediately Cammie was right behind him. "I'll help you," she said. "If you want me to."

Eza nodded.

Cammie closed the bedroom door behind them, seeming to suddenly notice the expression on Eza's face. "What's wrong? Are you okay?"

"I just thought I did a good job with the clothes." Eza chewed on his lip for a moment and then looked at Cammie. "I'm not upset that I did a bad job. I wasn't expecting to be good at fashion right away. I'm upset that I *really thought* I did well and then found out that I didn't."

"I hate that feeling too," Cammie said.

Eza was waiting for her to change the topic, to start talking about herself and a time when she'd felt that way or about someone she knew who'd experienced something similar, but she didn't. She was really just watching him, the way he watched her when she went off on a rant, as if she were waiting for him to finish his thoughts. "Are you...*listening* to me?" he asked, mystified.

Cammie shrugged, seeming suddenly self-conscious. "It seemed like the right thing to do," she said briskly.

"Thank you. It made me feel a lot better."

"Now, colors. You spend a lot of time outdoors, so you're pretty tan. Red is not going to mix well with tanned skin, and it's not the best for that sandy-brown mop on top of your head either. That purple you wore yesterday was great, and I think lighter purples might work too, something like a lilac color." Cammie was resting her chin on her open hand as she stood, swaying back and forth, obviously thinking out loud. "But you wouldn't want to do lilac the day after purple. That's not enough of a variation. Green would be fantastic for you."

"I like green," Eza said helpfully. "I wear it all the time at home."

Cammie's split-colored eyes fixed on him. "Did you just interrupt me?"

He *had*, and they both knew it. "I –" he began.

"You did," Cammie said in awe, a huge smile spreading across her face. "You cut me off."

"It was an accident," Eza protested. "I was trying to be helpful."

Cammie put her head down like she was trying not to laugh out loud, but was still smiling when she lifted it again. "One moment," she said, putting a finger up, then she stepped outside the room. "DAD! EZA INTERRUPTED ME!"

Eza didn't hear Barin's bellowed reply, but Cammie exploded into laughter and came back into Eza's room. "My dad likes you even more now."

"I'm glad, but I still need something to wear."

"I was *getting* there before I was *so rudely interrupted*," Cammie informed him with a dramatic flip of her hair. "Anyway, green is a great color for you. So is gold."

"Gold?" Eza said, his head filled with a vision of him walking around looking like a giant coin.

"Not, uh, whatever it is you're obviously thinking of. Not gold like jewelry. Gold like..." She thought for a moment. "Like that evening sunlight we saw together outside the palace in Tranquility."

"Oh, *that* gold." Instantly Eza knew what she meant, and he closed his eyes in concentration. The red shirt began to shimmer and then resolved itself into a gold with shiny metallic flecks in it. His pants wavered and turned a dark green that looked perfect next to the gold.

"*Yes*, Eza. Yes." Cammie took him by the shoulders and turned him slowly around. "That's exceptional, honestly. I'm very impressed."

"Cammaina Ravenwood, did you just compliment me?"

"Of course not. I'm the one who came up with the combination. I complimented myself."

"Do you accept compliments from yourself or do you get offended at those, too?"

Cammie giggled and gave Eza a gentle push away. "That was funny. Come on. It's breakfast time."

"I need to eat something. That wasn't a lot of magic, but doing it on an empty stomach...ouch."

Eza spent the walk across the living room trying to prepare himself for the raucousness of breakfast. Dinner the night before had left his ears ringing, so he was surprised when he sat down at the table and no one was speaking. That was welcome.

"Let us be grateful," Barin said formally.

"I'm glad for the food," Aed immediately declared.

"Me too," added Aileen.

"Me too!" shouted Cammie. "And I'm glad Eza's here."

"I bet you are," teased Aed.

Cammie tried to kick him under the table, but Barin laid a hand on her shoulder. "Not during the Gratitude," he said, then solemnly added, "I'm grateful for my family."

Barin looked at Eza, clearly expecting him to contribute something. Eza cleared his throat. "I'm grateful for your hospitality."

"We offer these thanks," Barin said.

Then things got loud.

Somehow Eza survived both the volume and the strongly seasoned egg-and-cheese wrap, though he drank what seemed like half of the family's pail of fresh water to try and get the spicy burn out of his mouth. It felt like the food was angry at him. He could tell the rest of the family was amused by his reactions as he tried to pretend nothing was wrong, but he couldn't hide the tiny bead of sweat that began on his forehead and trickled to his cheek before he nonchalantly wiped it away.

"Today is Sunday," Barin told Cammie, "which means you'll be expected at school tomorrow. I told your teachers that you were off on an independent study, so your absences were excused, but you'll have to make up the work."

"That was really smart, daddy," she said.

"I don't know what Eza is planning to do during the days when you're at school, so perhaps the two of you can think of something together today."

"Oh, we have plans," Cammie answered vaguely. "Come on, Eza. I want you to meet one of my friends, and then we'll go...explore the city."

Together they exited the house onto the narrow street. Shouted conversations bounced past them in every direction, the noise reflecting off the stone walls of the buildings and echoing back at Eza. His instinct was to cringe, to sprint away and find a quiet place, but he was supposed to be blending in, pretending to be an Exclaimovian.

"Nice day, isn't it?" Cammie asked him loudly.

"Beautiful!" Eza yelled back.

"Remember to swagger! Don't look around like you've never been here; stride like you own the place!"

Eza didn't even know what that was supposed to look like, so he swung his shoulders theatrically only for Cammie to double over, her hands on her knees in laughter. "You look like you're trying to get an apple out of your pant leg," she told him. "Just...walk with confidence, and do what you see me doing. Here. Give me your arm, or else people will ask questions."

"So...we need to touch each other, so that people *won't* think we're a couple?" He'd said the same thing the night before, but it was just so absurd that he couldn't help rubbing it in a second time.

Cammie gave a defeated shrug. "I told you I don't like the unwritten rules. But if you want to stay under

257

cover long enough to rescue those dragons, we've got to play the game."

Eza offered his elbow to Cammie. "Lead the way."

She did, and he followed her, trying to swagger. By the time he left here with the stolen dragons, his acting skills would be on par with Cammie's!

Cammie led Eza toward Declamation Park, the open space with two podiums set up in one corner. At any hour of the day and most hours of the night, there would be someone making a speech at one of the podiums – or, more commonly, two people or teams of people arguing furiously about something. One such debate was happening now, and appeared to have something to do with whether the new apartment housing blocks being built on the northeast side of town should be painted light orange or reddish orange. That was a normal Exclaimovian debate, Cammie knew. Most likely neither the man arguing for light orange or the woman arguing for reddish orange actually cared *even a little bit* about the position they were defending. It was a spectacle, the loud dramatic gestures and the witty turns of phrase serving to amuse and delight the audience. It was noise as entertainment, Cammie suddenly realized. It was noise devoid of content. Suddenly she understood what Eza thought when he saw such a scene.

But she hadn't brought Eza this direction to horrify

him. Rather, she was looking for someone –

"Alair!" she screamed at the top of her lungs, running to him. One of his familiar crushing hugs wrapped itself around her and she squeaked, "I can't breathe!"

"GOOD!" he roared. "Do you have any idea how worried we've all been about you? Your dad said you'd gone off on an independent study, but he wouldn't say where – and that's not like you, anyway, going off on an adventure, and –" Alair suddenly spotted Eza, who was striding quickly toward them. "Who's this?"

"This is Ezalen." Immediately Cammie thought it might have been a mistake to give Alair his real name, because Alair was smart enough to recognize what kind of name that was. Even as the thought crossed her mind, she dismissed it. She couldn't lie to her best friend.

"Ezalen, huh? Where are you from? That's an Introvertian name, isn't it?"

Eza was going to tell the truth anyway, Cammie knew, so she blurted it out before he could. "Yeah, Alair, he's from Introvertia. He came here because heard Exclaimovia was the greatest nation in the world and he wanted to see it for himself." Well. So much for not lying to her best friend.

"It's surpassed all my expectations," Eza said smoothly, and Cammie's eyes got wide as she tried her hardest not to laugh. He hadn't lied, but he'd made his distaste sound like a compliment!

"It's not real safe for Introvertians to be here these days," Alair said, his eyes narrowing. "I keep hearing rumors that there might be a war soon. You're not here to spy, are you?"

"Alair," Cammie interjected, "my father is General Barin Ravenwood. Would he let a spy stay in our house?"

"He's staying in your *house*?" Alair repeated in shock. "Wait, wait. You were gone for two weeks. Have you been with him the whole time? Did you leave me scared to death, staring at the ceiling unable to sleep, for TWO WEEKS because you were showing him around Exclaimovia the whole time?"

Cammie's lie had erupted all over her and she scrambled to save face. "It's not like that," she protested hurriedly. "It's – he's here because..."

She was hoping Alair was going to cut her off and continue on his angry rant so that she'd have a few more precious seconds to think of a story to tell him, but he crossed his arms on his chest and waited, looking at Eza and then back at her.

"I'm sorry I couldn't tell you," she said. "But like you said, there's talk of a war. His government sent him here, undercover, to see that we're a peaceful people. Only a few people know he's here. I was given the mission of showing him around."

"So where have you been the last two weeks? What

parts of the country?"

"It's still a secret, Alair. Please don't tell anybody. I could get into lots of trouble even for saying this much." Inwardly Cammie was breathing a sigh of relief. She'd put all the pieces of her lie back into a box and wrapped the bow of Alair's trustworthiness around it. She still felt awful for lying to him...

That's when the thought finally occurred to her. Cammie had just lied to her best friend in order to protect Eza.

She was so caught up thinking about this that she was only distantly aware of Alair, with a voice full of insincerity, asking Eza, "So you've had a good time with Cammie, then?"

Cammie's eyes went huge and she tried to get Eza's attention. It was a trap! If he said nice things about Cammie, they would sound like compliments, and Alair would think –

Eza noticed her, but so did Alair at the same time, and Alair was *way* better at picking up on subtle signals. If she tried to hint to Eza that he shouldn't answer the question, Alair would definitely notice. "Well!" Cammie interjected. "I haven't seen Keiko or Ilaria yet. I was hoping they'd be here too."

"I asked Ezalen a question," Alair said.

"We've had lots of fun," Eza agreed eagerly. "Cammie is very smart and very funny. I can see why she has so many friends here."

Ice surged through Cammie's veins as Alair stiffened. "Is that so," he said flatly.

Eza gave Cammie a look of panic, as if he had just realized what he'd done in giving her a public compliment. "She talked about how close the two of you were," he said, trying to recover.

Cammie threw her hands up and shouted, "Alair, you're being ridiculous. Why are you so jealous of this Introvertian? Do you really think someone like this could get in the way of what you and I have?" She desperately hoped Eza wouldn't take offense, that he would know she was only saying what needed to be said, but...

Alair shook his head. "Maybe you're right. Come on. Let's go find Keiko and Ilaria."

"Actually," Cammie said, "I have to show Ezalen a few more things before he goes home. But we'll spend more time together soon, Alair. I promise."

She led Eza back out of Declamation Park. That was *not at all* how she'd wanted her reunion with Alair to go. Anger flooded her, disappointment at herself for missing Alair as much as she'd missed him the last two weeks. Did he think so little of her, that he really believed she'd set aside everything she had with him and allow herself to fall for some *Introvertian* boy? She felt her ears getting hot and then –

A scream exploded from her lips and she lifted her

hand, flinging an enormous fireball into the morning sky. Dozens of onlookers applauded, as if she'd just put on some kind of street theater performance for them. Thinking quickly, Cammie bowed and thanked the crowd, then kept walking quickly with Eza. It was a good thing she'd had a huge breakfast, or else that kind of magic would have ruined her.

"Are you okay?" Eza asked her quietly.

"Don't talk to me."

Eza blinked and fell back a few paces. He had probably taken that personally, Cammie thought, but right now she couldn't care. Though, she had to admit, Eza had always treated her like a princess compared with what Alair had just done –

The catacombs ran underneath quite a bit of the central city, and the main entrance was not far from the main gate into the palace complex. The above-ground graveyard occupied an entire block, with a low stone building at the center that housed the staircase down to the lower levels. And the entrance...

That was interesting, Cammie thought, slowing as she neared the graveyard. Royal guards paced on the street outside the graveyard, and more stood at the doors of the stone building. Exclaimovians were perceptive people. Surely someone had asked questions about the fact that armed soldiers were apparently protecting the dead. That was...interesting...

Cammie stopped, waiting for Eza to catch up to her. "I think we found our dragons. What else would they be guarding?"

"Good point."

They stood there for a few moments, loud people shouldering past them and shouted conversations filling the air around.

"Now what?" Eza asked. "How do we...actually rescue them?"

"We need a plan," Cammie said. "Come on. Let's go back to my house."

But they had only been home a few minutes when a thunderous knock sounded on the front door. "What in the sun..." Cammie murmured to herself, opening the door. Most people would have just come right in without bothering to knock, so who could this be? Her jaw fell in shock when a detachment of royal guards shouldered their way into the house.

"Where's the Introvertian?" one of them demanded.

"Introvertian?" Cammie asked, feigning ignorance.

"We received a tip that an Introvertian was visiting. We have some questions for him."

"Introvertians are allowed in town," she protested, starting to panic. "Exclaimovia is open to visitors from all kingdoms. We pride ourselves on –"

"We have some questions for him," repeated the guard, his face hard. "And for you as well, since we're here."

"Who tipped you off?" Cammie shouted as the guards moved past her toward Eza, who was seated at the table and hadn't moved. "It was Alair, wasn't it?" She could feel herself starting to lose control again...

The guards didn't answer as they took Eza by the arms and ushered him out the door. One guard tried to take Cammie by her upper arm, but yelped in pain, pulling his hand back as if burned. "What in..."

"Don't touch me," Cammie said fiercely, following the guards out into the street.

Things had just gotten very, *very* bad.

EIGHTEEN

They'd kept telling Eza that he wasn't under arrest, but he was currently sitting in a windowless room with undecorated stone walls and a bare stone floor. Eza wouldn't have guessed there was a single room in all of Exclaimovia that wasn't painted bright colors or didn't have paintings on the walls or a brightly woven rug on the floor. This was a plain room that was *clearly* designed to make Exclaimovians uncomfortable.

Fortunately, Eza wasn't an Exclaimovian.

He kept reminding himself that he hadn't done anything wrong, hadn't committed any crime – yes, he was here to free his people's stolen dragons, but he hadn't made any attempt to do so yet. As far as any of them knew, he was just a visitor from a different kingdom, here to pay homage to Exclaimovia's greatness. And yet, if they decided to throw him in prison for the rest of his life, there was nothing he could do to stop them...

At last a man with a black patch over one eye entered through the door and sat down in front of Eza. "Name?" the man said.

Eza considered saying nothing, but suddenly realized that silence would make it seem as if he had something to hide. "Ezalen Skywing."

"Occupation?"

"I'm an army cadet, due back at the Academy in six days." *If you hold me longer, people will know I'm gone,* was the message he hoped the man got.

"What branch?"

"Studying to be a Ranger."

The man with the eye patch looked at him for a long time, his face almost expressionless. "Reason for visiting Exclaimovia?"

"Introvertians have a lot of very strong opinions about Exclaimovia," Eza said. "I wanted to see if those opinions matched reality."

That got a dry smile from the man. "And what have you learned?"

"Our people are very different," Eza admitted. "It's probably a good thing we don't live anywhere near each other."

"I think most of us would agree with that," said the man. "We find Introvertians to be cold and distant, while you no doubt find us to be loud and rude."

"There's nothing wrong with either of us being the way we are," Eza told him. "But all we want is to live in peace, for people to leave us alone so we're free to do things our own way, while all you've ever wanted is for everyone to do everything exactly like you."

Of course that was not a very smart thing to say to a

man who could throw him in jail for a long time.

"Who knows you're here?" the Exclaimovian asked.

"My father, who's also in the army."

"Does your government?"

"I'm not here under orders or anything like that."

The man with the eye patch shifted in his seat. "We believe you know more than what you're letting on, Ezalen Skywing. We believe you're here for a reason you haven't yet divulged. You've correctly perceived that our normal methods of interrogation would not work on you. If you were Exclaimovian, I would leave you alone in this cell for a few hours and you would tell us everything you knew before you went insane. But since you are Introvertian...we will have to get creative. I understand that Introvertians dislike small talk."

Eza said nothing.

"For the next four hours, you will be the royal dog walker. Everyone you see will want to make conversation with you. You will be relieved of your duties at any time if you simply choose to tell us what you know. This can be as brief or as lengthy as you want it to be."

"I have nothing to hide," Eza said calmly.

"We'll see about that."

Two huge golden retrievers awaited Eza in the kennel on the first floor of the palace. They seemed unsure of him at first, as if they'd never smelled anything like an

Introvertian before, but in a few seconds they were wagging at him and smiling in the goofy way that dogs seemed to. He bent down to pet them and they welcomed his hands, turning in circles and wagging so hard Eza thought for sure he'd have welts in the spots where they hit his legs.

A young man wearing royal regalia escorted Eza out of the kennel and through the gate of the palace complex. To Eza's immediate right was the graveyard with the catacombs entrance. He stole a glance in that direction. That was when the thought dawned on him: he didn't know where Cammie was, or whether it was safe to go back to her house when he was released. There was a chance he might have to sneak his way into the catacombs and rescue the dragons himself. How could he possibly do that? He could use his Artomancy, of course, but how?

Plots started forming in his head, but before any of them could coalesce, Exclaimovians were approaching him.

"Ohhhh, what adorable dogs!" one woman said, with a young boy in tow. "I haven't seen you walking them before; what's your name and where are you from?"

"Ezalen, and I'm –"

"LOOK, MOMMY, THE DOG LICKED ME!"

"Don't trip the nice dog walker, Kebrak. I'm sorry about Kebrak. Where did you say you were from?"

"Uh, well actually I'm –"

Another Exclaimovian came sprinting up and wrapped Eza in an enormous hug. Instinctively Eza thrashed away and stared with a mixture of anger and horror at the offender, a girl about his own age. "I'm sorry," he said. "That was rude of me."

"He's rude," the girl whispered.

"MOMMY, THE DOG KISSED MY FACE!" Kebrak shouted.

The young man in royal attire leaned toward Eza and whispered in his ear, "This can all be over any time you want if you just tell us what you know."

The term "dog walker" did not really apply to Eza. After two hours he had made it about half a block, with a mob of people twenty deep surrounding him in every direction, shouting questions about the dogs that he had no idea how to answer, grabbing his shoulders to get his attention, shrieking with joy when the dogs licked them, and trying to make small talk with Eza. He had the worst headache he could ever imagine a person having and wouldn't have been at all surprised if his head had cracked open so his brain could try and make a run for it. "This can all be over any time you want," the royal attendant kept purring in his ear.

The man with the eye patch had said this torture was supposed to last four hours, so Eza turned to make his way back to the palace gates. Somehow he made it. He arrived back at the palace just in time, his knees weak, unable to open his eyes all the way due to the incredible headache. Inside the gates, the man with the eye patch was waiting for him. Eza handed off the dog leashes and collapsed to the ground, shutting his eyes against the cacophony of noise that carried even over the walls of the palace complex after the gates were shut.

"Here in Exclaimovia, people fight each other for the honor of walking the royal dogs," said the man with the eye patch.

"Hrrrnnnnggg."

A glass of water was pressed into Eza's hands, and he drank it. "I hope that this experience will not color your perceptions of Exclaimovia," the man with the eye patch said quietly. "As a soldier yourself, I'm sure you understand that nations must do what they must do in order to stay safe. However, I'm afraid you will not be permitted to remain in Exclaimovia. We will escort you to the front gate of Pride and show you the way to the Very Large Forest. You must leave our kingdom at once."

Still sick and dizzy, Eza was placed on a horse and taken to the western edge of Pride. The city itself was several miles from Exclaimovia's border, so there were no guards at the city walls like the ones in Tranquility. Because of that, once Eza's escort turned and headed back to the palace, there was nobody watching to make sure he actually left the kingdom.

Flat prairies and tall switchgrass covered the first half mile outside the city, but past them he could see low hills and trees. If Eza could get there, he could find some food to forage, and maybe some water as well. Head still throbbing, he forced one foot in front of the other and squinted against the late afternoon sun. Eventually he reached the stand of trees and collapsed in the bushes. His backpack of tools and books and food was gone, still in Cammie's house. If he was spotted in Pride again, he'd just be kicked out once more – or worse, he thought miserably, since he'd be defying a direct order.

So was this it, then? Had he come all this way only to be turned back in defeat, to return home without the dragons – without ever even laying eyes on them? Eza couldn't do that, wouldn't allow himself to do that.

But what could he do?

His heart and his body were both sick as he put his head on the ground and closed his eyes.

Cammie's own interrogation had been significantly shorter. She had screeched demands at her inquisitor, a stern older woman with gray hair who was utterly unmoved by Cammie's fury. Several times Cammie had forced herself to calm down as fire threatened to erupt from her hands. After less than half an hour, her father had slammed open the door of the interrogation room, scaring the older woman half to death and escorting Cammie out the door and back to their house.

"Where's Eza?" she screamed at him as they walked.

"I don't know."

"What do you mean, you don't know? You're a general –"

"Not now, firebug."

As soon as they got into their living room, she rounded on him. "WHERE IS EZA?"

"They think he's a spy. They're asking him questions."

"WHAT'S GOING TO HAPPEN TO HIM?"

"I wish I could tell you, firebug. I really do."

Cammie paced, hands on her hips, shaking her head. "This is the worst day of my life."

The front door opened and Barin went to see who had arrived. Cammie recognized the voice. No, no, no. This was *bad*; she didn't want to see him right now...

"Cammie!" Alair said warmly, coming to her for a hug.

But Cammie put her hands on his face and shoved him away. "WHAT DID YOU DO?" she screamed at him.

Alair was leaning away from her, genuine fear in his eyes. "I was protecting you," he said, sounding wounded. "I didn't want that Introvertian..."

"EZA IS MY FRIEND!" Cammie screamed.

"Just...look," Alair said, moving in again for a hug.

But Cammie put her hands on his chest to push him away again, and this time Alair was the one screaming, two black marks on his shirt smoking from where Cammie had touched him. Cammie was staring at her hands in horror; they looked like they were on fire, the same way they'd looked right before she burned that dragon to cinders. "Get out," she told Alair with her head still down.

"Cammie..."

"GET OUT!"

Alair disappeared back out the front door, and Cammie took deep breaths, trying to get the fire to subside. She felt her father coming up behind her. "Don't touch me," she said, her voice cracking. "I don't want to hurt you."

"I'm proud of you," he said softly.

"WHAT?"

"Elemental magic is the pride of the Exclaimovian people. Many of us have learned how to use it, but for you to have that kind of ability without any training is very impressive. I'm proud of you. When you told me last night that you killed a dragon...I wasn't totally sure I believed you."

Cammie smiled in spite of herself. "That really happened. And the goats too."

"Train yourself, firebug. Learn to use that magic."

274

"How, daddy?"

"I'll hire you a magic tutor."

"I don't want to wait that long, daddy. I want to start teaching myself right now."

Barin looked at her for a few moments. "Wait here." He disappeared into his bedroom while Cammie watched after him, not wanting to be alone, but he came back in less than a minute with a book. "Here," he said.

"*Victory Through Elemental Magic,*" Cammie read. "This sounds fun."

"You've been to the family crypt before, on the northwest side of the city. There's a new wing under construction. It should be safe to practice your magic there." He smiled slightly. "And if you need to extend your independent study by a few days, I'll make the necessary arrangements. Here's the spare key."

Cammie hugged her father tightly, refusing to let go. "You're the best, daddy. I'll go right away."

"I'll come get you in three hours."

She knew she'd have to pack food to take with her. Cammie didn't own any backpacks, but she remembered that Eza had left his in the guest room. Her heart sank as she pushed the door open. The backpack was lying on the floor and Eza wouldn't be coming back for it. Their friendship was over. They hadn't even gotten to say goodbye.

The corner of Cammie's mouth tugged down as she

sat on the floor and picked the backpack up, hugging it like it was a person. It smelled like him – or it smelled like sun and outdoors, and he smelled like sun and outdoors too. That just made her feel worse. In a single day she'd lost Eza and lost Alair.

But – no. Surely Eza wouldn't just quit. He hadn't let anything stop him yet, had he? He'd find a way to get back into the city and free those dragons, and if he didn't, then Cammie would have to do it herself. She and Eza had known all along that getting the dragons back to Introvertia might be the only way to stop a war. The Introvertians might invade if the dragons were here – but they wouldn't attack just as punishment if the dragons were home safely. Eza had said Introvertia had never done anything like that, not in their whole history. Everything depended on the dragons going home.

And that meant everything depended on Cammie being able to use magic.

It was only that thought which finally got Cammie up off the floor, Eza's pack slung over her shoulder. In the kitchen she grabbed all the food she could find and filled up Aed's biggest canteen with fresh water from the pail. Then she was out the door, her legs carrying her toward the family crypt as she prayed she didn't encounter somebody she knew. Anyone she passed would have known something was up, though; her head was down, which was submissive body language and highly unusual to an Exclaimovian. But she passed through one of the market squares, past several blocks of apartment buildings and a neighborhood of smaller freestanding homes, and arrived at the Ravenwood crypt.

The Ravenwoods had been a wealthy and influential family for centuries, and their crypt reflected that. The building was larger than most of the houses in the surrounding neighborhood, painted in the brilliant gold, red, and black of the Ravenwood family crest. Cammie pulled the huge bronze key out of her pocket and slipped it into the keyhole, where it turned with a satisfying *thump*. The door sighed and creaked as it opened inward, and Cammie took a step forward, peering around her. Torches ringed the walls, but they weren't lit – why would they be? Paid crypt-keepers would light the torches when someone from the family was scheduled to come pay homage to the ancestors, but of course Cammie's visit was unplanned, and she didn't want anyone knowing she was here anyway. Closing the door most of the way behind her but leaving it propped open slightly – the thought of it somehow locking behind her was unsettling, even if her father would be coming to get her in a few hours – she took a deep breath and tried to use Eza's flint and tinder to light one of the torches.

It took several minutes of fumbling in the dark, but eventually the torch roared to light, and Cammie took it down to hold in her hand as she pushed further into the crypt. The entry chamber held statues of the family's important people from centuries past, and the next room held their marble burial boxes. Cammie had never been bothered by this place or the presence of the dead; she felt honored to pay her respects to them. Their hard work had helped create the life that she now enjoyed, where her family had money and her father was one of the most admired generals in the kingdom.

One hallway stretched off to the right, holding more burial boxes. Just as her father had said, a new wing was being excavated on the opposite side, off to the...northwest? Yes, that was right. She felt a thrill at herself for figuring that out; Eza would have been proud of her. Cammie stepped inside, looking at the bare dirt walls and floor that hadn't been overlaid with stone yet.

The thought of Eza made her upset again, but rather than dismiss the feeling or try to reassure herself, she kept a grip on the anger, holding it inside her the way Aed sometimes held in a burp until he could blast it right in her face. Her government was putting everyone in danger with this stupid plot to steal dragons, and now Eza had paid the price – and Alair, apparently going insane with jealousy...

Cammie couldn't hold the pain in anymore and blasted off a ferocious arc of lightning that smashed the dirt wall and fizzled. That felt good. But she'd been able to do magic when really, really upset for almost a week now. What she needed was to be able to summon it on demand, and to master it so she could use it without it weakening her.

She shoved her torch into the ground and sat cross-legged on the dirt, not caring if her gorgeous yellow dress got filthy. Out of Eza's pack came a spicy meat stick and *Victory Through Elemental Magic*. The first few pages talked about focus and concentration; Cammie skipped those, because she could already concentrate well enough to remember her lines and her blocking while she was acting in a play.

The book was...not what Cammie had expected. She'd been ready for something formulaic, with magic words like in the childrens' tales, or perhaps something mathematical talking about the precise geometric angles of her hands or her head. Instead, it was more...intuitive. It talked about seeing the energy inside of her, shaping magic deep in her body the same way she formed words with her mind, then guiding the energy outward into her arms and then to her target. Skeptical but willing to try anything, Cammie stuck her meat stick into the book to save her spot and then stood, closing her eyes and attempting to envision a lightning bolt inside her. Sure enough, there it was, and she could see it clearly, as if it were living in there right next to her lungs. Using her mind, she guided it outward, feeling a tingle as it entered her arms and traced its way down to her hands...

A tiny spark fizzled out of her fingers, like the ones she made when she shuffled across the carpet in her socks and then touched a doorknob. Cammie was so embarrassed that she giggled, then began laughing hysterically. If she was the only hope of freeing those dragons and preventing a war with Introvertia, then Exclaimovia was doomed.

After a few moments she regained control of herself. Maybe it would work better with fire, since that came more naturally to her. Again she closed her eyes, imagining she could see a sphere of flame inside her, feeling warmth as it surged down through her hands and then –

A fireball about the size of her fist sailed through the door and smashed the far wall, baking the dirt into a hard clay where it hit. Cammie stared at the spot in surprise, then went to take a look, putting her fingers on the dried dirt. "I did that," she murmured to herself. A slow smile spread across her face, and she repeated it with satisfaction: "I did that!"

Delighted humming filled the empty chamber as Cammie skipped back to where the book was and tried again, and again, and again. Fire was definitely easiest, but Cammie was eventually able to make a passable lightning bolt as well. When she tried water, the stream was so strong that it turned part of the far wall into mud, which sloughed to the ground and started oozing toward

Cammie. Panicking, she grabbed her book and fled into the entry chamber, peeking in after several minutes to make sure she hadn't just started an avalanche. The mud hadn't gotten very far, though, so Cammie went back into the room to keep casting spells. Fire, then more fire, then lightning, then more fire, none of it as strong as it had been when she'd killed that dragon or even when she'd accidentally burned Alair, but a start was a start...

"How's it going, firebug?" came a voice from behind her.

Cammie screamed and flame exploded from her hands at the floor where she happened to be pointing. "DADDY! YOU SCARED ME TO DEATH! What are you doing here?"

"I said I was going to come get you after three hours, remember?"

Cammie's mouth fell open in surprise. "It's been THREE HOURS?"

"It sure has! Now, show me what you've learned. I want to be proud of my baby girl."

So Cammie demonstrated her fire and lightning spells, eagerly turning back to Barin to see his reactions. She was surprised to see the look of concentration on her father's face. "That's...exceptional," he said quietly. "Most Exclaimovians wouldn't even make it halfway through the chapter on concentration in three hours."

"I'm not most Exclaimovians," Cammie said proudly.

"No," Barin agreed. "You're not.

But even as the words were coming out of Cammie's mouth, she realized how true they were, in more ways than she'd meant. After all, she'd just spent three hours completely by herself and mostly in silence except for her occasional grunts and screams. Surely her father must have had the same realization. Was her secret out? Did her father suspect that she'd run away the first time because she wondered if she was a little bit Introvertian?

"Your teacher knows you'll be absent tomorrow, and maybe the next day, too," Barin said. "Come on, firebug. Let's go have dinner."

NINETEEN

Eza awoke the next morning feeling much better, at least physically. The second he opened his eyes and remembered where he was, though, he felt a crushing emptiness, a despair like he'd never experienced before. He was dozens of miles away from home, with nothing to do except return in utter failure. The thought made him not even want to move, even though he also wanted to be home as soon as possible. Stuck between those two conflicting thoughts, he forced himself to take deep breaths and think. Well, one thing was for sure. There was no point in him wearing these ridiculous Exclaimovian colors anymore.

He sat up and moved his hands, and his clothes shimmered into his normal Introvertian attire of forest-green shirt and gray pants. Before they'd even finished changing colors, a rainbow-colored oval opened next to him, making a *fwoosh* sound, and a person stepped out.

Instantly Eza was on his feet, reaching for his scana, which of course was not on his belt. He dropped into a ready position, prepared to fight with hands and feet if he had to.

It was Gar.

"What..." Eza mumbled.

"Most people are a lot more excited to see me," Gar announced. "I'd have thought you would be too, considering."

"How..."

"Magic," Gar said, smiling as if he'd just made the world's funniest joke. "No, really. Artomancy instructors always begin by casting a teacher-student spell, which shows them what spells their students are casting and where they are at the time. I did the same before I started teaching you, so that I could track your progress. I saw you in Pride, and I didn't see any spells I thought a person would have to use to free a bunch of dragons, and then I saw you outside the city. I figured something had gone wrong, and..." Gar held his hands out. "We have no dragons, and we have you looking like someone dropped a house on you. So I'm guessing I was right."

"Yeah," Eza answered, not wanting to put up with Gar's self-congratulations but also thrilled to have some company. Being alone was great, but being alone while miserable was no fun. "That's about right. They found out I was an Introvertian and kicked me out of the city."

"Clearly a reasonable action from people who have nothing to hide," Gar said, his voice thick with sarcasm.

"Well, we don't allow Exclaimovians into our kingdom either, so..."

"Right, but that's just who your people are. You're reserved by nature, and if you suddenly weren't, that would be noteworthy. The Exclaimovians are open and welcoming by nature, so if they're suddenly not...well, that means something."

"What do you care?" Eza asked, the despair returning. "You said a war between Exclaimovia and Introvertia was no concern of yours."

"I did, and it's not." Gar exhaled, as if trying to figure out how to condense all of his greatness into a single-sentence response. "Look, I just traveled over twenty miles by rainbow door in only two jumps. Ten miles at a time. There are two, maybe three Artomancers in the whole world who can do that. I'm so good at what I do that it's been a long time since anything challenged me, and...I think this whole business of helping you steal your dragons back sounds like fun."

"You want to help me?" Eza asked in disbelief.

"And here I was thinking you were intelligent. I'll say it a little slower. Yes, Ezalen. I want to help you get your dragons back."

"Just because it sounds fun?"

"For the love of beets, son, do you always torment the people who are trying to do you a favor?"

"Only Cammie," joked Eza. Putting up with Gar was a small price to pay if it meant having such an excellent spellcaster on his side. "Let's do it. What do you have in mind?"

"Artomancers are masters of disguise. I taught you

the clothes thing, but you'll be able to do way more than that when you're properly trained. Watch." Gar rubbed his fingers together, then acted like he was flicking something at Eza. "Look at your hair."

"I don't have a mirror."

"Who leaves the house without a mirror?"

"Someone who's captured by the Exclaimovian royal guards and then hustled out of the city with only the clothes on his back?"

"Uh." Gar cleared his throat. "Yeah, you got me there. Here." He handed Eza a small mirror.

"My hair is black now!"

"No, it's still light brown. I didn't change your hair, just the way light reflects off it. That's...twelfth term, I think. We didn't quite get that far together."

"And my eyes are blue!"

"For the love..." Gar buried his head in his hands. "No, son, they're still green. It's a trick of the light."

"Let me do the clothes myself," Eza said, trying not to be offended at Gar's brusqueness. "Cammie and I were talking about a color scheme yesterday."

Gar waved at him and Eza turned his shirt lilac, making the cut a little longer so the shirt flowed. His pants stayed gray, but more of a lighter, silvery gray as opposed to the muted shade Eza used in the woods. "What about your clothes?" Eza asked.

"Mine?" repeated Gar, looking down at his black

robe.

"Nobody in Exclaimovia wears black robes, not even to a funeral."

"Fine." Gar spun in a circle, a cloud of glitter appearing in the air around him and fluttering to the ground as he halted, one arm up and one arm down as if showing himself off. His shirt was a ruffly crimson, shot through with gold accents, and his pants were tight and black, decorated with crimson and gold braiding.

Eza doubled over in laughter. "Are you kidding?!"

"Watch. I'm going to get a million compliments."

"Exclaimovians don't give compliments, Gar."

"Oh. Hm. Well, I will draw the envy of their men and the interest of their women, in whatever culturally appropriate form or fashion those things are shown."

"If that's what you have to tell yourself," Eza said, trying to stifle his laughing.

Gar was still admiring his clothes, and finally tore his gaze away to look at Eza. "By the way, if we're going to pretend to be father and son, I might have to put my arm around you and pat you on the back, things like that. I know you Introvertians get weird when people touch you, so I wanted you to know it was coming."

"I'll do what has to be done."

"That's the spirit," Gar said with a smile. "If anyone asks, your name is Garreth. That's what I want my son to be named, if I ever get around to settling down."

"There's got to be somebody out there capable of handling your enormous ego," Eza said.

"That wasn't very Introvertian of you. I think that Exclaimovian girl is rubbing off on you."

Eza didn't want to, but he couldn't help chuckling. "We do tease each other about that."

"Unless you have more gratuitous insults to get off your chest, I say we make our way into the city."

"I might think of a few while we're walking, but that's all for now."

Shoulder to shoulder, they circled around to the north gate of Pride. Eza had to admit defeat; quite a few Exclaimovians they passed did indeed gaze approvingly at Gar's outfit. The Artomancer himself was clearly loving the attention, and he threw a paternal arm around Eza's shoulder and whispered, "I told you so."

They made it to Cammie's house without Gar drawing too much attention to himself, and Gar strolled up to her door, knocking on it several times. Cammie answered the door, peering up at the Artomancer. "Hello!" Gar announced with a warm smile. "Do you have a moment to talk about our lord and savior, the Dragonroaster?"

"Wh–" Cammie spluttered, blinking in confusion several times. Only then did she glance over at Eza, doing a double-take. "EZA?!"

"Shhh," he said. "I'm –"

But Cammie had already launched herself at him, wrapping him up in a hug tighter than any he could ever remember. "I thought I was never going to see you again," she whispered.

"I thought the same thing," he said, squeezing Cammie.

The hug went on for so long that Gar cleared his throat. "Nothing for the guy who arranged this happy little reunion in the first place, hmm?"

"The thing is," Cammie said, her arms still around Eza, "you're the worst, so..."

"I'm also here to help you rescue those dragons, so if you're finished being ungrateful, perhaps we can get moving."

Cammie finally pulled away from Eza. "Let me get your backpack," she told him. "Come on inside while you wait."

It only took her a few seconds to return with the backpack, which Eza happily took back from her. "So," Gar said, "I'm assuming you and Ezalen have been seen together in the city over the past few days, correct?"

"Yes..."

"Which means we should probably disguise you as well. If you just had attention drawn to yourself for spending time with an Introvertian, it wouldn't do at all for you to be seen with two other strangers so soon afterward, would it?"

The look on Cammie's face said that she was not at all pleased to concede he had a good point. "Fine."

Gar looked over at Eza. "Would you like to try?"

"Try what? I don't know how you did the hair thing."

"Look at her hair. Really *look* at it. Examine the way the light reflects off it. Take in how it falls around her shoulders. Just...try to *lose* yourself in it. Then reach out with the new color you want it to be. It's the same idea as what you do with the clothes, but more complex. It'll take all your concentration."

Eza met Cammie's eyes, and it was hard to tell which of them was more skeptical about the whole thing.

"If you really make a mess of it, I can always fix things," Gar reminded him helpfully.

"True," Eza said. "Cammie, what color do you want?"

"Pink," she said immediately. "I've always wanted pink hair."

Eza closed his eyes, then opened them again, emptying his head of every thought except for Cammie's hair, the same way he did when he was trying to listen to Neemie or Aleiza. Then he reached out and touched her long braid, feeling the texture in his fingers. *Pink* came to his mind, and he guided the thought out through his fingers and into Cammie's hair...

The new color started where Eza was touching her braid and radiated out over the rest of her head. Cammie reached behind her and pulled the braid in front, examining the color. Eza held his breath. A huge smile broke out on Cammie's face. "It's *perfect*," she said admiringly. "I have to go look in the mirror."

She vanished from the living room. Eza looked up at Gar and asked, "Did you do that?"

Gar shook his head. "That was all you, friend. I mean, you were taught by one of the most gifted instructors ever to practice Artomancy, but that particular spell was all you."

Cammie reappeared and threw herself into Eza's arms again. "I love my hair," she gushed. "It's so pretty."

"It was pretty before, too," Eza said.

Cammie poked him in the side. "Watch the compliments, mister."

"Listen," Gar said, "you two are an adorable couple and all, but you seem to have a remarkable lack of urgency when it comes to, you know, actually rescuing dragons."

"We're not a couple," Cammie snapped.

"You can do that define-the-relationship talk on your own time, okay? Dragons. Let's go."

"Maybe it's better if we wait until nightfall," Eza suggested. "You had enough people staring at you earlier, and now Cammie has hair that you could stick at the top of a lighthouse."

"Fine," Gar said grudgingly.

"In the meantime, Cammie can tell us everything she knows about the catacombs, which is where we think the dragons are being kept."

"We went down there on a school field trip a few years ago," Cammie said. "It's where all the old kings and queens are buried."

"Which direction do the tunnels go?" Gar asked.

"Excuse me?"

Gar closed his eyes in frustration. "We don't have to go through the front door. I can use my rainbow door spell to take us straight down through the street and directly into the catacombs. But I have to know where they go. If I make a door down in a place where there is no tunnel, that won't help us."

"Um," Cammie said. "Well, after we went in the front door, there was a long staircase down –"

"How many stairs?"

"Forty-one. Then there's a big round chamber with other hallways branching off it."

"That'll do. I can drop us into that chamber. From there...we improvise."

"Good," agreed Cammie. "Now go eat some food or something. I made stew for lunch and there are leftovers. Eza and I have to talk."

"I'll never say no to free food." Gar wandered off toward the kitchen.

As soon as he was gone Cammie hugged Eza again.

"You're clingy today," he told her with a smile.

"I was so scared," she admitted, resting her head on Eza's shoulder. "I lied to Alair to protect you, and he showed back up here thinking he'd done me a favor by getting rid of you. I never knew he could be jealous like that. So that friendship is ruined, and I thought you were gone forever..."

Eza gently rubbed the back of her neck. "I'm here now."

"I really hope we can get those dragons back to your people."

"Me too."

Gar had reappeared in the doorway between the living room and kitchen. Cammie's back was to him, but he met Eza's eyes and mouthed, "Not a couple."

Eza mouthed back, "Go away."

Gar smirked and retreated into the kitchen.

At last Cammie pulled away and looked into Eza's eyes. "Are you hungry?"

"I should eat something. I have a feeling there's going to be a lot of magic happening tonight."

"Let's go see if Gar left any stew."

Eza was a patient person, but the three-hour wait until nightfall was excruciating even to him. He could only imagine what it must have been like for Cammie, who hated waiting for anything. Normally he would have loved to pass the time by letting Cammie tell stories, but she seemed reluctant to open up with Gar around. Instead, they were both treated to a nearly endless monologue from Gar, telling stories in which he inevitably saved the day through some clever and skilled use of Artomancy. Eza listened halfheartedly; the stories really were interesting, but did the guy really *have* to be so full of himself?

"Right," Cammie said as soon as it was dark outside. "Let's go. Follow me and try not to be conspicuous." She glared at Gar as she said the last part.

Cammie led them on a roundabout route toward the palace complex, and they emerged to the rear of the graveyard. In the pale moonlight they could discern the silhouettes of the royal guards far off by the entrance. Gar seemed lost in thought, wandering away from Cammie and Eza as if counting something. He stopped in the middle of the wide avenue, drawing bewildered glances from a few passing Exclaimovians.

Only then did Eza begin to fully grasp all the different things that could go wrong. What if Gar was spotted making his rainbow door? What if he dropped them into solid rock instead of into the entry chamber? What if there were dozens of guards in the catacombs? What if the dragons weren't there at all?

It's a bit late for all this, he scolded himself. *Stay focused.*

Impatiently Gar waved Eza and Cammie over to himself. "We need to act like we're here for a reason," he said. "Pretend we're talking about something important."

"Something *unimportant*," Cammie corrected. "Exclaimovians debate about irrelevant things all the time."

"Fine," Gar said.

Cammie put her hand on her hip. "If chili doesn't have beans in it, it's not real chili."

"WHAT?" spluttered Gar. "Why would anyone lovingly prepare the best ground meat they could procure, delicately season it, and then put *beans* inside it?"

"Because without beans it's not chili," Cammie said heatedly. The corner of her mouth was turned up ever so slightly, and Eza could tell she was playacting and enjoying herself. "It's just a meat bowl. Nobody ever went to their parents and said 'Mom, can we have meat bowl tonight?'"

"They've obviously never had my meat bowl."

"Aha! So you admit that meat bowl isn't chili!"

"I admitted nothing of the sort," said Gar indignantly.

Eza was a third wheel in this conversation, so he closed his eyes and reached out with his mind, seeing if he could make contact with Aleiza. *There* – she was faint, almost imperceptible at such an incredible distance, but she was there. Eza could tell she was pleased to hear from him again, and that she'd been worried about him. Quickly he looked around, showing her where in the city she was, and trying to convey to her that she should come and wait at a safe altitude until he came out from underground. He had no idea how well she'd understood him; the mind link was so fuzzy, and Eza had never given such specific instructions even to Neemie, whom he'd known for a lot longer than Aleiza. If Aleiza misunderstood him, and came to land in the graveyard while looking for Eza...

Cammie and Gar were still going after each other, and kept up their discourse for the next fifteen minutes, during which time nobody on the street paid any kind of attention at all to the loud dispute going on. At last Eza was sure no one was nearby, but even as he opened his mouth to say something to Gar, a rainbow door appeared on the street, shining brightly in the darkness. If anyone saw –

"Go fast," Gar said.

Without a second thought Eza jumped through the rainbow door, landing gently on the floor of the catacomb entry hall. Cammie hit the ground next to Eza a second later, wobbling a bit as she did and leaning on him for support. Through the door, Eza could clearly make out Gar's voice muttering a curse...

And then the rainbow door vanished.

"He didn't come through?" Cammie asked, fear trickling into her voice.

"Something must have gone wrong," Eza said. "We don't have time to wait around for him, though. He knows where to find us."

"Hey, you!" a voice sounded from behind Cammie and Eza.

Instantly a flash of lightning lit up the room, momentarily blinding Eza, and when his vision cleared he saw a royal guard lying on the ground and twitching.

"You did that?" Eza asked in shock.

"Yeah. He's not dead...I think. I tried to hold back."

Eza nodded admiringly. "You've been busy while I was gone."

"A little bit," Cammie agreed. "Come on. The bigger chambers are down this way."

Cammie led Eza down a long hallway which opened into a broad room. Along the left wall were what looked like small rooms, burial chambers that would normally have been filled with marble coffins but at the moment were full of –

"Dragons," Cammie said with wonder in her voice.

They were crammed twenty to a chamber, with barely enough room to move. As soon as they saw Cammie and Eza, they began protesting at the tops of their voices. Obviously they were used to bad things happening whenever a person poked his or her head into the room.

"How are we going to set them free?" Cammie asked, looking at the iron jail doors that had been hastily set up across the front of each burial chamber.

"I don't want to just yet."

"*WHAT?*"

"It doesn't look like they know we're friendly. I need to see if I can get through to them so they don't attack us after we let them go."

Cautiously Eza approached one of the jail doors and reached out with his mind to the nearest dragon. He could immediately feel surprise; the dragon was not expecting this strange person to be able to communicate. Then dozens, *hundreds,* of other dragon voices began cascading into his head, and Eza was overwhelmed, nearly falling over from dizziness before regaining control enough to close off the mind link.

"Did you get through?" Cammie asked eagerly.

"I think so. Now to get them out."

"I could try to make an earthquake and see if that gets the doors off their hinges."

"Great idea, but I don't like the thought of this place collapsing on us." Eza frowned. "Oh...hey. The doors aren't locked."

"WHAT?"

"They're latched, but there aren't any locks. I guess that makes sense. It would probably get annoying to unlock all these doors every time, wouldn't it?"

"Well, unlatch them, then!"

Eza did, trying to reassure the dragons through the mind link, but the confusion and excitement of so many dragons in one place was like an explosion inside his head, and he had to close it again. He desperately hoped they saw him as a friend and not as food...

Hesitantly, he eased the first cell open, and the dragons burst out, looking thrilled to be free. Some of them nuzzled him with their snouts as they passed, and he smiled. They were grateful.

"That's about a hundred," he said when all the dragons in the room were loose. It was almost funny to watch them all milling around, as if someone had invited them to a party and they were trying to figure out what it meant to mingle. Not that Eza had any experience mingling, of course. "Where are the rest?"

He opened his mind link again, picturing a dragon and asking "Where?" Dragons were always fiercely protective of their own; it was Neemie's concern for these ones that had sent Eza and Cammie on this adventure in the first place, after all. Instantly thirty of the dragons made a sprint for the door at the far end of the room, which was made of solid metal and barricaded shut.

Eza cast a rainbow door in front of it. He saw more dragon pens on the other side of the door, but no guards – at least not at first. Suddenly he could see two of them, pointing at the rainbow door and asking, "What is *that*?"

The dragons, though, didn't seem to have any interest in going through...

"I'll take the lead," Cammie said. "Just...make sure they're right behind me, okay?"

She leaped through the rainbow door and instantly a dozen of the dragons piled in behind her, with the rest in close pursuit. Through the portal he could hear screams and the sound of a colossal fight, and his heart started to beat faster. Was Cammie okay? Dragons were still pouring through the portal; Eza had never held one open this long, didn't know when it was going to collapse. He felt himself straining under the effort, his legs starting to shake. If he exhausted himself and passed out here, like Cammie had done in the wilderness...

Finally all the dragons had passed and Eza slipped through the door himself, shocked by the sight that greeted him. The dragons had been blocking his view the whole time, and only now did he see the thirty Exclaimovian royal guards dead on the ground, uniforms ripped by dragon claws and faces scarred with bite marks. The dragons were chittering excitedly; the thought of revenge against their captors had clearly gotten them going. "That was really brave of you," Eza said to Cammie as he started unlatching the closest jail doors. "And that's not a compliment. It's an observation."

"It's funny," she said as two jail doors swung open

and Eza went to work on the next two. "I should probably have been scared, especially when I stepped through and there were thirty guards coming into the room and I had no idea if the dragons were going to follow me. But I wasn't scared, because all I could think of was what would happen if we failed and your people went to war to get their dragons back. I was more afraid of *that* than whatever was waiting for me in this room, so I went for it."

By now there were about two hundred dragons milling around a room that was obviously too small for all of them. Eza didn't know how many dragons had been stolen, but there were four hundred third-year students at Carnazon, so the total number was probably at least that, and possibly higher. Sure enough, the dragons pulled him onward, this time down a wide spiraling staircase. "Look," he said out loud, trying to convey the same message through the mind link, "it's really not necessary to have *all of you* go..."

But the dragons wouldn't be deterred; they were moving with single-minded focus. Once again, the sounds of screaming and fighting drifted up toward Eza as the dragons poured down the staircase, and it took nearly five minutes before he and Cammie were able to follow the horde down to the bottom. Eza was not prepared for the sight that awaited him.

The round room was *massive*, so large Eza could

hardly have thrown a rock from one side to the other. The entire outside was ringed with cages like the ones upstairs, each cage stuffed with dragons. But in the center of the room were thirty or forty poles, each with a dragon chained to it, as if the Exclaimovians had been trying to teach them fighting moves. It wouldn't be possible to ask the Exclaimovians themselves; every single guard in the room was unconscious or dead. These dragons were not messing around, Eza thought.

He had to deliberately block out his mind link; there were so many dragons in one place now, all of them clamoring for his attention, that he could barely even keep his own thoughts straight. Some of the chained dragons seemed malnourished or abused; a few looked like they'd had scales yanked out and others had what appeared to be burn marks on them. Cammie rushed toward the ones that looked the worst off, using her elemental magic to spray water into their mouths. The looks of gratitude on their faces melted Eza's heart, and he immediately started opening the doors on all the cells around the outside of the room.

"Seven hundred dragons, give or take," Eza said. "Getting them out of Exclaimovia is going to be...very interesting."

"What's your plan?" Cammie asked.

"Uh...just run for it, I guess."

Cammie smiled nervously. "Run the whole way out

of the city? Did you forget who you're talking to?"

"Leave that part to me."

"Great. I will just be here taking up space, then."

"Hey, you're useful. Gar wouldn't have known where to drop us if not for your great memory."

"Hmm. True."

Eza opened his mind link just long enough to let the dragons know it was time to go back upstairs, and the hundreds of voices quickly obliterated his defenses. He blinked quickly a few times and dropped to one knee, closing the link off as the dragons headed back to the staircase. What he really wanted was to try and get a hold of Aleiza again, to see if she was in position above them yet, but he wasn't sure he'd be able to make out her voice through all the noise and he didn't want to get overwhelmed again. They'd just have to hope for the best.

There were so many dragons that Eza and Cammie had to wade through them in order to get back to the spot in the entry hall where Eza would need to cast the rainbow door back to the surface. This was where it would have been *really* helpful to have Gar back, because Eza had no idea how far the door would need to go. Sixty feet should be enough...but if that was too much, there would be a long fall back to the road, instead of the gentle plop that Gar had given them when they'd come down. However, if he didn't make the door far enough, it would end in solid ground – Eza didn't know what would happen if he did that, and he didn't want to find out.

"Sixty feet it is," he muttered to himself. "I'm going first, Cammie. Give me five seconds and then come after me."

He motioned the rainbow door into existence just over his head and then leaped. There was a disorienting sense of being sucked upward and then he was falling five feet to the ground, landing a bit heavily but not painfully. Apparently the dragons didn't plan on waiting the five seconds, because they spewed out of the rainbow door and up into the night sky. A few of them had atrophied wings from being so long in the cells, and those ones wobbled their way back to the ground, scurrying around and looking to Eza for leadership.

A crowd of Exclaimovians had begun to gather, along with several guards. In a flash the dragons were spiraling down toward anyone wearing the royal uniform, knocking them off balance and tearing with claws. Then the crowd was fleeing in a massive stampede, people hurtling every which way as dragons milled around aimlessly in the sky and outside the palace grounds.

Eza's entire body was screaming with the effort of holding the rainbow door open, but at last the torrent of dragons slowed to a trickle and then Cammie was leaping out as well, holding precariously to the rim of the portal. Eza threw his arms around her and heaved her out, and she landed on top of him with a heavy thud. "Sorry," she said.

Try as he might, Eza couldn't think of the right witty comeback, so he just hauled Cammie up to her feet. As he did, Aleiza came screaming out of the sky, swooping above the rescued dragons with a ferocious roar. Instantly the dragons snapped into something resembling a formation, following Aleiza as she led them off to the west. That left Eza and Cammie alone with the dragons who were too weak to fly, so Eza popped open a rainbow door and jumped through it with Cammie.

The rainbow door only took them about sixty feet down the road – apparently that was the furthest Eza could go, so it was a good thing they hadn't been further underground – but with enough little jumps like that, it would save Cammie from having to sprint too far. The dragons on the street followed in a disorganized mob, but it would still take them about ten minutes to make it to the gates –

"Trouble," Cammie said. In front of them, a line of royal guards had formed across the road.

"We'll rainbow door past them," Eza suggested.

"They'll chase us down!"

But then a flight of dragons blotted out the stars, and Aleiza led hundreds of them down from the sky, smashing into the line of royal guards. Panicked screams filled the street, and Eza opened his mind link just long enough to urge the dragons onward again. Another well-placed rainbow door took him and Cammie past the carnage where the royal guards had been, and in a few more minutes, Eza and Cammie and several dozen dragons hustled through the western gate of Pride with Aleiza, Neemie, and the other dragons soaring overhead.

For whatever reason – disorganization or fear – the Exclaimovians didn't offer a defense, and it wasn't long before Cammie, Eza, and their vanguard of dragons were out of Exclaimovian territory and into the Very Large Forest. *Fwoosh* went a rainbow door, and then Gar was next to Eza, who slowed down in surprise.

"You're late," Eza said.

"Late!" Gar repeated, guffawing. "I suppose you think it was *easy* to confuse the entire Exclaimovian military so they didn't pursue you out of the city."

"You mean it wasn't easy?" Cammie needled him sarcastically. "It actually challenged your considerable intellect?"

"Of course not. I meant it would have been difficult for you." Gar surveyed the dark sky and the dozens of dragons hopping along on the ground. "Then again, maybe it wouldn't have been. You did all this yourselves?"

"That's right," Eza told him.

"I am...actually impressed. When the guards

responded suddenly and I had to leave, I assumed you two would get yourselves into a tough spot and I'd have to come do everything. I'm pleased to see that I was..."

"Wrong?" Cammie asked, delight in her voice.

"I had not fully..."

"You were wrong," Cammie told him, a huge smile on her face. She clapped her hands excitedly. "You were wrong!"

"Savor the moment, child. It doesn't happen often." Gar grinned as well. "But yes. I underestimated your capabilities, and I stand corrected."

Cammie stuck out her tongue at him. "I stand corrected," she repeated in a singsong voice.

Gar shook his head, still smiling. "I'll stay with you until you reach Introvertia. I doubt the Exclaimovians would pursue you into the Very Large Forest, but if they do...well, you'll want me around."

Gar took over the rainbow-jumping duties from Eza, and gradually the mob of dragons and people worked their way closer and closer to Tranquility. The distance would have taken them two full days to travel on foot, but with Gar's rainbow jumps covering a hundred yards in every step, they were nearing the gates of Tranquility in just three hours.

Eza knew the dragons had been cooped up for...well, however long it had been since the Exclaimovians had stolen them. He opened the mind link to all seven hundred dragons at once, immediately regretting it as the noise and chaos invaded his mind. He pushed back just long enough to encourage them that it was only a little further to go until they were home, and the relief that flooded back through the mind link was almost overwhelming.

"Hold on," Gar said, putting a hand on Eza's shoulder. "Let me do something for you."

Eza felt a slight tingling on his hair and in his eyes and immediately figured out that Gar was returning him, and his clothes, back to normal. Cammie's hair, too, flickered back to its normal dark brown. Eza could see her lips twinge in disappointment. "Well, folks," Gar said, "it's been real. Thanks for letting me help your little mission. I hope you prevented a war and all that. And you," he added, pointing at Eza, "we'll be in touch. I know you have classes and all that, but I'm not done making you into one of the greatest Artomancers the world has ever seen. Not quite on my level, of course, but *one* of the greatest."

"Thanks, Gar," Eza said.

"One final thing," Gar added. "Have either of you heard of an Artomancer named Kavora?"

Eza looked in confusion at Cammie, who shook her head. "No," Eza answered. "Why?"

"He's an...acquaintance of mine. I'm looking for information on him. If you hear of anything, please find a way to contact me, okay?"

"We'll do that," promised Eza. "Thanks again."

With a *fwoosh*, Gar disappeared.

Eza dug around in his backpack, pulling out his Ranger cloak and wrapping it around himself. Then he offered Cammie his arm. "Shall we?"

Cammie put her hand inside his elbow and the two of them walked the final half-mile toward the Tranquility gates, with dragons overhead and bounding along on the ground. They had almost reached the gates when a company of Introvertian soldiers came rushing out, slowing as they saw Eza approaching. "Cadet," the commanding officer said, spotting Eza's cloak. "What's the meaning of this?"

"These are our dragons that Exclaimovia stole. My friend and I stole them back...with a little help."

The officer peered at Cammie. "That girl is Exclaimovian."

Eza felt Cammie move closer to him, and he put his arm around her protectively. "She's a hero of the kingdom and will be given the respect she deserves."

There were several seconds of silence, punctuated by the flapping of dragon wings and an annoyed roar from Aleiza.

"Right," said the officer. "So. I'm just going to take you both directly to the king and queen and let them figure this thing out."

TWENTY

It was well after midnight by now, but King Jazan and Queen Annaya were seated in the throne room when Eza and Cammie entered, somehow looking not at all tired. The rest of the room was just about as full as Eza had ever seen it, packed with important generals and other army people. Over there was Captain Onanden, whose half-truth to Eza had kicked off this whole adventure. Cammie sat next to Eza, her leg jiggling furiously on the ground. "Are you okay?" he asked her.

"What if they send me back and I get in a lot of trouble?" she whispered.

"The king and queen are kind people. I don't think they'd let that happen."

Cammie nodded, but took Eza's hand for reassurance anyway, her fingers sweaty against his.

"Honored guests," Queen Annaya began, a warm smile reaching all the way to her dark eyes. "The two friends you see before you have returned from an adventure with a tale that must be heard to be believed. Please yield your ears to Ezalen Skywing, third-year student at the Dragon Academy, and Cammaina Ravenwood of Exclaimovia."

Eza extended his arm to Cammie; she would do a far

better job telling the story than he ever could. She rose to her feet, bowed to the king and queen, and began with her initial discovery about the stolen dragons and her decision to visit Introvertia. Every few minutes Eza could feel wondering eyes on him, and he kept nodding along, letting the astonished listeners know that yes, things really had happened exactly as Cammie was describing them, and no, she was not exaggerating.

An hour and a half later she had finally reached the conclusion. "And now I'm standing in the throne room," she said with a flourish, taking a bow.

The king and queen led a polite round of applause. "Truly an astounding tale," King Jazan said approvingly. "Cadet Skywing and Miss Ravenwood, the kingdom stands indebted to you for your acts of bravery. Please, name your reward and it will be given to you."

The offer of reward was ceremonial, Eza knew. The correct response was for the person who'd just done the brave deed to protest that no reward was necessary, that the satisfaction of doing one's duty to the kingdom was quite enough. But these were exceptional circumstances. Eza stood, and if he'd thought people were looking at him in shock before, that was nothing compared to the way they looked at this young man who was about to buck tradition. "If it please the king and queen," Eza said, doing his best to sound formal but humble, "Miss Ravenwood has risked everything to help the Kingdom of Introvertia. She has committed an act of treason by aiding us. It would be unthinkable for us to turn her away, to send her back to her people; she could be put on trial and imprisoned or killed. The reward I ask is that she be granted asylum here in Introvertia, that she be permitted to live with my father and me since we are the only people she knows in our kingdom, and that she be enrolled in my class at the Dragon Academy." A murmur of surprise was beginning to circle the room, but Eza finished his thought. "I believe the king and queen would agree that this is the only compassionate choice considering how much Cammie has sacrificed for the good of our kingdom."

Eza heard several quiet protests, including "An Exclaimovian, here?" in what was obviously not a tone of approval. But King Jazan and Queen Annaya merely glanced at each other, and then the Queen motioned down with her hands. The room instantly quieted. "The king and queen are pleased to grant Cadet Skywing's request for asylum for his friend. How old are you, Miss Ravenwood?"

"Sixteen, Your Highness."

"And are you prepared to take an oath of allegiance to the Kingdom of Introvertia, to renounce your citizenship of Exclaimovia, and to abide by all the laws and customs of Introvertia?"

The word *renounce* seemed to make her flinch, and

she glanced at Eza, as if looking for reassurance. He smiled gently at her. This was the only way.

"I am, Your Highness," she said confidently.

"Then let the royal records show that Cammaina Ravenwood is granted full Introvertian citizenship, with all the rights, privileges, and responsibilities thereof. Let the records further be updated to reflect her immediate enrollment at Carnazon."

The look of gratitude and relief on Cammie's face was overwhelming, and she wrapped her arms around Eza's neck, planting her face in his neck. He could feel wetness on his skin, and Cammie whispered quietly in his ear, "Thank you."

Eza rubbed Cammie's back for several seconds until he suddenly became aware that everyone was staring at them. Cammie chose that moment to pull back from him, wiping happy tears from her eyes and beaming at Eza. "The royal audience is dismissed," King Jazan said. "The two cadets will please remain for a while longer."

The throne room cleared out, and the king and queen approached Cammie and Eza. King Jazan extended a hand to Eza, who shook it gratefully, and Queen Annaya offered Cammie a hug. "The matter of the stolen dragons had been in front of me for two weeks before you discovered it," the king said. "We hadn't yet come up with a plan to rescue them that was more likely to *prevent* a war than to start one. The success of your adventure was a great relief to many of us who wanted to keep the peace."

"You don't think Exclaimovia will attack anyway, do you?" Cammie asked with worry in her voice.

"I don't know what Exclaimovia will do," the king admitted. "But our hope is that they will be pragmatic about it. They stole our dragons, we stole them back, and that ought to be the end of the story."

"But sir, the dragons are so tightly guarded. How were Exclaimovian agents able to steal them from us in the first place?"

"I'm not prepared to answer that question publicly yet, Cadet. Perhaps in the coming days." King Jazan smiled. "One other thing. I notice that Miss Ravenwood's story involved both of you doing magic. Introvertia is still a non-magical kingdom, so you will be required to refrain from practicing magic from this point forward. Am I understood?"

Cammie cleared her throat. "Your Highness, I noticed something about Neemie. That's Eza's father's dragon. She seemed...drawn to magic. Whenever I used my elemental magic, she kept wanting to be near me. I don't know what that means, but I wonder if it's important."

The king and queen looked at each other again. "We'll look into it," Queen Annaya promised. "For now, I believe we've taken enough of your time." She pressed a handful of coins into Cammie's hands. "Please enjoy a meal tomorrow at any restaurant you choose."

Cammie gave a curtsy. "Thank you, Your Highness. For everything."

"Thank you for the safe return of our dragons," King Jazan said. "I hope you enjoy life here in Introvertia."

Cammie woke up the next morning wondering if the whole dragon adventure been a dream. It *felt* like one of the good dreams she always had after she'd been up late reading a book. There had been action, and magic, and danger, and heroes and villains...

But the feel of this bed was unfamiliar, and when she opened her eyes, a plain wood pattern on the ceiling greeted her. This was *definitely* Introvertia, and that meant everything was real. The dragons were safe in Introvertia, just like she and Eza had wanted all along. There was probably not going to be a war.

Her mouth tugged down. And that meant she was a traitor and an exile, and *that* meant she wouldn't be able to see her family anytime soon – or maybe ever. Loneliness overcame her, and she forced herself to say it out loud: "It was worth it." She'd freed hundreds of dragons from a miserable fate, and had kept Introvertia from launching an invasion to get them back. It was the right thing to have done, and it was worth it. Just...if it did cost her the chance of seeing her family again, that was a *really* steep price.

She wasn't the one who'd made the choice to do the wrong thing, though; her people had done that. Once she'd found out, the only question was whether she had the courage to put things right or whether she was a coward who was willing to let other people – and dragons – suffer so that nothing bad happened to her.

That made her feel a little better, so she swung her bare feet out of bed and made her way down the stairs to see what was cooking for breakfast. Eza had probably been up since dawn again, and sure enough, there he was, working a trio of pans on the hot stone cooktop.

"Hey," he said without turning around. "I'm making you something."

"How is your hearing so good? I wanted to surprise you."

"This is what happens when you spend time around silence," Eza teased. "Here. It's a spicy egg-and-cheese wrap like the one we had for breakfast at your house."

"Spicy?" Cammie asked doubtfully.

"Try it."

Cammie did. "This is pretty good," she confessed.

"Try it yourself."

"Oh, not a chance. I made myself one without the spices."

"You did this one just for me?" Cammie asked, looking down at the wrap on her plate.

"Sure did."

That was very thoughtful of him, and for several moments Cammie didn't know how to react. "Thank you," she said at last.

"You're welcome," he said, eyes back on the cooktop. "Are you feeling okay?"

Cammie stuffed her face with the spicy wrap so she didn't have to answer right away. If Eza were Exclaimovian, he would have gotten bored of waiting for her to reply, and he'd have started telling a new story while her mouth was full. But Eza wasn't Exclaimovian, and he waited patiently for her to finish.

"Do you think I can learn to be happy here?" she asked.

Eza immediately slid the hot pans to the stone countertop so the food would stop cooking, then sat across from Cammie at the table. His green eyes were creased at the corners; he was concentrating fully on her, with his ears and his eyes and his whole body. "I do," he said. "You told me all the things you didn't like about Exclaimovian society. You don't have to follow those unwritten rules anymore. You don't have to second-guess whether you're allowed to say certain things or whether you're allowed to talk to certain people. You don't have to play those games. Yeah, you'll have to learn how to listen without interrupting, and how to keep from blurting out everything that comes to your mind, but those aren't bad things for a person to learn, are they?

And none of those things change who you *are*. They just change how you express all the things that make you wonderful."

Cammie was so focused on his words that she didn't realize he'd given her a compliment. She was even more surprised when her usual skepticism and defensiveness failed to appear. "You think I'm wonderful?" she asked.

"You are. Don't you know that?"

"Well...I don't want to sound like Gar, but yeah, I guess I do. It's always nice to hear it, though." She smiled. "Thank you, Eza."

"When you finish eating, let's go walk around the city again. I know I gave you a tour once, but maybe it'll look different if you're thinking of it as home. I can show you the art museum, the theater –"

"There's a theater?" Cammie blurted. "I'd love to get back into acting!"

"There are three or four in Tranquility alone. I –" Eza cut himself off and frowned. "I was going to say that I could loan you some clothes and use my Artomancy to change the color and style for you. But the king and queen said we can't use magic now that we're back in Introvertia."

"That's a little disappointing, isn't it? I mean, we worked really hard to learn magic. Are we just never going to get to use it again?"

"I don't know. I hope we get to keep studying

it...somehow."

"Me too." Cammie slid her hands across the table toward Eza. "You know...we made a pretty good team."

A huge smile came to Eza's face and he turned red. "I thought so, too," he told her, taking her hands.

It seemed like a really long time before either one of them moved. At last Cammie squeezed Eza's fingers and stood. "I'll get changed, then. It sounds like we have some clothes shopping to do!"

Eza blinked in surprise. "Say what now?"

"The king and queen gave me some money last night, remember? And since your clothes don't fit me, and you can't use magic to change them..." She put an arm across her forehead dramatically. "I'm afraid we have *no choice* but to go clothes shopping together."

"Okay," Eza said happily.

Cammie's eyebrow arched. "You agreed way too quickly. What kind of game are you playing?"

"We don't play games here," he reminded her. "I just felt like you're going to be doing a lot of unfamiliar things today, learning your way around a new city, going places you've never been before. So if clothes shopping will make you happy, then I want to go with you, even if it's something I wouldn't normally enjoy."

"You're really going to do *everything* to make me feel welcomed, aren't you?"

A lopsided grin came to his face. "That's the plan."

Twenty minutes later the two of them were stepping out into the cool spring morning, sunlight on their faces and the smell of pine drifting on a light breeze. It didn't take Cammie long to find a clothing store she liked, and she roamed the aisles with childlike excitement. Most of the clothes were typical Introvertian earth tones, grays and browns and greens, but there were also lighter blues like the sky and deeper blues like the ocean, and a few things that were dark purple like nighttime. It wasn't exactly an Exclaimovian palette, but Cammie put together six outfits, smiling with approval at each one and then at Eza as they walked out of the store. "It was fun watching you enjoy yourself," he told her.

"I liked the challenge, honestly. Having fewer colors made me more...creative. It's like when you write a poem or a song and it has to rhyme, and that makes you think harder than if you just wrote whatever you wanted."

Eza nodded with satisfaction. "I like that attitude."

After a brief stop at Eza's house to deposit Cammie's new clothes, with the sun still gleaming above them in a clear blue sky, the two of them strolled all over the city. Eza showed her the art museum, the history museum, the three theaters...and the Music Square four or five times. Cammie had said she had a perfect memory, so Eza was fairly sure she was making a map of the city in her head, and somehow she kept finding a way to get them to cut through the Music Square, lingering there for as long as Eza would let her.

At last they were cutting through the Reading Square, past the palace, on their way to Mr. Cappel's bookstore to tell him everything that had happened. As they neared the palace, though, one of the guards outside stopped them.

"Cadet Skywing?"

Eza stopped in surprise, wondering if he'd done something wrong. "Speaking."

"Wait here, please."

TWENTY-ONE

"Is something wrong?" Cammie asked quietly, fear gripping her heart. What if the king and queen had changed their mind and she was about to be sent back to Exclaimovia?

A messenger came out of the palace, placing a folded letter in Eza's hands. "The king thought you would want to see this."

There was an Exclaimovian wax seal on the back of the letter, but the seal was broken, meaning the letter had already been opened and read. Eza unfolded the paper and Cammie leaned over his shoulder, reading the words out loud.

"Be it known to all that King Dorran III of Exclaimovia does hereby issue this proclamation of banishment against Cammaina Ravenwood, daughter of Barin Ravenwood, for the crime of treason. From this moment, the traitor is no longer welcome within the borders of Exclaimovia, and any Exclaimovian found to be giving aid or comfort to her will be similarly considered a traitor. She is to be cut off, entirely and permanently."

Her voice caught in her throat at that last sentence. She felt Eza stiffen, as if debating whether to put his arm around her or whether it was better not to touch her. She leaned against him, clutching the letter with both hands, and felt Eza hugging her.

"That's it, then," Cammie said. "It's official."

"I'm sorry," he said, turning to face her.

"Would you have done the same thing, Eza? Would you have betrayed your kingdom in order to help Exclaimovia, if you knew it was the right thing to do? Even knowing you'd never see your family again?"

His green eyes met hers. "To do the right thing, to prevent a war? Yeah. I would."

"I know you would. So don't feel sorry for me, okay? I'm upset that my people reacted the wrong way to me doing the right thing, but I can't control that. And if this is the way it has to be...then this is the way it has to be." She looked around at the wide expanse of the Reading Square, then at the whitewater of the Rapidly Flowing River. "I can't change things, so I'll just have to make the most of them."

"Then I'll help you enjoy life here however I can," Eza told her. "I want you to feel at home."

That brought a smile to Cammie's face. "You know...I think I just might."

Dragon Academy Intake Test

Greetings Cadet,

Today is an exciting day for you! You're about to begin training to become a dragon-companion, one of the legendary protectors of the Kingdom of Introvertia. Please complete the following test to the best of your ability, as it will determine your assignment to either Victory, Harmony, Sun, or Excellence Company.

Cadet, it's very important that you understand there are *no right or wrong answers on this intake test*. No company is more valuable than the others, and no company is useless. All four companies, and the personality types they represent, are important to the kingdom. Do not answer according to what you *think you should answer*, or what you think *other people would say about you* (except the question that asks you to do so). Answer what *you feel is true about yourself*.

Good luck!

Question 1: You're about to play a card game with your friends. What is most important to you?
A. I want to win! Why play if you're not trying to win?
B. I want everyone to get along. If people take the game too seriously, feelings get hurt.

C. I want to play my very best. Even if I don't win, I can still be proud of giving it all my effort.
D. I want all my friends to have a good time. That may mean we play a game I don't want to play, but if they're enjoying themselves, that's okay with me.

Question 2: You've just been placed in command of a squad of your fellow students. What do you focus on in your first few weeks of training?
A. Tactics and techniques. That's what will give us the best chance of victory.
B. Building relationships. We'll fight harder for each other if we have close friendships.
C. Assigning roles. People have to know their own strengths so I can place them where they'll do best.
D. Finding humor. If my squad is a place people can laugh and have a good time, they'll naturally want to be their best for their friends.

Question 3: You and another student are debating a question of tactics. The other student is saying things that the professor said were incorrect. What do you do?
A. Win the argument! They need to admit that I'm right and they're wrong.
B. Find something else to talk about. The professor can correct them; it's not worth arguing over.
C. Debate as well as I can. It doesn't matter if I convince

them, but I want to make great points.

D. Stop the argument and go do something fun with them. It's hard to argue when you're laughing!

Question 4: You're scheduled to do a mock swordfight against a student who injured herself in training last week and isn't fully healed. How do you approach the fight?

A. My job is to win, so I will. If I were hurt, I'd expect her to do the same!

B. I would talk to her beforehand to make sure I'm not going to hurt her feelings if I beat her.

C. I'd ask to postpone the fight until she's healed. I want the best possible test of my ability.

D. Win, but try to make it funny. If I have to beat her, I can at least make we'll all laugh about it later.

Question 5: You and one of your best friends are both up for a promotion. How do you handle the competition?

A. I want that promotion! I've worked hard to earn it, and my true friends will be happy for me.

B. If the other student wants it so badly, they can have it. I'd rather have a friend than a fancy title.

C. I'm going to give it my very best, but I can't control whether my commanding officers choose me or not, so I won't worry.

D. I only want it if it's going to be more enjoyable than

what I'm doing now. If it's more stress and more pressure without being more fun, I'd rather not be promoted at all.

Question 6. You're in charge of decorating for the Spring Formal dance, and one of the other students is questioning your choices. What do you do about that?

A. I was placed in charge for a reason, so I need to make sure my orders are carried out. I don't like how it feels when I get second-guessed.

B. I want everyone to feel like their input is heard and appreciated. It's no problem for me to modify my plans if it means the rest of my team feels valued.

C. I'm going to do the best job I can. I want everyone to like my choices, but if they don't, that's okay.

D. I want everyone to have fun serving on my team. We all need to loosen up and stop taking things so seriously.

Question 7: The center forward on your ringball team has been playing poorly for the last few games and is not scoring goals. You think it might be time for him to be removed from the starting lineup and replaced with another player. What do you do?

A. Replace him! We play to win, and it's not fair to the rest of the team to leave someone in the starting lineup for sentimental reasons.

B. Talk to the center forward, his replacement, and the

other players. There has to be a way to do this without people's feelings getting hurt, and drama hurts our on-field performance.

C. The team has to be its very best, and the player should recognize that he's not playing well. Perhaps he would be better suited to a different position?

D. Practices need to be more fun. He's probably nervous about how he's been playing, and if he loosens up and stops overthinking, he'll start scoring again.

Question 8: Cammie Ravenwood, the loud Exclaimovian, has been assigned to the squad you command, and not everyone is happy with that. How do you react?

A. If her magic makes the squad stronger, nothing else matters! We'll use every advantage we have, and my squad-mates need to adapt.

B. Cammie is working hard to meet us halfway. We should be patient with her and kind to her so that she feels welcomed and at home.

C. I may not like her, but I can become a stronger person by being around her. Maybe she'll help me become more patient or tolerant.

D. I bet if we go play some games together, do something goofy, or find a way to laugh, that conflict will go away.

Question 9: One of your friends has challenged you to a competition doing something you're not very good at.

What do you tell her?

A. If I know I'm not good at it and have no chance of winning, what's the point?

B. If it will make her happy, I'll do it. Maybe I'll look a little silly, but if she smiles, it's worth it.

C. I'll do it! I'm not good, but maybe she can help me get better, and I always want to better myself.

D. If I think I'll enjoy myself, then why not? If it doesn't sound fun to me, maybe we can find something else to do that we'd both enjoy.

Question 10: What makes you feel the best?

A. Looking into the faces of my friends as we've just won the Company Games together. Nothing compares to the rush of victory!

B. Close relationships with people I trust. Nothing compares to the rush of being around people who love and understand each other!

C. Getting better at something. Nothing compares to the rush of pushing my own boundaries, learning new skills, and finding out what I'm capable of!

D. Having fun and enjoying life. Nothing compares to the rush of laughing so hard you can't breathe!

Question 11. Introvertians don't talk behind people's backs, but if your friends were going to discuss you without you being in the room, what would you want them to say?

A. You're someone they can always count on; whatever you say you'll do, you find a way to do, because you don't know how to be defeated.

B. You're someone who always has a kind word, a bit of encouragement, or a thoughtful gift for your friends.

C. You're someone who's always curious, who always wants to learn new skills and get better at the things you do, and who wants your friends to be the best they can be too.

D. You're someone who always makes them laugh and always does fun and crazy things; there's never a dull moment around you.

INTAKE TEST RESULTS

Tally up how many times you answered with A, then B, and so on. Your highest score determines where you are assigned:

A represents Victory Company.

B represents Harmony Company.

C represents Excellence Company.

D represents Sun Company.

In rare cases, a cadet may not exhibit a preference, and may have equal or nearly equal scores across two, three, or even all four companies. In such a case, the cadet may choose, with the following two pieces of guidance: (1) the cadet's answer to Question 11 is generally the best tiebreaker, and (2) the cadet should talk to members of the companies he or she is considering, to get a feel for where his or her personality would be the best fit.

Remember that all four companies are vitally important not just to the Dragon Academy but to Introvertian society as a whole. Be proud of who you are, because when you're fully alive, Introvertia is a better place!

> General Anra Leazan
> Director, Dragon Academy
> Carnazon Fortress
> Tranquility, Introvertia

Dragons of Introvertia

A Personal Request from the Authors

If you're still reading, it's because you loved (or at least tolerated!) *Dragons of Introvertia.* Book reviews are extremely important to authors, and the more reviews we get, the more people will have the opportunity to fall in love with this book just like you have!

Would you please take two minutes to visit this link and leave an Amazon review? It would mean the world to us!

Leave a review for *Dragons of Introvertia!*

More than anything, we hope you had fun reading the book! If you can't get enough, here are a few more links you can follow:

Our Facebook group: Dragons of Introvertia
The Wind Before Rain (*Dragons* book 2) on Amazon
A Fury Like Thunder (*Dragons* book 3) on Amazon

Keep on being awesome!

James and Bit

The Adventure Continues!

Dragons of Introvertia Book Two
The Wind Before Rain

Eza and Cammie's daring rescue of the stolen dragons has raised more questions than answers. Will Exclaimovia be content to merely banish Cammie, or are more sinister forces at work to maneuver the two kingdoms into a war anyway? Is there any way Eza and Cammie can keep training their magic even though Introvertia is a non-magical society? And for that matter, once Cammie started casting spells, why did Neemie the dragon suddenly want to be around her all the time?

The kingdom full of introverts may desire nothing more than to peacefully mind their own business, but it appears war is coming to them whether they like it or not – and they may have no choice but to make an alliance that none of them want to make...

DragonsOfIntrovertia.com
Facebook.com/DragonsOfIntrovertia

Made in the USA
Coppell, TX
27 December 2024

43529661R00198